C000006687

Elementals

About the Author

Matthew Alec, born and raised in Manchester before moving to Cambridge, is the proud inventor of the world of *Elementals*. Recently graduating from college with two goals; get a respectable job and create a fictional universe, he is proud to say both have now been accomplished.

Days are spent running around a hospital attending cardiac arrests and nights are filled with an imagination that runs wild and begins conjuring magical happenings.

Elementals will be the beginning of a series that dives into this mystical world.

Who knows what will happen?

Matthew Alec

Elementals

Olympia Publishers
London

www.olympiapublishers.com
OLYMPIA PAPERBACK EDITION

Copyright © Matthew Alec 2017

The right of Matthew Alec be identified as author of
this work has been asserted in accordance with sections 77 and 78 of the
Copyright, Designs and Patents Act 1988.

All Rights Reserved

No reproduction, copy or transmission of this publication
may be made without written permission.
No paragraph of this publication may be reproduced,
copied or transmitted save with the written permission of the publisher, or in
accordance with the provisions
of the Copyright Act 1956 (as amended).

Any person who commits any unauthorised act in relation to
this publication may be liable to criminal
prosecution and civil claims for damage.

A CIP catalogue record for this title is
available from the British Library.

ISBN: 978-1-84897-711-2

(Olympia Publishers is part of Ashwell Publishing Ltd)

This is a work of fiction.
Names, characters, places and incidents originate from the writer's imagination.
Any resemblance to actual persons, living or dead, is purely coincidental.

First published in 2017

Olympia Publishers
60 Cannon Street
London
EC4N 6NP

Printed in Great Britain by CMP (uk) Limited

Dedication

Dedicated to my Uncle Adam and Grandad Alan.

Remembering you is easy

I do it every day

It's just the pain of losing you

That never goes away.

Loved forever and missed always.

Acknowledgements

The driving force behind most of my actions is my family. I have to give a wholehearted 'thank you' to all, both present and departed, for always being there and waiting with bated breath to hear any news regarding my work. My parents, Kathryn and Martin, for their undoubtable love. If I grow up to become anything like them then I will consider my life a success. My beautiful sister Lauren, who has always been my number one fan – thank you for all the proofreading. You are the best sister I could have.

My thanks extend to my family across the country, starting with two ever-loving grandparents; Gail and Alan, three amazing aunts; Liz, Janine and Helen, two dedicated uncles, Adam and Bill. The list continues with many younger cousins, Karis and Jessica, and an older cousin, Catherine – who is an inspiring author herself – before moving onto distant relatives, be they in the UK or Australia. Not to forget dearly departed great grandparents and great aunts/uncles. My love goes out to all of you no matter how many miles separate us.

This book came to be during some free time on a school day and developed into so much more. My first thanks go to all my schoolmates who cheered me on, the teachers who supported me (even the ones who said my writing was below par) and all those who gave me encouragement.

My best friend, Harmony, has been a rock for me many times – my eternal gratitude goes out to you.

As I matured and moved into the working environment, I met many people, all different ages, who taught me a multitude of things. Special thanks has to go to my wonderful colleagues, the Physicians Assistants, who work tirelessly to provide a service to the sick. Our staff room, despite being no bigger than a shoe box, holds many happy memories – times filled with joy, tears, anger, frustration, tear inducing laughter and stomach turning stories.

Special mentions to my colleagues and friends Emily W, Gemma, Cardine, Charlotte W-K, and Catherine K, who have all not only provided me with brilliant car journeys but also many words of wisdom, brilliant days out, hours of laughter and so much more. I am very grateful for all you have done.

As mentioned in my dedication, I need to take a special moment to call upon three members of the family who passed during my lifetime, Uncle Adam, Grandad Alan and Great Grandad Jack, who have all helped me become the man I am today. I thank you, miss you, and love you.

Chapter 1

Evelyn

It happened again. The same nightmare.

It's the exact same one that I get every night, the stupid forest, the eerie mist, that immense gut wrenching feeling of fear and that voice. The soft, whispering voice, calling my name throughout the darkness urging me to walk towards it. Being the stubborn seventeen-year-old that I am, I naturally ignore it. The dream never lasts long as before I can make out any real details, I am forced back into the land of the awake. I sit bolt upright in my bed, cocooned in my bed sheet, and stare into my bright room. With light pink walls, rich pink carpets and fluffy pink teddy bears you can really tell that my parents wanted a girl.

My mother's voice pierces the silence and draws my focus back to the present moment. "Hurry up sweetie you don't want to be late on your first day back." Her voice comes calmly through my door. Damn, it suddenly dawns on me that today is the first day back to school after what could be considered the most glorious summer of my life.

I begrudgingly leap out of my comfortable bed and walk towards my wardrobe and stare at the many colourful and extravagant clothes that my doting mother gets me in an attempt to make me 'fit in with all the trends'. Dressing to impress others has never really been my main focal point when choosing what I wear. The clothes that I choose are ultimately ones that I am most comfortable in; be that a hoody and sweats or a blue lace dress and knee high boots.

Actually, I would never be caught wearing sweats or a blue lace dress in public.

I eventually decide on a simple red t-shirt coupled with my favourite black leather jacket and black skinny jeans. Now the choosing of shoes is an almost perilous decision for most girls my age but I simply grab my black wedges and, after the quick-change act, I stare at myself in the mirror. With light blonde hair that falls past my shoulders in naturally messy curls and both my eyebrows and ears covered with thick bangs, smooth and fair skin that look like fresh milk, probably due to my supposedly Scandinavian heritage, eyes that are a striking blue but splashed with little flecks of green and lips so red and full that I do not have to wear lipstick. I get compliments all the time but I rarely listen to them. Looking good doesn't matter to me as I refuse to be one of the image obsessed teenagers that my school already has so many of.

Well actually, there is one thing that I could not leave the house without.

My pendant.

My pendant is a solid egg shaped piece of silver intricately decorated with small green swirls that interlink around the pendant like a spider's web wrapped around the metal. At the front of the pendant, there is a small ruby that when it is hit with light it casts a soft red glow. Now I have had this necklace for as long as I can remember and I have never been able to open it. The front half and the back half of the pendant look as if they are welded together, and after many hours of trying to prize the halves apart I gave up.

Then it catches my eye. The small plant pot on my windowsill.

Looking at my watch and seeing that I have a couple of minutes to spare, I walk over to the windowsill and pick up the plant pot and sit with it on my bed. After a few seconds of me staring intently at the small green plant I slowly extend my arm and spread my fingers. The familiar feeling of warmth spreads all around my body until it accumulates in my hand. The little green plant starts to tremble until a brand new leaf sprouts from the stem, adding to the new group of leaves that I routinely create every day, as a way of exercising my powers. The plant continues to grow until a knock at my bedroom door breaks my concentration and the now bigger plant stops growing.

"Evelyn Frances Harp, I will not tell you again." Okay, as my mum is using my full name, I can tell that she is getting kind of pissed now.

"I'll be down in a second!" I yell as I hastily grab my bag and return the plant pot back on the windowsill and, after a lingering look; I shut the door, leave my room and descend the stairs into the busy kitchen.

It's all stations go at my house, with my younger sister Lisa colouring in and talking to our cat, Mr Truffles, whilst my mother rustles around in the cupboards and my father perches silently at the table reading this morning's newspaper. The members of my family are carbon copies of one another. We all have blonde hair and pale skin with the exception of a few grey hairs on my dad and the slightly darker blonde hairs evident on my mother. My younger sister on the other hand is the spitting image of me. It's like looking into a mirror eleven years into the past.

My mother and father seem to be in the middle of a heated conversation when I enter the room, something along the lines of being late home and picking up dinner. I rarely listen to what goes on in my house.

"I just hope that once in your life you can get out of work early enough to be home for dinner," my mother mutters whilst her head is buried in a cupboard above the sink apparently trying to find something that does not want to be found.

"And as I always say, the time I finish work actually has nothing to do with me."

I think it's my time to leave the house before there is a full on war.

"I am going now!" I shout above the volume of the TV, radio and my six-year-old sister.

"Okay, sweetie, have a great day," my mother replies as I am leaving the kitchen and walking towards the front door.

I swiftly exit my house and head straight to my lime green little Volkswagen Beetle, named Bessie, parked on the front curb, and drive off into the most boring place in the world.

Ravens Valley.

Originally called 'Corvos Vallis', which directly translates into 'The Ravens of the Valley', it was soon shortened into Ravens Valley due to the prevalence of the bird.

It is the kind of town that you see on those old-fashioned postcards; with every single house next to each other and exactly the same. Every single piece of grass in the front garden is cut to the perfect height and the white picket fences stretching as far as the eye can see. It really is picturesque. At least for the first few times you look at it because after that it gets very annoying. If the houses weren't boring enough, the people are even worse. The men go to work each day to complete mundane tasks and then return home to doting wives in 1950s pinafores who have spent all day baking and looking after their brood of children. The whole monotonous situation is enough to make you sick. This town might not be as boring if there were things to do. But there aren't.

Apart from Ravens Church and the few shops and the small hospital, the town really is empty. Driving to school every day only further enhances my unparalleled desire to leave the town that time obviously forgot.

Pulling into the busy car park of Raven's High, I observe the many students rushing around to greet each other on the first day back after summer break. Fake smiles are plastered on the faces of girls who are trying their hardest to appear excited to see their friends whereas the guys only grunt and pump fists and then begin to act like chimps in a new zoo. Pulling into my usual spot in the car park, I exit my car only to see my favourite person. Both my partner in crime and my best friend; Luke Morgan. I constantly have to correct people when they assume we are brother and sister or that we are dating. Well, in their defence, we look strikingly similar and we are always together. Luke has light blond hair that he wears short at the sides but longer at the top so he can mould it into ruffles that fall to his eye level, and full red lips like mine. However, Luke is six foot one with a footballer's body whereas I am about five foot ten with a slim, but slightly athletic, body. People often refer to Luke as a hunk, which is understandable due to his strong jawline and his statuesque physique, but after being best friends for all of our lives, and not to mention our parents constantly reminding us that we saw each other naked in the swimming pool when we were infants, we both agreed to remain best friends.

I walk towards him with a huge smile and extend my arms for a hug when he speaks.

"How's my little witch doing?" he shouts with a huge cocky grin.

"I am not a witch!" I furiously exclaim whilst punching Luke in the arm.

He winces before saying, "I'm sorry but how many people do you know that can control flowers and plants?"

Okay, he has a point there.

"Well, have you made any plants grow recently?" he inquires.

"I made my plant grow a new leaf this morning," I quietly tell him.

Luke is the only person that knows about my secret. I mean it's not like I can just announce to my parents, 'Hey I'm your freak of a daughter and I can make plants grow'. I have always thought of telling my parents but I can imagine the shock and the horror closely followed by my arrest by the government and being dissected like an alien in a secret facility in the desert.

I would have been perfectly happy if nobody knew my secret. I mean, I would have told Luke eventually if he hadn't have barged into my room a few years ago uninvited whilst I was making the vines on my trellis snake through the windows and spread along the walls. The moment he walked in I lost control, the vines fell down, and Luke demanded an explanation so I had no choice but to tell him the truth.

I have absolutely no idea where my abilities come from. It's just that I feel this pull whenever I am near nature and I can feel the energy that plants emit. I can control them and will them to do whatever I want but the amazing thing is that sometimes I have this empathic bond with certain plants that allows me to feel what they feel.

"Earth to Evie." Luke's voice snaps me out of my walk down memory lane.

"Don't call me Evie." Luke has it in his head that I will automatically like every nickname that he gives me and now it looks like I have to add 'Evie' to his long list of names including; Snowy, Mother Nature, Plant Girl and my least favourite at all is The Dirt Woman.

"C'mon, we better be going to class," Luke says whilst dragging me off into the school. It's at that moment I realise that I really do hate my school. It's full of two faced, pretentious, self-centred, arrogant back stabbers and it looks like the worst of them is heading my way.

Pandora Mallory.

She strides down the hallway with this unparalleled air of confidence whilst at the same time emitting the stench of arrogance. Her glossy, golden hair falls perfectly down to her shoulders and her pinched face is plastered into a very fake smile that rarely leaves her face. Pandora is the sort of person who will push you in front of a speeding train if it meant that she could remain the Queen Bee at the school. I literally despise the girl and she is walking right towards me, eyes fixed like a hawk looking at its prey.

 "How are you both doing?" she asks but I have a strong feeling that she doesn't actually want a response.

"Well, I ..." I begin only to be crudely cut off by her.

"I am having a super-cool welcome back to school extravaganza at my house tonight and I would like to invite you both," she states in her 'butter wouldn't melt' voice.

God I hate this girl.

"There is no dress code but I'm sure that you can wear something better than that." She gestures to my outfit and goes on to talk in the most patronising voice I have ever heard.

I am about to lunge forwards until Luke grabs my arm, restraining me, and calms the situation. "We'll be there, Pandora."

"Well, I look forward to seeing you there, then." She gives me one last look up and down before sauntering off to probably go victimise someone else.

"Please let met turn her into a weed," I plead with Luke.

"Can you even do that?" he asks.

"No... But there is always hope!" I refuse to let Miss Good Girl get the best of me.

"Everyone knows that she is only popular because her dad is the principal and her mother is on the council. Now this school year will be over before we know it and me and you will be out of this crap town and be moving on to better and brighter things," Luke says speaking positively.

He always knows how to cheer me up. Before we turn to walk off, the lights start to flicker on and off, causing the students in the hallway, including myself and Luke, to look up and questionably stare at the lights until, after a few seconds, they return to the previous state of constantly on.

"Oh great, the school is falling apart around us," I mutter as we start to walk.

"Maybe you can ask your best friend, Pandora, to put a word in to her daddy?"

"Or maybe I should turn you into the weed?"

"Now now, come on, we better get going before we are late," he urges whilst once again dragging me down the hallway.

We promptly arrive into the stuffy classroom that is already filled with students lounging around their little wooden desks. Me and Luke squeeze through the narrow gaps between desks and take our normal seats at the back of the room. I really haven't missed this room. I feel so cramped, so trapped, as this room is basically a prison cell.

It looks like one as well. The walls are a dirty dank green colour that has become chipped and cracked over all the years that the school has been here. At the front of the room, there is a large blackboard with an equally large wooden desk a few feet in front of it. The walls contain posters and inspirational quotes that fail to inspire anyone. The most valuable piece of advice that you can give to someone in Ravens Valley is probably, "Get out as soon as possible."

On cue, our teacher, Miss Watts, arrives seconds after Luke and I, and the room quickly falls deathly silent and every student starts to sit straight up in their seats, hands firmly planted on the desks, just like marionette dolls and Miss Watts is the puppet master. She stands in front of us, her beak of a nose protruding from underneath her eagle-like eyes, with a stern look smeared across her face. Someone should really take her shopping because she is wearing a tweed jacket with a matching tweed skirt that clings to every inch of her large body. She has somehow managed to force herself into a pair of horrendous black pumps that squeeze her ankles so tightly they give her a funny little wiggle when she walks. Her straw-coloured hair is pushed up into a messy bun with the exceptions of a few strands which have managed to escape and fall messily down that eagle-like face of hers.

"Class has begun!" Her shrill voice echoes around the room causing everyone to flinch, but remain looking forward, so as not to deviate from the eye contact that she has created with the class. So naturally, I look out of the window.

I aimlessly gaze out onto the sports pitch and the adjoining woods. The woods have been here since before Ravens Valley was even called that and majority of the town was built around them. The tall trees stand proud amongst the almost colourless grass stretching high into the skyline and I long to be there, well I'd rather be anywhere but here. I am about to face the front, albeit begrudgingly, when something catches my eye.

A tall man stands at the front of the forest. He seems to be staring straight at me through the window. The sunlight pours through the window causing me to close my eyes and turn away. When I feel the heat of the sun leave my skin, I crane my neck to look out of the window to see that the man had disappeared.

Chapter 2

Evelyn

I desperately try to get Luke's attention, who seems to be staring at his lap, in order to alert him to the presence of a very strange man who was staring me down and can apparently disappear on a whim.

After deducting that Luke is not staring at his crotch but is in fact looking at his phone underneath the desk. I decide to rip a slither of paper from my notebook, role it into a ball shape, and launch it at Luke. My impromptu paper bullet hits Luke on his temple and he seems to look around as if the piece of paper was thrown by a ghost.

"Pssst!" Evidently, I have to resort to being a child in order to get his attention. He quickly looks towards me.

"Did you see that man?" I whisper.

"What man?"

"The one out the—" I try to finish my sentence, only to be interrupted by the increasingly shrill voice of Miss Watts who seems to be staring at me whilst pointing her stumpy, fat finger at the blackboard, which contains some sort of weird looking equation.

"Well then, Evelyn, what's the answer?" she shrieks.

I stutter for a few seconds before Luke comes to my rescue.

"It's negative six," he proudly announces before ushering a quick wink in my direction. I mouth 'thank you' back to him but Miss Watts apparently isn't as thankful.

"If you wish to answer a question you shall raise your hand and not be so disobedient in my classroom again, Mr Morgan." Her voice echoes around the room, leaving a ringing sound in my ear.

"Sure thing, Miss Watts," Luke cockily replies before turning back to me. "So, what man?"

"Never mind, I'll tell you later." I don't want either of us getting into trouble on the first day back. Instead of paying attention, I sit back in my seat and think about the man in the forest. At first I wonder what he was doing standing in the forest but then I start to think about what he was wearing. This man was freakishly tall and wearing a sharp, black suit that deeply contrasts his pale skin that was wrinkled and almost withered. I try to think in more detail but the memory is already leaving my mind.

My train of thought is disrupted by the ringing of the school bell informing us that class is over. Everyone in the class quickly packs their belongings in their bags and hastily leave the room. Luke and I are the last two to leave and we both head straight to our lockers, adjoining of course, and start to collect the books for the next lesson.

"So what were you trying to say earlier?" Luke absent-mindedly asks whilst his head is in his locker.

"It's just I saw a man in the forest out of the window," I murmur.

"Probably just the janitor."

"In a black suit?"

"Maybe he wants to make an effort, who are we to question the janitor's fashion choices?"

I jokingly shove Luke, say goodbye then head to my next lesson. I have biology in the science lab whereas Luke has English literature somewhere in the north building. We only have a few lessons today, as it's the first day back after the long break.

I walk down the bustling hallways of my least favourite place and walk into my classroom to see my least favourite person sat at my desk.

"Pandora, what are you doing?" I ask.

"Oh, hi, sweetie, I just wanted to remind you that you and Luke are both invited to my little soiree tonight." There it is again, that stupid smile coupled by an obnoxious little gesture as she waves both her hands into the sky to put emphasis on the word 'soiree'.

"And as I tried to say earlier, before I was cut off, I will think about coming." I shove past her and take my seat.

"Now sweetie, I want to make this work, I mean we do take a few classes together, and I don't think that our time will be well spent if we are at each other's throats all the time." She speaks to me like everything is my fault!

"Listen here, Pandora, I have no gripes with you and we won't have any problem. Now get your backside off of my desk." Wow, I am actually proud of myself for standing up like that. You go, Evelyn!

"Well you can't say that I didn't try talking to you." With that, she leaps off my desk and slinks to her seat where she proceeds to fake laugh with her fake friends whilst occasionally casting a few dirty looks towards me. She only hates me because I refuse to follow her every word like the puppet master she thinks she is.

Our biology teacher, Mr Winters, begins the lesson and after a few minutes of taking notes on the interesting process of mitosis, I notice the lights starting to flicker again.

So this has happened twice now in two different rooms. Either the school is falling apart or something is wrong. I don't know how to explain it but I have these horrible feelings deep down inside of me. A very, very bad feeling.

"Mr Winters, can I please be excused?" I ask politely. I just really need to get out of this classroom.

"Sure, make sure you take the hall pass." He gestures to the small laminated piece of card hanging on the wall next to the door. I swiftly leave my desk, exit the room, and head to the bathroom down the corridor.

I enter the toilets and the sharp, white lights cause me to squint whilst a wave of nausea hits me. I stagger to the sink and hit the cold tap sending a strong jet of cold water into the basin. I fill my cupped hands with cool water and splash it onto my face whilst the nausea subsides.

What the hell is happening to me?

I grab a handful of tissues and wipe my dripping face then stare at myself in the mirror. I look the same but something is different, like I have changed, but I can't see it. I am about to leave the bathroom when I get the same feeling as earlier, the one that I felt in the classroom.

"Come on, Evelyn, you can do this," I say to myself whilst leaving the bathroom and ignoring the feeling deep inside.

I return to the classroom, take my seat and scrawl down any work off the board that I missed. After what seems to be an eternity of Mr Winters warbling on about cell division and some other stuff that I wasn't listening to, the school bell went, signifying the end of class and the start of break time.

I grab my bag and rocket out of the room, before anyone has even managed to get out of their seats and head straight to my locker where I eagerly wait to meet Luke.

On cue, he walks round the corner, smiles, and heads straight towards me.

"You feeling okay?" he concernedly asks. "You look pale."

"Not really, I have been feeling bad all day. I had to leave Winters' class because I felt sick." I inform Luke of how my last class went, including my run in with Pandora.

"Well, I am glad you stood up for yourself," he proudly announces. "Next time you should fling some dirt at her or something."

Apparently, that's his idea of humour.

Me and Luke head to our usual spot on the front field and slump against the base of a large tree. I tell Luke of all the bad feelings that I have been getting sporadically throughout the day, all the while absent mindedly playing with my pendant. After hearing the full story, Luke gives me some of his best thoughts and ideas on the situation.

"Could be trapped wind? I mean I get that all the time." Judging by the look he is deadly serious.

"Are you kidding me, Luke? I am telling you about this deep internal feeling that has got me so confused and kind of upset and you think that it is trapped wind!" I would hit him if it wasn't for the slightly hurt expression on his face. "I'm sorry, Luke, I just feel really bad today."

"Is it related to your powers?"

"I don't think so; I haven't been practising them, really."

"Well, there you go! It's probably all that pent up energy you have inside of you, urging to get free."

"You think so?" I ask.

"Of course, look you have a free period next so why don't you head into the forest and just let some of your witchy powers loose." He seems so pleased with himself, like he just got full marks on a test.

"Luke, I think that's the best idea you have had in a long time."

His smile is practically beaming.

"But if you make one more witch reference I will send a horde of thorny roses to get you whilst you are in the shower." I threaten as I walk away. Even though I had my back to Luke but I can only imagine his reaction.

I quickly run to the forest and stop at the entrance. There is a gravel path that runs through the entire forest about five feet in width that follows a snaking pattern. I stop directly in front of the large woodland and I can feel the siren call of the forest. I follow the gravel path deep into the heart of the trees.

After about fifteen minutes of walking, I stop and survey my surroundings and deduce that I am alone. I plant my feet firmly in the ground and slowly extend my arms. I can feel the heat and energy pulsating from every tree in the vicinity. I can feel the depth of the ground below me and the height of the trees above me. I call upon the familiar feeling of warmth inside me and let it spread across my body. The heat gathers in my hands as I feel myself connect to the leaves on the trees, and like a moth to the flame, they all detach from the trees and dance in the air as they circle around me. The rapid motion of the leaves as they whip around me should make me feel sick but instead, the feeling is euphoric. I send out a command for all the leaves to halt, and as if time has frozen, every leaf hangs in the air motionless.

That's when I see him.

I relinquish control over the leaves and they all silently float to the ground and lay there. It's the same man I saw earlier standing at the entrance to the forest except now I can see him much more closely. He is wearing the same black suit as before, which looks like it is covered in a fine layer of dust. His whitewashed skin seems to hang loosely on his face giving him a saggy look, but his sunken and sallow eyes seem to have receded into their sockets giving him the shocking resemblance to a skull. The eyes themselves seem too completely devoid of colour and instead have settled for grey.

I don't know what to say to the stranger; after all, he has just seen me levitating hundreds of leaves, so he is bound to be in shock.

He is greedily staring at me, eyes fixated on my face, as if he was looking at a piece of meat, or a prized possession.

"Urm... hello." I shakily raise my hand into a little wave.

He remains both silent and motionless for a few seconds until I see his pale lips crack open and a single word slither out.

"Earth."

He speaks like he has a mouthful of sand, like a man who hasn't had anything to drink in a long time.

"Yes that's where I am, fancy joining me?" Why am I making a joke? Am I seriously expecting a laugh from him?

He slowly lifts his arms and extends a long, thin and bony finger in my direction and, as if I was suddenly placed in the middle of the Arctic, I get very cold, very quick.

"Yeah, I'm going to go now if that's okay." I slowly start to retreat, the gravel crunching beneath my shoes, not for one moment taking my eyes off him.

After gaining about twenty feet between us, I carefully turn around and, now at a much quicker pace, head towards the exit of the forest. I throw a cautious look over my shoulder to see where the man has gone, only to see he has completely disappeared. Again.

I stop dead still and turn around a few times to try to catch where he may be hiding. The only noise I can hear is the rustling of the leaves in the wind and my own heartbeat thunderously booming inside my ears.

After a few more seconds of staring into the thick foliage of the forest, I ready myself to run back to the school and inform Luke of this ghastly experience.

The cracking of a twig suddenly draws my attention to the left, only to hear a thick rustling on my right side. Okay, now I am getting really scared. I rotate full circle and still no sight of the Grim Reaper.

"Three... two... one..." I whisper out loud, counting down the seconds until I will sprint straight to the school.

I turn steadily on my feet and shoot forwards only to run full pelt into what feels like a brick wall. I fall to the ground with a thump as all the wind is knocked out of my body. I look up to see what I hit, although I most likely know what or who it was. Grim Reaper is towering above me, completely unphased by me rocketing into him. I slowly crawl backwards, hand clasping at the gravel on the floor, and try to get back to my feet. Grim Reaper starts to extend both his arms, into a zombie-like position, and closes his eyes. He starts to mutter something that sounds like a million words all being said at once.

I take advantage of the momentary pause and stagger to my feet and just start running with no apparent sense of direction. After heading straight into thick branches that claw at my skin and tug at my clothes, I eventually find myself back on the gravel path and try to gather my bearings. My deep breathing is now the only noise in the entirety of the forest. I slowly take one step after another, quietly cursing as the crunch of the gravel could give away my position, and try to figure out a way back to school without Grim Reaper seeing me.

That's when I feel the sharpest, most painful, feeling ever, resonate in my right shoulder, as if five needles had grabbed me and put me in a vice grip. The pain sears through me and causes my legs to go weak and my vision to blur.

It feels like I am being electrocuted from the inside out. I shakily reach my hand up to my shoulder to feel what the source of the pain is and my hand lightly brushes what feels like five, cold as steel, thin bones wrapped in withered and cracking leather.

I turn my head and see the Grim Reaper looming above me with his hand clamped on my shoulder and his emotionless eyes locked onto mine. I grimace at the thought of what he will do next.

I dig down deep within myself trying to summon any strength that I can muster and call out to the surrounding thorny branches on the trees and will them to follow my thoughts and cause them to lash out, tear at his skin, and latch on to any of the Grim Reaper's exposed flesh. The frenzied attack of the thorns on the Grim Reaper causes him to unleash me from his death grip and throw me face first onto the ground.

I quickly roll over and stare at the Grim Reaper, who is being held by the neck and wrist by a mass of tangled branches. He once again stares directly into my eyes, but it's almost like he is looking through me, rather than at me.

I crawl back a few inches before staggering to my feet. Before I can stop myself the words have already poured out.

"Who are you?" I hiss at the Grim Reaper. I try to sound strong but there is a hint of fear quelling at the back of my throat.

His deadly white face stays unemotional as his pale lips crack open, revealing yellow teeth that bear strong resemblance to fangs and a single word slither out.

The same word.

"Earth."

Okay now I have had enough.

"I don't care who you are, but you made a big mistake attacking me in the middle of the forest," I announce whilst trying to appear much braver than I currently feel.

He still remains silent so I call out for the branches to tighten their grip and a single flicker of pain spreads across Grim Reaper's face.

"Okay, so now that I have your attention, I want to know exactly what you are doing here and I have absolutely no problem hurting the man who just tried to kill me!" I shout whilst taking tiny steps toward him until I'm about a foot away from him.

With his withered face and dead eyes, he really is something that nightmares are made from. Perhaps I should change his name from Grim Reaper to Nightmare Man.

"Tell me!" I scream at him.

And it's at that point that he reacts for the first time. Just one emotion that twitches onto his ghostly face.

A smile. A smile that is not produced from joy, but rather a smile of pure hatred or arrogance. A smile similar to that of a hunter who has just caught his elusive prey.

"Something funny?" I question, not once taking my eyes off of him.

His lips crack open one more time and instead of words slithering out, a sharp, ear splitting, scream pierces the silence causing me to jump and retreat in fear.

I turn on the spot and sprint as quick as I can towards the school whilst the scream fades into the background and, after gaining a safe distance between myself and the Grim Reaper, I relinquish control over the branches that held him in place, not for one second slowing down or stopping, in the hope he will leave Ravens Valley and return to whatever asylum he escaped from.

I reach an entrance to the school and fling myself through the doors, sprint down the hallway and head straight for Luke's classroom.

Chapter 3

Evelyn

I hurriedly push open the door to the English room that Luke is currently residing in, only to meet the gaze of twenty-five silent students who are confused as to why a random person has suddenly flung herself into their classroom. I quickly scan the room until my eyes lock onto Luke's face, which holds a mixed expression of confusion, surprise and shock, as he stares directly at me.

"Sorry Mr. Jefferson, please can Luke be excused from class?" I hopefully pant to the equally confused looking teacher.

"Is it an emergency, Miss Harp, because we are in the middle of a very important lesson?" he inquires.

"Yes, sir, I promise I will return him in a moment," I plead to the stern looking man.

"Well, if you insist." He turns from looking at me to looking at Luke, "Mr Morgan, you are excused,"

Luke quietly grabs his bag and shuffles out of his desk, quickly walking towards me where I lightly grab his arm and drag him down the hallway, the classroom door loudly slamming behind us.

"Are we really only going to be a moment?" he asks.

"No." Well there is no point lying to him. I finally halt in front of the doors that lead to the courtyard that is located in the centre of the school. The courtyard is a large, perfect square that has an even bigger stone water fountain in the centre in the shape of dolphin, now heavily moss covered, squirting water into a small pool at the base. The courtyard has a few benches scattered around, some located underneath the overhanging roof, providing shade and a quiet place where me and Luke can sit.

"Mind telling me why you just dragged me out of class... and why do you look like that? Have you been rolling in the forest?" Luke quietly asks whilst eyeing me up and down. I take a second to think about what he could be referencing before leaping up and heading towards the water fountain and staring into the pool. My blonde hair is now dishevelled and the new home to a small amount of leaves and twigs. My face has a small smattering of dirt near the chin and a few little scratches that were caused when I was caught in the crossfire between the branches and Grim Reaper. My red top and black jacket are covered in mud and gravel but my attention now falls to my right shoulder. The jacket and top now have four, round, claw-like marks that also seem to be burnt.

I turn back to face Luke, who looks bewildered at me, and I slowly walk to him and take my seat once again.

"I was just attacked," I whisper.

"What... Evelyn are you okay?" Luke cries out in fear.

"It was the man from earlier. The one I was telling you about."

"Wait, do you mean the janitor?" asks a confused Luke.

"No! Honestly, Luke, he wasn't the janitor. He was creepy and he looked a little bit like death; to be honest, he smelt like death as well,"

"So some random man attacks you, in the middle of the day, during school hours?"

I can smell the disbelief seeping from his words.

"Luke the Grim Reaper followed me..."

"Wait a second; who is the Grim Reaper?" he confusedly asks.

"That's my name for him. He looks like the Grim Reaper," I solemnly answer.

"Okay, now you have me interested. So this Grim Reaper is following you?"

"Yeah, he followed me into the forest and he saw me... well... he saw me using my powers," I whisper.

Luke's eyes widen in shock as he leans in close and stares directly into my eyes.

"What did he say?"

"Well, that is the point, Luke. He didn't say anything. The entire time we were in the forest he didn't mutter a single word... well, unless you count 'Earth'."

"Earth?"

"Yes, 'Earth'. He said it twice, I think. You know, just before attacking me," I say with a slightly smug tone to my voice. After all, Luke doesn't really seem to be believing me!

"So he attacks you, ruins your jacket, and makes it look like you have been in a fight with a tree?" Luke splutters whilst trying to wrap his head around the fact that some creepy man was attacking me all the while he was sitting in his classroom daydreaming about God-knows-what.

"Actually, he is the one who got into a fight with a tree." Luke furrows his brow and a look of confusion smacks itself across his face.

"He hurt me so I whipped out a can of Whoop-ass. I made all the trees and branches nearby grab him while I made a run for it," I explain to Luke how I ran as fast as I could to the school and then straight towards his classroom.

Luke leans back on the bench, absentmindedly moving his ruffled blond hair that had flopped over his eyes, still trying to encompass the information that I had just offloaded onto him.

After a few moments of silence I stand up and, once again, head back to the water fountain where I take my jacket off and stare intently into the freshly made marks in the shoulder. The four smouldered claw

32

marks stare back at me as if to smugly say 'Oh hi, we are just going to stay here in order to remind you that you were just nearly killed'.

The tense silence is broken by the sharp ringing of the school bell, signifying the end of the school day, causing the courtyard to be filled with rushing students who are eagerly waiting to go home but first must have a chitter-chatter with their friends.

"C'mon Luke you can come round mine and we can carry on our conversation," I say whilst walking over to Luke who hasn't actually moved from his spot.

"Wait, I have football practice until four today." I over-exaggeratedly roll my eyes. "But you can stay here until I am done and *then* we can carry on our conversation."

"Fine, text me when you are done and I'll meet you," I begrudgingly say whilst he smiles and jogs off to join his football teammates.

I slowly start walking towards my locker in order to grab my things and then I will most likely go to the library and get some work done while I wait. I head through the doors into the dreary school, straight down the corridor, and turn the corner only to abruptly walk straight into the very angry looking Mrs Watts. So that's twice today that I have walked into a monster.

"Watch where you are walking, Ms. Harp, you could have knocked me off of my feet," she shrieks.

"You'd need a bulldozer to do that," I mutter under my breath.

"Excuse me, Ms. Harp?" she enquires.

"Oh, nothing, I said I am sorry for walking into you," I lie.

"As you should be; now be gone with you," she says while swiping the air with eagle like claw as an indirect way of ushering me away. Obviously, I oblige her and run down the corridor.

"And no running!" echoes her voice down the hallway.

I have a little giggle to myself and then look down to my watch to note the time.

"It's not even three o'clock yet... okay, that gives me enough time to—" Before I can finish my sentence, I am shrewdly cut off by a deep male voice.

"Talking to yourself, Evelyn? You know that is the first sign of madness, right?"

Quickly turning around I come face to face with Ethan Jessop who has a sincere grin plastered across his face.

Ethan Jessop. The British transfer and newly appointed head of the football team, currently stands in front of me looking all rugged in his football uniform, with his dirty blond hair descending past his perfect cheekbones and settling on his broad shoulders.

"And interrupting people whilst they are mid-thought is just plain rude," I stammer whilst trying not to get weak at the knees. It is safe to say that I have a little... well... tiny... almost minuscule crush on Ethan.

"What are you still doing here?" he questions me whilst staring intently into my eyes.

I, on the other hand, seem to be slowly losing myself into his mud-brown eyes.

"I am waiting for Luke to finish practice so that he can come round my house," I once again stutter.

"Oh, yeah, I forgot about Luke," he whispers whilst a look of sadness spread over his face.

"Only to do homework and stuff!" I announce a little louder than I expected.

"Good!" His face perks up a bit. "Do you mind if I ask why on earth your face is covered in dirt?" he ponders. "And not to mention those little cuts on your chin?"

"Oh... well... I... fell... That's right, I fell outside, earlier... clumsy me!" I stammer whilst trying to come up with an excuse for my appearance as well as trying to brush my tangled hair with my fingers in order to make myself look presentable.

"Well, you still look beautiful, even covered in dirt," he says, letting the compliments roll of his tongue and straight into my eagerly awaiting ears.

"Well," he continues, "I should be going now but I was just wondering if you wanted to come see some friends of mine play their music down at the hall on Friday? There are only a few of us going so it should be a right laugh," he calmly announces while I am staring at him like a dog with a bone.

"I would love to." Play it cool, Evelyn. "What time shall I be there for?"

"Oh, don't worry. I will pick you up around seven-ish," he proudly announces before heading past me, not before sending me a smouldering look.

"See you then, Evelyn," he states whilst disappearing around the corner.

I take a few seconds to gather myself and try to stop my heart from beating like a drum when I realise that there is something on the floor. I bend down to pick it up and upon further observation, I realise it is a piece of paper with small diagrams and names and arrows on it. Ethan's football plays.

I swiftly turn on the spot and steadily walk down the corridor in order to catch up with Ethan and return the football plays to him. After a few moments of walking, I stop near a large window that shows the sports field and upon further examination I see Ethan in all his beautiful glory leading the team, including Luke, through a set of rigorous routines. Staring out of the window my gaze eventually travels from the players on the field, to the field itself. The large grassy area, mown down and intricately painted with white lines that represent sporting fixtures, like the shape of the running track or the halfway line. The field is currently being pounded by the football boots from the boys and the stomping dance routine from the cheerleaders, when I start to feel a dull aching sensation in my stomach, like someone tightening a knot deep down inside me.

I turn around and start to walk back towards the lockers, trying to ignore the sensation within, only to be hit by an even stronger wave of the stomach pain. I double over whilst a gasp escapes from my mouth. I try to stand up but the searing pain prevents me from moving. I manage to lift my head and, through tear filled eyes; stare down the hallway to see what could possibly be causing the most unimaginable pain I have ever felt in my entire life. The corridor is completely empty, excusing the few pieces of litter aimlessly rolling on the floor like tumble weeds and the slightly ajar locker doors blocking my already stifled view, when, in the distance, the faint sounds of footsteps echo around the corner and directly into my ears. The approaching sound seems to get louder when I am able to decipher small details like the fact that the ominous sounding footsteps are, in fact, not your regular shoes, but they are instead a pair of high heels. And I bet my life that they are bright pink and attached to a vapid, repugnant, human being.

The footsteps reach their climax when they turn round the corner, and through my blurred eyes, I see a pair of pink high heels, slowly walking towards me in a perfect model strut. The shoes sit comfortably on a pair of little feet complete with perfectly painted toenails. Somehow managing to lift my head from the floor, after hearing that the footsteps have finally stopped and a shadow has been cast over my crumpled form, as I gaze up at the looming figure to see Pandora Mallory, dressed in a hot pink, ruffle filled, dress, complete with matching headband and purse, with that pearly white smile plastered onto her face, her delicate hair pulled back into a neat ponytail and her hand placed on her cocked hip.

"Got our self into a spot of bother have we Evelyn?" she smugly questions.

"Are you going to help me, Pandora?" I spit at her through the searing pain.

"To be honest with you, I am truly enjoying watching you squirm like a little spider trapped in a glass," she says whilst putting emphasis on the word 'trapped'.

"What the hell is wrong with you, Pandora?" I cry through the unfaltering pain.

"Nothing is wrong with me; in fact, I am feeling better than I have in a long time."

"Pandora... you're deranged."

"Oh I am not deranged. I am powerful, and I am more than you will ever be, and there is nothing you can do to stop me, little girl," I can feel the venom in her words.

She slowly takes her hand off her hip and squats down so her face is now in line with mine. At first sight, Pandora may seem to be completely normal but something has changed. I gasp in horror as I realise what has happened to Pandora. Her eyes, normally a light blue, have become a deep grey, with a thick glazing over them, like mist trapped inside a crystal ball.

"Pandora, what happened to you, what's wrong?" I shout at her trying, but failing, to illicit an emotional response from the real Pandora.

"Nothing is wrong. I am here to set things right. I am here to fix the cracks that you are yet to cause."

"Do you really need to speak in riddles? I am in enough pain as it is!" I laugh through my gritted teeth.

"You have no idea, do you?" she asks with a hint of disbelief in her voice.

"Idea about what?" I question all the while noticing that the deep searing pain within seems to be nullifying, albeit slowly, and allowing myself to gather some strength.

"Who you really are!" she spits, making directly eye contact with me, and allowing her cold fingers to gently stroke my cheek.

"And who am I then?" I ask, trying to buy some time.

"You, little girl, are a piece of the puzzle," she states while snatching her hand back from my face.

"Since when are we playing a game?" I wittingly retort.

"Oh, there are no games any more. Only you and I and your pathetic friends,"

"My friends? What... Luke?"

"No, not that bumbling excuse for a man... your *other* friends," she impatiently replies.

"I have no idea what you are talking about." And for the first time I am being serious.

"Stop playing coy with me!" she shouts.

"I have told you already, and I'll tell you one more time, I don't know what you're talk—"

My words are cut off by a loud shriek erupting from Pandora's mouth whilst the quick movement of her body flying back blurs my vision.

"Enough is enough!" she screams as she raises her hand high into the air.

"Wait!" I scream, "I can take you to my friends!" I lie in the hopes it will prevent her from exacting whatever damage she was about to commit.

"So now you decide to tell the truth. Well, honestly I am a little confused, and upset, as why you would feel the need to lie to me," she smoothly replies.

"Because you are right; you are much more powerful than I am, Pandora," I state whilst dragging the word 'much' out in order to illustrate my point.

"Yes, I am. Now get moving," she requests.

Suddenly, as if it never happened, the pain deep inside of me ceases to exist. I finally stand up and face Pandora only to be roughly shoved to face the other direction.

"Well get moving, I don't have all day!" she yells.

I start walking down the hallway, heading towards the end of the corridor, all the while trying to come up with a plan. I can't run away nor can I fight her because she can all of a sudden give me unimaginable cramp! With the thought of the pain on my mind, I decide to buy myself some more time.

"So Pandora, since when can you make people literally fall at your feet?" I ask over my shoulder.

"Oh, I have always had that power, amongst many, but I consider it my speciality," she cockily replies.

"Okay... since when have you have the power to make me feel like I am dying?" I rephrase my question.

"I've had powers since the dawn of eternity. There is nothing and no-one more powerful than I," she smugly states. Maybe it really is Pandora because it sure does sound like something she would say.

"Well I will give you that one, Pandora." I roll my eyes when I am suddenly struck with an idea.

"They are here, Pandora... behind that door," I say, pointing at the janitor's closet, waiting for her to move to open the door.

Pandora takes two steps forward, and before she can even react, I race forward towards the fire exit doors that face the football field in the hopes that I can run onto the field and gain some attention or help. I push the cool metal bar that opens the door and the little corridor is flooded with light. I start to scream 'help' at the field of football players only to have a cold, yet delicate, hand harshly clasp over my mouth and a thin arm wrap around my waist, yanking me away from the door, and throwing me onto the hard floor.

"That was your last chance," Pandora coldly says, her face void of emotion, whilst outstretching her hand and causing tiny little sparks to accumulate on her perfectly manicured fingers. The little volts of electricity float around her and ultimately join to become one huge ball of bright, flickering, electricity in her hand.

Chapter 4

Evelyn

The glowing ball of electricity lingered in Pandora's hand for a few seconds before she lifted her arm, ready to fling it towards my cowering figure, when she is violently thrown to the ground by a red blur.

I breathe a sharp sigh of relief and stand to see my saviour face to face. The figure turns around and I am greeted by the extremely flustered, and not to mention worried, Luke. He glares directly into my eyes and we hang silently staring at each other until he makes the first move, throwing his arms around my neck and pulling me in close for a very welcomed hug.

"What the hell was that?" he quietly breathes into my head, which is leaning on his sturdy chest, with strong tinges of worry lingering in his voice.

"That was Pandora," I bluntly answer, unable to quell the fear in the back of my throat and stop the shaking inside of me.

"Thanks for that Captain Obvious... But since when can she become a human battery?" he jokes.

"I don't know Luke. Why don't we ask her?" I reply whilst throwing a glance in the direction of Pandora's crumpled body.

"Well do you want to wake her up, because I damn well don't want to?"

"Honestly, Luke, you did just tackle her to the ground," I retort.

"And it was actually the most satisfying thing I have done all day." He grins.

"Well being terrorised by Pandora wasn't exactly what I call fun."

"Let's see why she did it then!"

We both turn to face Pandora, still lying snug on the floor, and after repeated urging, Luke slowly extends his arm to shake her. A heavy silence lingers in the air. I hear Luke gulp before finally planting his firm hand on Pandora's clothed arm.

"Pandora?" he whispers whilst giving her a little shake.

"Maybe she's dead..." I suggest.

"Oh my God. Please don't say I killed her. I'm not even that strong," he whined as he retreats his hand.

"I am sure you didn't kill her Luke. She is pro—" Before I can finish my sentence, Pandora erupts with a huge shriek before sitting bolt upright.

"You pushed me!" she screams, staring at Luke.

"I... I... I..." Luke stammers, struggling to come up with a response.

"How dare you! These clothes probably cost more than your house!" she hissed.

"Oh, goodie, our Pandora's back!" I mutter, sarcasm spilling from my voice.

"I never went anywhere you bumbling idiot. Now why did you push me? What am I doing here anyway!" she confusedly asks.

"You tripped Pandora and Luke tried to help you up," I lie whilst extending a hand to help her up.

"Tripped on what?" she asks while batting my hand away. "I do not need your help, Evelyn."

"I don't know. Maybe your ego?" I innocently answer.

Once standing and regaining her composure, Pandora starts to bat her clothes down to remove the dust and run her hands through her tangled hair in an attempt to gather any modesty she has left.

"Pandora, can I ask you a question?"

"What?" she sharply answers.

42

"What is the last thing you remember?" I enquire.

"You mean besides being body slammed by the little elephant over there?" she angrily retorts, gesturing at Luke.

"Firstly; he tried to help you, and secondly; I meant before you fell. What is the last thing you remember?"

"Well everything is a little foggy but I remember walking to my locker, I needed to grab my diary as it has all my party plans in it, and then... urm..." Her face contorts in confusion as she struggles to finish her sentence.

"Did you see anyone?"

"There was someone. I don't know what it was though. It wasn't... well, it wasn't..."

"It wasn't what, Pandora?" I ask, getting more forceful with each question.

"It wasn't solid. It came around the corner and I screamed and it covered my mouth, but I didn't feel anything, I just couldn't talk anymore," she whimpers.

I almost start to feel a little bit of sorrow for Pandora. This wasn't her fault.

"Everything went blurry after that. It's like I was looking through fog at everything and I couldn't do anything about it. Evelyn, tell me what happened to me?" she begs.

"I don't know Pandora. Let's go," I say whilst ushering her down the hallway.

"Do you think you will be okay to drive?" Luke worriedly asks.

"Oh, I will be fine. Besides, I have a party to plan," she smugly answers, tossing her golden locks over her shoulder and putting on her false smile.

We finally reach the car park and Pandora sulks off, without a goodbye, and sits behind the wheel of her pearly white Mercedes Benz, a gift from her doting parents, and rolls the window down.

"I'll see you guys later. Thanks for helping me," she mutters under her breath, before speeding off out of the car park and into the distance.

"That must have been painful for her to say," Luke jokes.

"I was nearly barbecued just then," I announce, making no effort to laugh at Luke's joke.

"I know. What the hell was going on?"

"That wasn't Pandora, but I have no idea who it was." I shrug.

"Well, luckily I was here to save the day," he proudly states.

"I am being serious, Luke. First it was the Grim Reaper and now a fully possessed Pandora."

"Possessed?" he questions.

"Yeah. Like full blown body possession."

"Wow. Is this like that movie I watched where all those ghosts invaded that school and those teachers got possessed and the students had to fight them off but in the end all the kids were sent to, like, limbo or something?" he excitedly yells, getting far too carried away with his story.

"Can we be serious, please?" I shout.

"I thought I was being," says a solemn Luke.

"I'm sorry, Luke," I guiltily reply. "It's not every day you get attacked."

"It's not every day you get attacked twice."

We eventually reach my car and get in. Pulling out of the school, we take the quickest route back to my house, which involves taking the long, always empty, road through the outskirts of the town. After a few moments of silence, Luke starts to question me about Pandora until I brush him off and decide to change the topic. Luke keeps me up to date with all the football news, much to my chagrin, and the conversation soon turns to Ethan.

"He asked me out earlier," I absentmindedly say whilst keeping my eyes firmly fixed on the road.

"What!" Luke yells with enough force to make me flinch and swerve, narrowly missing a squirrel that was happily crossing the road, before he nearly became road kill.

"For God's sake, Luke. Did you want to give me a heart attack?" I yell.

"No! But Ethan asked you out?" he questions me all the while continuing to shout.

"Luke calm down, what's the problem?"

"Nothing," he responds, finally quietening down "I just don't think that you should go out with him."

"And why is that?" I enquire.

"Because he is the football captain. He dates cheerleaders... and you are just... well... you."

Is he being serious? I slam my foot on the brakes causing Luke to lurch forward in his seat, narrowly missing bumping his nose on the windscreen, and turn to give him an evil glare.

"I am just me?" I seethe towards him.

"It's not an insult, I promise, Eve." He panics as he tries to dig his way out of the hole he made.

"I am free to see who I want and when I want okay!" I yell. I feel my temper start to boil and, as if someone gave me a shot of adrenaline, I feel my power start to swell and brew, connecting to the ground beneath my car, causing a small tremor to shake the road. The once straight and tarmacked road now seems to be cracked and crumbling, sending large chunks of rock and stone shooting high into the sky and allowing fissures to spread along the road like the cracks in a glass. The tremor seems to grow, and show no signs of stopping, as my car starts to tilt towards one side, where I have appeared to cause a miniature sinkhole. The deafening sound of rocks cracking and crashing seems to only quieten down when I hear Luke's voice.

"Evelyn, you need to calm down!" he yells, over the crunching sound, the fear in his voice extremely evident.

"I can't!" I scream ,"It's out of my cont—" Before I can finish my sentence, we are violently thrown to one side by a large chunk of rock, causing Luke and I to smack around the inside of the car.

"Not my car!" I scream, only to make the earthquake more violent, it seems.

The tremors seems to grow to the point where a nearby tree uproots itself and comes crashing down, narrowly missing my car, which would have been impaled by the many pointy and heavy wooden branches.

"Evelyn, please!" screams Luke. "You need to focus on my voice!"

I start to inhale and exhale loudly in an attempt to calm myself. I feel my power over the ground subtly start to quell and dissipate, allowing myself to regain a little more control and composure over the situation. With a few more deep breaths, I can feel my hold over the earth completely disappear and all tremors and cracks cease to grow. After a few seconds of silence, which seems like an eternity, I hear Luke's terrified voice pipe up from next to me.

"I am not cleaning that up."

Instead of coming up with a witty or argumentative come back I, instead, start to crack up with laughter.

"What's so funny?" Luke questions my fit of giggles.

"I don't know. I have never, ever, done that before. I have never had that much control over something!" I gleefully announce.

"Please don't do it again," Luke urges.

"I'll try."

"Note to self: do not talk about Ethan to Evelyn," he jokes.

I shrug him off with a simple wave of my hand whilst I try to decide the safest way off the road. Driving forward is out of the picture thanks to a large tree now firmly planted there and reversing seems like it would be a tricky task due to the chunks of rock depositing them on the road like a minefield. I decide to risk it, and shifting my car into reverse, I narrowly start to manoeuvre around the rocks and fissures in the ground until I get to a stretch of road that is unharmed and safe.

"What happened Evie?" asks Luke, a worried look on his face.

"I don't know. It was like I wasn't in control of my powers. They kind of just... grew," I admit.

"Well, that makes a large leap from making your window plant a little bigger," he states.

Once again, I ignore him, while I turn the car around and head back towards the town. After about ten minutes of silent and extremely awkward driving, we finally pull into Luke's driveway. We both climb out of the car, and whilst Luke goes inside to greet his parents, I inspect the damage inflicted by the earthquake. The side of my lime green Beetle is now splattered with thick mud and tarmac and a large dent has grown, thanks to a chunk of rock, causing a hollow to appear in the metalwork, not to mention completely ripping off my wing mirror. I touch the contorted metal and the cold, sharp, steel shocks my body back into reality where an extremely important thought comes to mind.

My parents are going to kill me.

Before I have time to process the horrid image of me being shouted at by my parents I hear Luke calling me in from the doorway. I turn to see his solid form leaning on the doorframe.

"Finished fondling your car?" he cockily asks whilst a toothy smile spreads across his young face.

"Oh, shut up," I joke whilst walking towards his door. Upon the entry to his house, I am greeted with the familiar smell of cinnamon and honey, due to the award winning muffins his mother makes, which instantly soothes me. This house became a second home to me and vice-versa with Luke, because of the amount of time we spend around each other's houses. As if on cue, Luke's mother, Marissa, appeared around the corner carrying a set of her mouth-watering, delicious muffins on a baking tray in her hands. She flashes me a thousand watt smile as she sets the tray on the counter. Marissa is in her late thirties with a short golden bob that perfectly cups her sweet face. Your first thought upon seeing Marissa would be a stay at home mother who does nothing but bake but she is instead a famed, and well sought after, doctor down at the local hospital who randomly decides to bake muffins for some of the people in the ward in her spare time.

"Hello, Evelyn dear," she says, her smooth voice coming across more of a whisper, as she scoops me up in a delicate hug.

"Hi, Marissa," I reply. I used to call her Mrs Morgan but after years of her telling me to call her Marissa, I finally gave in.

"Oh dear, darling, you seem to have ripped your jacket!" she states, almost apologetic. "I am sure I could stitch that up in a matter of minutes."

"I will probably just put it in the bin when I get home. It's old anyway and I didn't like it," I lie.

"If you insist, darling," she whispers as she flashes me one of her *if-you-say-so* smiles.

"I am on my way out now anyway, so you two have fun," she calls as she scoops on her coat and heads out of the house.

"Can we go now?" calls an impatient Luke as he rushes in from the bottom of the stairs and straight into the kitchen where he scoops up a few muffins and heads straight back to his bedroom. After shouting goodbye to Marissa I head to his room with him, shut the door and tentatively listen to make sure I hear Marissa's car pull off the driveway.

"Okay, now that we are alone, can we discuss the elephant in the room?" asks Luke, giving me direct eye contact.

"You mean the state of your bedroom?" I ask. His room is a complete mess. With posters of TV shows and bands that litter the walls and clothes that litter the floor I am amazed he can find his way around. In the far corner of the room there is a large wooden desk, complete

48

with laptop, with a matching wooden chair, which currently has a pair of jeans thrown over it. His large king sized bed takes up most of the space, closely followed by his wardrobe and matching drawers. I sit down, cross-legged, on his bright blue bed and stare intently back at him.

"Sorry," I apologise. "Go on."

"I am talking about how you have been attacked twice today, by two different people, at two different places," he worriedly says.

"I can't help it. I am a danger magnet," I joke.

"Seriously, Evelyn. You are my best friend and you have been attacked and there was nothing I could do about it."

A look of sorrow slaps itself across his face.

"Luke, there is nothing you could have done. Besides you knocked out Pandora!" I tell him, trying to make him smile.

"It's not the same!" he says, slightly raising his voice. "That man could have done anything to you!" he sobs.

"Luke, I can take care of myself," I proudly announce.

Before I can continue trying to calm Luke, I feel a small shaking on my chest.

"I know, bu—"

I rudely cut Luke off with a swift shush as I stick my hand town my top, causing Luke's eyes to bulge and his head to turn away and look at the wall, and fish my pendant out. Luke turns back to face me and we both stare intently at my pendant.

"I promise it just started shaking," I tell him.

We both return to looking at the pendant where it starts to shake a little more forcefully now. It rolls around my extended palm until it shoots into the air and hovers delicately. Luke opens his mouth to say something before the slight sound of a crack silences him. My pendant ceases to hover and falls to the bed with a light thud.

I lean in close and scoop up the cool metal when I feel something is wrong with it. I hold it up close to my face and my eyes widen with shock whilst I leap off the bed and turn away so my back faces Luke and I can get a better view of the pendant in the light.

"Evie. What is it?" he asks, his voice shaking with a mix of apprehension and confusion as he tries to peer over my shoulder and look. I turn around to look Luke straight in his face where I fearfully announce what has me in such shock.

"It's opened."

Chapter 5

Evelyn

"What's opened?" asks Luke, with a perplexed look on his face.

"My pendant," I reply, feeling just as confused.

"Your sealed shut pendant. The one that has been shut, and no matter how many times we have tried to open it, still remained welded in place. That pendant?"

"Yeah, that's the one."

"Sure," he says with a strong essence of disbelief in his voice. "Let me see it then," he replies as he yanks the pendant from my hand and brings it up to his face.

"Any closer to your face and you'll end up eating it," I say sarcastically.

Luke runs his thumb across the silver swirls and, albeit reluctantly, hands it back to me.

"A seal has definitely appeared." He sounds almost a little annoyed at himself for being wrong.

"Thanks for that, Captain Obvious," I cockily reply as I run my own thumb across the new seal.

"So are you going to open it?" whispers Luke. "Like, open it up fully?"

"Stop rushing me!" I yell, as Luke retreats back into his crossed legged position on the bed.

"Sorry," he mumbles.

"No, I am sorry, Luke, I'm just overwhelmed by all this," I whimper.

"You don't need to be," he replies. "I'm here to alleviate your burden." A sweet grin spreads across his face.

"Thank you," I softly say.

I sit back on the bed with Luke, directly in front of him, and roll my pendant in my hand.

"So you're going to open it then?" says Luke, although it comes across more like a fact rather than a question.

I stop rolling my pendant and keep it flat on the palm of my hand, facing upwards, and I place my fingers on the top.

"Here goes then," I state as I try to prise it open.

The cool metal refuses to move.

"Well, open it then," chimes Luke.

"I'm trying!" I gasp whilst putting a little more force into my pull "It's not opening."

"Here, let me try," Luke says as he grabs hold of it and tries to open it, once again with no result.

"Well, it is obviously broken," he groans.

"You aren't going to amount to much with that defeatist attitude, you know, Luke."

After a few more haphazard attempts to open the pendant I too give up.

"Maybe it just cracked instead of opening," I suggest.

"Explain the ghostly floating," Luke asks as he raises his eyebrows and stares at me through his long eyelashes.

"I don't know!" I reply, slightly angered at my incompetence at opening my pendant.

I continue rolling it around in my fingers, completely absent-mindedly, when I feel this slightest bit of movement. I freeze all movement and draw my pendant up to my face.

"Now who's going to eat it?" grumbles Luke.

"Oh shush," I silence him. "I think we tried opening it wrong." I give up trying to prise it open and instead turn the top half in a clockwise position. The metal willingly turns, just like you would expect when you turn the little door on a locket. Once I have turned the top half of the pendant all the way around I see the content of the hollowed inside.

A thin, shiny, single piece of metal.

"A staple?" questions a confused Luke.

"It's too big to be a staple," I reply whilst I prod at the metal, which effortlessly rotates under pressure.

"So it spins?" questions Luke again.

"Oh my God Luke, how could we have been so stupid?" I shout, as Luke looks more confused than ever.

"It's a compass!" I yell, proud at myself for, once again, getting it right.

"Oh!" replies Luke as if he knew all along. "Pointing to what though?"

"That I don't know," I reply as I slouch further down into the bed.

"Well, you know what this means, don't you?" Luke says as he perks up a little bit.

"No," I groan back.

"We are going on a quest," he announces with a huge grin on his face.

We ultimately decide to leave the house and venture to the town centre where the compass-pendant hybrid can work its magic. Luke grabs a handful of biscuits from a tin, which is his idea of preparation, whereas I grab one of his mother's cream coloured jackets, due to the weather taking a turn for the worse, becoming overcast and cloudy.

"It's going to rain," Luke mumbles, his head in the fridge as he forages for food.

"How could you possibly know that? You are too busy scavenging."

He turns around and flashed me one of his 'I-know-everything' looks.

"Right, then. We should really get going," I say as I impatiently tap my foot.

"What are you expecting to find... you know if we follow the compass?"

"I don't know. I mean after everything that has happened; being attacked, twice, must lead to something, even though I have no idea what that something is. But I need to find out why. I am just a normal person Luke and I didn't ask for this, nor did I want any of it, but I'll be dammed if I let it win," I reply, letting my inner warrior come out.

"Whatever you say, Boss. I am behind you one hundred percent!" He smiles and he gestures towards the door.

We open the door and quickly venture outside to see that the 'bad weather' we saw mere minutes ago has been replaced by something much worse. The sky, which was originally a calming pale blue, is now a thick and heavy grey colour, which is covered with dark clouds that not only make the sky look murky and bruised but also stretch as far as the eye can see, suspending Ravens Valley in what appears to be a huge shadow as the clouds prevent any sunlight breaking through, as if they were an impenetrable barrier. The howling wind savages the town and rips around all the trees, which causes them to violently sway and whip through the air, sending large discarded branches rolling down the street and into houses and cars. The once light rain has now become a blustering torrential downpour, which covers the ground in a thin veil of water and sends small, murky, makeshift rivers cascading down the streets. The tempestuous grey sky irregularly flashes a brilliant silver that surrounds the town in a dazzling light, which resonates deep into the eye. The sharp burst of lighting is swiftly followed by a thunderous boom which shakes deep into the ground causing car alarms to go off in the distance. Luke and I pull our hoods over our heads and race out of the comfort of his warm home and into the midst of the violent storm, the rain sticking to us, clinging to our skin, soaking us to the bone.

"Are we still going to the town centre?" Luke yells over the roaring winds.

"Yes, we can go the short way though," I shout back, as we head down the street, following the direction from the compass which has suddenly come to life and is spinning violently.

"I don't get why we couldn't drive," Luke asks.

"Maybe it is because my car was just destroyed in a little random earthquake."

"And whose fault was that?"

"Oh, shut up," I reply as I shove him and we set off running down the street, the crashing sounds of the storm all around us.

"Where the hell did this come from?"

"I have no idea, Luke," I shout due to my face being painfully pelted with raindrops.

"I don't know why I am surprised considering what else has happened today. Magic pendants, possessed teenagers and now random hurricanes. I am starting to think that I should move house," he giggles to himself as we push forward through the heavy rain.

"As soon as we graduate from school we can get out of this mundane hell hole," I mumble.

"Of course we are," he says whilst he flashes a genuine smile in my direction. "So where is your magic necklace leading us?"

"This way." I point as we enter the Town Square.

If there wasn't a hurricane currently surrounding us I would say that the Town Square is extremely beautiful, well as beautiful as you can get in Ravens Valley, and one of my favourite places. The Town Square is literally a square with thick paving stones cutting the bright green grass into four sections, each with a water fountain placed in the centre with accompanying benches. In the centre of the square lives a huge iron statue of a raven with its thick and heavy wings spread wide because, apparently, naming the town Ravens Valley didn't give enough of a clue that this town seems to have a little obsession with their feathered friend.

We start to cross the square when a crackle of thunder booms above us and a slither of lightning rips across the sky.

"Wow!" Luke screams as he throws himself forward and starts to cower under one of the extended wings of the raven statue.

"Scared?" I mock.

"No. I just happen to not like lightning," he retorts.

"So you stand under a metal statue... during a lightning storm." I start to laugh as I see his eyes widen in fear and he speeds out from under the metal bird.

"Can we please just get out of the rain, Evie? I'm freezing and I don't like being wet."

"We can pop into the café on the corner for the time being," I tell him as we start to jog towards our destination.

We enter the well-lit and unsurprisingly warm café to find it full of people, who evidently had the same idea as we did, who are hiding from the blustering winds. We squeeze through the hustle and bustle of people and find a small vacant table in the far corner next to an extremely unhappy looking elderly woman sipping a very strong coffee.

"So now what?" questions Luke as he shakes his wet hair like a dog.

"Wait for the storm to pass, I guess," I retort as I shield my face from his vigorous hair shaking.

"Do you want a drink because I am freezing and I am about to become a human ice cube?" he asks as fishes some coins out of his pockets and dives into the mob of people who are also waiting for their warm drinks.

I absent-mindedly gaze around the room, all the while rolling my pendant between my fingers, when my eyes land on the elderly woman sat next to me.

"Can I help you?" I impatiently ask her.

In return I get a shrug as she turns back to looking into her coffee mug. I quickly reach into my pocket and whip out my phone and stare into the reflective screen in an attempt to sort myself out. I comb my fingers through my curls and straighten my fringe when I see Luke squeeze out from the ever-growing mob, holding two steaming mugs.

"Wow, that queue is long. Here you go," he says and he hands me one of the mugs containing a latte. "I know you like your coffee milky."

"Thanks," I reply as I swallow the strong liquid and allow the warmth to flow through my cold body. "Oh God, that is good."

"I hate to be the bearer of bad news but we literally have no idea what we are going do. I mean we are running around during a storm following a magic pendant in the hopes to find something," Luke glumly says with his head in his hands.

"You don't think I know that, Luke?" I raise my voice as I start to get slightly angry at our situation. "I did not ask for any of this."

"I know you didn't, Evie," he replies as he smiles sincerely.

I go back to observing the people in the room where I see a young woman with light red hair squeeze through the crowd that Luke just ventured in. The only reason she catches my eye is the fact that she may be the only non-blonde in this entire room. Another problem with this town is that there is no cultural diversity. It's like everyone is a clone of one another with the same blonde hair and blue eyes with the extremely rare chance of maybe seeing a dark blonde or a set of brown eyes. This redhead wanders through the crowd, casting intense looks around the room before she halts and waits in the queue to get a drink.

"Have you ever noticed how similar we all are?" I ask Luke.

Yes!" he yells. "I was watching a movie where everyone was actually a clone of one person and he was like the king of this little town and then all the clones turned on him and eventually the cloning machine broke and no more clones could be made," he tells me as if I am the weird one for not knowing about this movie.

"I just meant that there are a lot of blondes in town, Luke."

"Maybe there's a convention?" he answers as he starts to laugh.

"Well, she wouldn't be invited," I say as I point to the direction of the redhead to find that she has disappeared from the crowd.

"Who wouldn't?" he asks as he turns his head and surveys the room.

"There was a redhead over there." I point "She was wandering around."

"Maybe the blondes ran her out of town." He starts to laugh again.

"Maybe." I smile.

"I am just going to go to the toilet, then we can get back on our magical quest," Luke jokes as he leaps out of his seat and bounds to the bathroom.

After a few minutes of me staring into my coffee, continuously stirring it with my spoon, I hear Luke's chair scrape against the floor.

"Ready to get going?" I ask as I lift my head, only to be greeted by a worryingly pale Luke, his eyes wide in a mix of fear and confusion.

"Luke, are you okay?" I fearfully ask.

"The man that attacked you earlier. The one with the suit and creepy face," he coldly replies.

"Yeah, the Grim Reaper. What about him?" I confusedly ask.

"Was he wearing a black suit?"

"Yes."

"Bald?"

"Yes."

"Does he share a shocking resemblance to a dead man?"

"Kind of. He did look a little bit like a corpse. Luke where are you going with this?" I ask, getting slightly annoyed at the sudden influx of questions.

"I think... I think..." He begins to talk as I raise my eyebrows in an attempt to speed him along with his sentence.

"I think that he is standing outside."

Chapter 6

Luke

"What do you mean he is outside?" Evelyn asks.

"I saw him from the bathroom window. He is just standing out on the grass, facing the front of the café," I reply, fearfully.

Evelyn's eyes widen in shock as she leaps out of her chair, sending it flying back into the table of an unsuspecting couple who spill their drinks on themselves, and starts walking towards the glass window.

"Evie, wait!" I yell, after I quickly apologise to the couple. I jump out of my seat and jet off after her. She reaches the window and presses her palms flat against it and leans so close her breath starts to condense on the glass. The heavy rain smacks against the window, which completely blurs out and chance of seeing outside.

"Right, I am going out then," she says whilst turning to face the door and extending her arm to open it. Before she has chance to grab the door handle, I quickly grasp her wrist and pull it away from the door.

"So what are you going to do?" I enquire "You going to go and confront the man who viciously attacked you earlier?"

"Yes," she bluntly replies.

"Well, okay then."

"Good." She pulls her arm free of my grip.

"But..." I stop her again before she leaves the café, "I am coming with you."

"Luke, you should stay here and wait for me until I come back."

"Excuse me?" I scoff at her.

"Well, what if he gets violent?" she retorts.

"Like he hasn't already," I smugly reply. Try thinking of a reply to that.

"Well, I need to stop him."

"I don't care. I am not going to stand around and wait in here sipping coffee and making idle conversation while my best friends goes and plays with the Grim Reaper. I am not as useless as you think," I exclaim, all the while getting angrier at the lack of belief my friend has in me.

"It's not that I that I think you are useless!"

"Then let me help you!"

"Luke, if you got hurt I could never forgive myself."

"I am not as fragile as you think, Evie," I confidently reply.

"Can you do this?" she asks as she directs her gaze towards the ornamental potted plant on the counter-top near the till. The plant starts to tremble slightly before a small pop causes a mass of soil to be expelled everywhere, covering the shocked people in the queue with bits of dirt. A young teenager, who is furiously pushing buttons on the till and trying to deal with the angry customers in the queue, starts profusely apologising.

"You don't need to show off Evie, I know full well what you are capable of."

"I am not showing off. I am trying to show you that I can take care of myself," she defiantly replies.

"You may be able to move little plants, Evie, but I can do this," I say, and before she can do anything else, I quickly open the front door and head out into the rain to face the Grim Reaper.

"What the hell are you doing?" I hear Evie scream behind me.

"Using my initiative," I call back.

Evie yells something behind me but her words are drowned out by a boom of thunder and the heavy splashing of rain on the ground. The heavy rain still pours down the street, flooding the sewers, and sloshing over the curb.

I scan the area to see where the Grim Reaper is standing, when my eyes catch a quick blur of red dive behind a nearby building. I start to jog towards the blur, the grass squelching beneath my feet, when I hear Evie urgently scream my name. I turn on the spot only to see the Grim Reaper standing mere inches in front of me. I can see, out of the corner of my eye, Evie racing towards us.

"Who the hell are you?" I ask.

His cold, grey eyes narrow, as he looks me up and down. His pale and chapped lips crack in the corners and a disgustingly sinister smile is plastered on his whitewashed face.

"I said—" Before I can finish my sentence, the Grim Reaper shoves me away with a simple flick of his wrist. My body flies a few metres through the air as if being pulled by an invisible cord only to hit the wet ground with a squelch. I slide along the slippery ground until finally coming to a stop.

"Luke!" screams Evie as she finally catches up to me. She crouches down and frantically runs her hands all over my body.

"Are you okay?" she worriedly asks.

"He knocked the wind out of me, that's all. Evie, get out of here," I gasp.

Evie stands and turns to face the Grim Reaper. He just stands solemnly staring at her.

"Get out of here. I will hurt you," she bravely announces.

"Evie, please," I cough.

Evelyn takes a step forward towards Grim and calmly asks him again.

"Leave."

Obviously ignoring her, he starts to walk toward us but, before he travels any real distance, Evie raises her right hand and then clenches her fist. At first nothing happened, both me and Grim staring intently at her waiting for something to happen. Her arm starts to tremble and her eyelids clamp shut.

Still nothing.

"Evie... shouldn't something be happening?" I whisper from behind her. I slowly rise from the ground and stumble over to Evelyn's shaking body, the rain still falling down heavily. I clasp my hands on either side of her face in an attempt to help pull her back to reality.

"Evie!" I yell.

Her eyes shoot open and her hand falls down to her side before she lets out a single sigh. Her already pale face has taken on a sickly white hue and her eyes have become bloodshot.

"Evie, what were you trying to do?" I question.

"That," she replies.

I look over to the Grim reaper to see that he has dropped at least a foot in height. The slightly squelchy ground has completely liquefied and turned into what seems to be makeshift quicksand. The strands of grass surrounding the mud have grown in length, weaving around his waist and wrists creating tightly woven cuffs that chain his hands to the floor.

"You can create an earthquake no problem but making some mud nearly gives you an aneurysm?" I joke.

"Yeah, well, I was extremely angry then."

"And you aren't now?"

"Stay on task, Luke."

"Oh, right," I reply as I turn to face Grim, who is politely waiting in the mud, staring at us silently. The rain continues to pour down, luckily obscuring us from any prying eyes that may be peering from shop windows.

"Maybe if we put some fertiliser on him he could grow into a sunflower?" I suggest.

Evie just glares at me.

"Sorry."

Grim slightly turns his head to the right, as if he has trouble understanding what we are saying. I squat down and look straight into his cold, dead eyes.

"Do you speak English?" I ask.

Nothing.

"Parlez-vous Anglais? Sprechen Sie English?" I ask again.

"I don't think he speaks English, Luke. Let alone French or German," Evie comments.

"Well, that's good as they are the only foreign words I can say. Well, that and 'un petit canard achète une toilette'," I proudly announce, using clear diction and showing off my vast array of French vocabulary.

"A small duck buys a toilet?" asks Evie, giving me one of her looks.

"I thought I was ordering a hamburger," I reply, furrowing my brow in confusion.

"No."

"Well, that explains all those funny looks I got on that trip to France last year."

"We have a maniac half buried in the mud, this town is moments away from flooding and you want to stand around and talk about ducks that need to purchase toilets?" she yells.

"You're right. I'm sorry," I apologise.

"No, you don't need to apologise to me. I'm just a little worked up," she says, looking down at her feet.

"Okay, then," I announce, putting my thinking cap on, raring to go, "We should make a run for it now. It's pouring down with rain and we are both soaked to the bone. Let's go back to mine before we freeze to death."

As if on cue, an icy wind howls across the green, sending shivers down my body and blowing Evelyn's hair around her.

"And what about him?" she says pointing to the half-submerged man in the floor.

"Well let's just leave him. I'm pretty sure that he can wiggle out of the floor after we get a head start. I'd rather not be here when he gets out."

"Fine." She turns on the spot. "But we better get running."

Before I have a chance to turn and run a deep tugging feeling, like a rope around my stomach, prevents me from going anywhere.

"What if he comes back?" I croak.

"What?"

"What if he comes back again and you are on your own? What if he comes back and takes me out of the picture?" I ask, paranoid.

"Luke, if he comes back, I will be ready."

"And if you aren't?"

"What's with the lack of trust here, Luke? I told you that I will protect you!"

"That's a bit rich coming from you. You were more than happy to go in all guns blazing a moment ago. Just remember that I don't need protecting! I am not the one he is after!" I shout, my temper getting the better of me.

"Then I will take him down." She stares into my eyes. Hers are full of determination whereas mine are purely worry for my friend.

As Evelyn opens her mouth to come back with a follow-up point she is lifted into the air and thrown back down a few metres away. She tries to grab on to anything but the force just slides her along the floor.

"Evie!" I shout before I run towards her to help.

Before I can reach her, she is lifted high into the air again and hovers there for a moment.

"Let her go," I say as I spin to face the Grim Reaper who is now no longer buried in the floor but instead standing a few metres away. Covered in mud. Looking very angry. A sick smile appears on his face and he clicks his fingers, causing Evelyn to fall from the height. Her flailing body plummets to the ground and lands with a very discomforting thud. I sprint over to her to see if she is okay only to see some blood trickling from her nose. She staggers to stand up and wipes the blood away with her sleeve.

"Evie, stay still!" I frantically say as I catch up to her.

"Luke, get back," she whispers.

Her usual blue eyes have been replaced with a dark hue and she no longer appears to be as helpless as she was a moment ago. Her body radiates intense power.

"How do you like it?" she asks, looking straight past me and into the Grim Reaper.

He doesn't even have time to say a word before the long blades of grass weave their way up his body and firmly wrap around his neck. He is violently pulled to the squelching ground and the grass blades drag him backwards across the filthy floor. She is literally wiping the floor with him.

"Evie!" I bellow as I try to break her concentration and see if she is okay.

"Get back," she motionlessly replies.

"Evie, please, we need to go," I plead.

She clenches her fists and raises her arms up slowly as the grass mimics her movements. The blades slash quickly towards the Grim Reaper. They whip and tear at his skin yet I cannot see a single drop of blood, instead what seems to be some sort of sand pours from the wounds. "Evie, it isn't working. We need to go," I beg.

She manages to snap out of her vindictive rage long enough to make eye contact with me.

"Stop," I order her.

Her hands fall down to her side and she huffs with regret.

"What the hell was that?" I question her, surprised at the attitude change.

"I don't know. It was like I wasn't in control any more. My powers sort of just took control and led the way."

Again she looked into my eyes. I remained silent as I stared passively back at her.

"We can't just leave him. He could hurt someone," she says.

"You aren't a killer."

"I'm pretty sure he isn't human."

"Don't do this."

She doesn't answer me. Instead, she tightens the grass on Grim Reaper's neck, causing his eyes to bulge, and he starts clawing at the makeshift noose.

"Evelyn!"

"He needs to be stopped." She doesn't even sound like my best friend any more.

"Not by you!" I shout.

"By who then?"

"Me," announces a female's voice from behind us. Both of us snap around in surprise.

Standing in the pouring rain is the girl from earlier. The redhead.

Chapter 7

Luke

This girl is hot. Like really hot.

Despite the heavy rain, I can still see her beautiful features. Long red hair frames her heart-shaped face and falls down elegantly across her shoulders and down her back. Her piercing blue eyes have orange flecks that dance across them, making them look like rust, and her slightly red, parted lips show perfectly white teeth. The only mar on her alabaster skin is a light scar on the top of her lip and she even makes this look hot. She looks like a supermodel. Even though we are standing in the middle of rainstorm, she looks just like she just stepped off the page of one of those girly magazines that Evelyn reads.

"She's smoking," Evelyn mumbles.

"I am so glad that you agree," I splutter.

"No, Luke, she is literally smoking."

Small wisps of smoke twirl off her statuesque body and dissipate in the cold air, just like when you pour cold water into a hot pan, and her hair shows no sign of being wet, nor do her clothes, as she stands facing us.

"Who are you?" asks Evie.

"My name is Jessica," she says, the words rolling off her tongue just like silk.

"You shouldn't be here. It's not safe," Evie warns.

"Don't go yet, though," I whisper almost pleadingly.

"I'm here to help you. I need to talk to you," Jessica states.

"I don't need your help," Evie growls.

"Are you sure about that?" She points in the direction of the Grim Reaper who has broken free from his ties and is crawling towards us. He is just like the zombies in that film I watched recently.

"Luke, get back!" Evie shouts as she raises her arms to defend us but I can see that she still isn't strong enough to fight.

"I've got this," announces Jessica as she pushes her way through Evie and I and faces the now fully standing Grim Reaper.

She raises her right hand and the wisps of smoke become thicker and heavier as they move around her pale skin. The air around her hand starts to wave from heat before a red flame appears and dances along her palm. The flame grows until it's the same size of a football. She hurls the flame at the Grim Reaper who recoils in horror and hisses in retreat.

"What the hell are you?" shouts Evie.

"That's rich coming from you. Didn't you just bury that man?" smirks Jessica. This woman just radiates power and authority.

The Grim Reaper seems to stare us all down before slowly edging back towards the edge of the grassy field. He turns around and seemingly disappears into the heavy rain that still pours from the sky.

"We need to talk," says Jessica.

"Yeah, we do. I want answers!" Evie yells, running a hand through her dripping hair.

"In time I promise. Do you have somewhere we can go?"

"Back to mine," I say. I'm just happy to get out of the rain.

"Let's go then."

Evie starts walking whilst I struggle to tear my eyes from the astounding beauty who is literally the hottest thing I have ever seen.

⚘

We enter my house and shake the rain from our sodden bodies. Well Evelyn and I do; the redhead just stands there looking as dry as a summer day.

"Are you going to tell me what is going on now then?" Evelyn crosses her arms and eyes up Jessica, who similarly matches her gaze. Both girls look like they are taking part in a staring contest and there can only be one winner. I have no idea why they seem to have so much resentment for each other because they only just met.

"Well, I am just going to make some cocoa because I am about to freeze to death," I announce as I back off towards the kitchen. I'm just afraid the house is about to be either flattened or burnt down. I set to making the cocoa whilst Evelyn rings her hair out on a nearby towel and Jessica paces around the adjoining sitting room.

"Dammit, I think the storm has blown the fuse, the electricity is down," I glumly announce as I struggle to get the kettle to work.

"Let me help," says Jessica as she strides over towards me. She pours the instant cocoa powder into the mug and fills it up with cold water from the tap. She wraps both of her hands around the mug and focuses.

"Are you going to break my favourite mug?" I stare in anticipation.

"Don't worry!" she laughs as the water starts to boil and steam fills the air. Her hands seem to emit the slightest of orange glows and the air buzzes with heat and warmth.

"All done," she smiles as she places the boiling mug of cocoa in front of me.

"You know that I am freezing too, right? You could hold my—"

"Luke!" Evie shouts and cuts me off.

"Hands, Evie. She could hold my hands." I raise my arms defensively towards Evelyn so she doesn't crush me.

"Don't sweat it. You're cute." Jessica looks me in the eyes and gives me a half smile.

Evelyn scoffs in the corner and drags me to the couch in the sitting room. We plump our damp bodies on the seats and Jessica follows us over and takes a seat in my dad's armchair. Evelyn sits with a stern look plastered on her face whereas I, on the other hand, am still blushing from the *cute* comment that Jessica just made.

"Do you want to tell me what is happening?" Evie asks.

"Have you ever wondered why you can do what you can do?" Jessica shifts in her seat. "How you can control the earth or how connected you feel to nature?"

"Of course I have. I just never knew why." Evie looks down as if she is ashamed.

"You are special. You are a part of something much bigger."

"The government?" I ask as I take a sip from my cocoa.

"No, not the government." Evie swats my hand.

"The forces of nature themselves. You are one of the chosen few who are destined to save the lives of billions," Jessica announces like she has done this a hundred times before. Save the world, I mean.

"Can you cut the storytelling and get to the point?" Evie shouts. I can tell she is getting irate because her palms are twitching and her bottom lip is sticking out just like a child who isn't getting what they want.

"You are a Guardian."

"Excuse me?" Evie leans in as if she must have misheard Jessica.

"A Guardian... you guard things," I try to explain although I am trying to gasp the job title myself.

"Not exactly, but you aren't far off." Jessica once again shifts in her seat and is now leaning towards us as if she is going to tell us a secret.

"We are very special people, Evelyn. We were chosen millennia ago to protect the world from the evil it doesn't even know of. That's why we have gifts." With that statement, Jessica flings her arm in the direction of my fireplace, causing a mighty blue flame to erupt from underneath the logs, and causing both myself and Evie to flinch away from the jet of fire, which eventually dwindles to a calm flame that fills the room up with a welcomed warmth.

"You don't need to show off. We can all do something special," Evie scolds. I do detect a hint of jealousy though.

"I'm not showing off. I am trying to prove that I am like you. I may even be the only person, in the entire world, who fully understands what you are going through right now. I had no one to help me when I first got my abilities and I was so scared and so alone. I would have killed for someone to stay with me and tell me that everything will be okay and to not panic." Jessica's voice starts to tremble as if she is calling upon a bad memory.

"The only person?" Evie asks as if that is the only piece of information she got from that conversation.

"Actually, that's a lie. There is someone else but you will meet *her* soon." She smiles elusively.

"There are more people like us?" Evie stands up "Where the hell have they been?"

"I said you will meet her soon. But there are only four of us."

"Were there more?" I ask.

"Once." Jessica's voice cracks when she whispers the word.

"What happened to them?" I push further.

"They died. Not all at the same time though. The Guardians stretch back through history."

"And now they are all dead. What happened?" Evie seems to be facing away from us as if she cannot bear to listen to our conversation.

"Most died from old age. Some died in other ways." Jessica's voice falters and I swear tears are forming in her eyes.

"I want to know more," Evie's voice pitches in from the corner.

She moves from the corner and stands in front of the fire. Her body becomes a silhouette and she casts a shadow over me. I suddenly feel very small and very powerless.

"There are some things that even I cannot explain. You need to wait to ask more questions if you want better answers."

"Why?" Evie scoffs "You are here so you can tell me."

"It's not my place," Jessica rebuffs her.

"Then whose is it?" Evie shouts. I jump at this sudden flare in temper.

"Calm down," I say as I gesture for her to sit down.

"I don't want to, Luke. I want to know what the hell is going on and no one is telling me. I found out today that there are more people like me and I am not alone, yet I am beginning to feel lonelier than ever."

"You have me!" I stand up to meet her eyes.

"You aren't alone, Evelyn," Jessica chimes up from her seat.

"Why can't you tell me what is going on?" Evelyn makes eye contact with Jessica who reclines in her seat.

"Because it is not my place. The spirits will show you."

A cold chill rolls down my back.

"The spirits. Are they here now?" I whisper as I look around in fear.

"They aren't poltergeists, Luke. They just give us guidance." Jessica smiles at Luke's sudden paranoia.

"Spirits?" Evie questions, almost struggling to believe what she just heard. "Oh my God, there are spirits now?"

"There always have been. Have you ever thought that just because you cannot see it, it doesn't mean that it isn't there? The spirits have always been here since the dawn of time and—"

"Stop!" Evie screams. She raises her hands to her head and slowly rubs her temple, as if the challenge of processing all of this information if physically painful and exhausting.

A heavy silence fills the space in the sitting room. The wind howls outside and the shutters rattle. Evie lifts her head, the fire casting a menacing glow across her face, and squares off with Jessica.

"I do not know who you are but you are mistaken if you think that you can come in here and start spouting off about ghosts and Guardians and you expect me to listen to it!" The authority pours from Evelyn's rosy lips.

"Actually, I think it was spirits and not ghosts," I mumble and Evie gives me a death stare. "Sorry," I mumble.

"I'm not expecting you to believe me. I just want you to open your mind to the possibility that there are greater things out there that are too big to even comprehend," Jessica states.

"I'm sorry, Luke, but do we even know that we can trust this girl. We just let her into your house and we don't know anything about her, apart from that she believes in ghosts and can toast a marshmallow without the campfire," Evie sarcastically questions.

"Spirits," Jessica mumbles under her breath.

"She saved us, Evelyn."

"I don't want to be a part of this bigger mystery okay Luke. I am struggling to fit in at school as it is and I certainly do not want to be any more different!" she fearfully says, "I just want to be normal!"

"You have no choice," pipes up Jessica.

"Excuse me!"

"Whoa, Evie, calm down. We don't want another accident like earlier," I warn.

"What happened?" questions Jessica.

"Evie got a little bit upset and caused an earthquake."

"Where?" enquires Jessica.

"On the road over near the school," I state.

"We need to go back," Jessica says as she jumps up from her seat and heads for the door.

74

"Wait a second. Why?" Evie asks in confusion.

"Because in moments of great stress we can amplify our powers. And somewhere that you unleashed a large amount of your energy then you can tap into it"

"Why would I want to do that?" Evie questions.

"I thought you wanted to chat to the spirits," Jessica coyly answers.

"Well, my car is kind of out of commission at the moment." Evie blushes.

"Well, then we can take mine," Jessica shouts as she exits my house.

We get out of Jessica's small red car, after an extremely awkward and silent journey, and stand at the end of the road that was destroyed a few hours ago. The rain has dwindled to a light patter and the gale force wind has instead become a heavy breeze.

"So what do I have to do?" Evie questions as she strides over the tree that she ripped out earlier.

"Sit down and close your eyes," Jessica instructs Evie as she pushes her down on the fallen tree,

"Now what?" I ask as Evie closes her eyes.

"Silence, please, Luke," Jessica scolds me.

I bite my lips as Evie tries to stifle a smile. She has always found it funny when I get told off, probably because she just assumes it is her right to tell me off and no one else's.

"Now breathe, Evelyn. Focus on the earth around us. Feel the energy that you released earlier. Channel that energy through you and feel yourself being carried off. Let the warmth lift you."

I look around half expecting Evie to float off, or at least the ground to crack, but she just stays firmly planted in her seat. I wait a few more seconds before her face starts to crease in confusion.

"Is she okay?" I worriedly ask Jessica.

"She will be. Just let her disappear."

"What does that mean?"

I don't even need an answer from Jessica because Evelyn's eyes whip open and startlingly show that her normal crystal blue eyes have gone and have instead glazed over with a thick black mist. She continues to stare into the distance, like she is looking at something that isn't there. Her white skin starts to become transparent, allowing me to see the road behind her, due to her now ghost-like appearance.

"Where the hell is she going?" I shout in fear that my friend is about to disappear forever.

"She's meeting the spirits."

Chapter 8

Evelyn

No way.

I'm in the forest. The exact same forest as the one that I dream about every night. I can feel the cool mist sweep across my face, the wind caress my hair, and the leaves crunch underneath my feet. A few moments ago, I had my eyes closed sitting on a tree and now I'm in the middle of God-knows-where.

"Hello?" I call into the vast expanse of trees and mist. The cool wind whistles around the trees pulling leaves from the ground twirling them around my body. There seems to be no end to this forest, instead the trees roll on for miles with only the thick mist to stop them disappearing into oblivion. I reach out to touch a nearby floating leaf but my hand harmlessly passes through it. I quickly recoil my hand, clutching it to my chest, in a mixture of fear and confusion.

"Jessica!" I yell, hoping that she came along for the ride with me. I continue to walk through the forest aimlessly, and despite me not being able to touch anything, the leaves continue to crunch beneath me and rustle around my ankles.

"She isn't here," a calming voice calls from behind me. I jump from the sudden shock of this voice echoing through the silence, I quickly turn and stare at the person who spoke.

A woman, around her forties, stands looking peacefully at me. Her calm face shows the faintest of smiles and her long brown hair plummets down her sleek body and pools on the floor around her. Her piercing grey eyes stare directly through my body and into my soul, and she's dressed in a floor length blue gown that's decorated with millions of diamonds, that glitter like drops of rain in the moonlight. This woman is ethereally beautiful.

"Who are you?" I croak, my voice trembling.

"Gwendolyn," she responds.

Her voice echoes through the forest making the wind pick up and send a flurry of leaves in our direction. This time the leaves make full contact with me and I brush off the ones that desperately cling to me.

"What is going on?" I ask.

"It's about time you learn the truth, child." She slowly moves towards me. "You must have so many questions."

"No, not many," I sarcastically comment. Gwendolyn speaks with a calm, English accent, making her soothing words come across even smoother.

"Well, allow me to answer the ones that you have." She holds her hand out towards me and I fearfully place my hand into her open palm. "You have a right to know what your destiny is."

We walk in silence for a few moments along a footpath that leads towards two smooth stumps in the middle of a leaf filled clearing. We each take a seat, with Gwendolyn sitting with a sense of royalty about her, and I lean in, eager to learn more, waiting for her to tell me what's going on.

"There are things in this world that exist without your knowledge, only choosing to make their presence known when needed, and living alongside us for years. The image you see in the corner of your eye or the monster that you think is under your bed. They are very real and they live amongst us."

"The bogeyman is real?" I raise my eyebrows in confusion.

"He is not known by that name, but yes, my child. However, there are many things in this world that are much more dangerous." She closes her eyes as if to recall a memory. "Millennia ago, there was an evil like never seen before. He slept for years under the earth until the presence of man awoke him. He was set free to pillage villages and incite wars amongst mankind. This man fed upon the evil, anger, hatred and suffering of the world. This demon had a name."

"The Grim Reaper?" I question, referring to the man who had tried to kill me at least twice already.

"No, not the creature that you have so aptly named. This specific demon was called *Avarice*."

"I know that name." I struggle to remember where I have heard it before but the word pulls at the back of my brain like a bad memory that you cannot forget.

"The word *greed* is based upon his name."

"That's where I remember it from." It suddenly twigs inside of my head where I recall the name. "It's one of the seven deadly sins."

"And the most powerful, I may add," she calmly says, but a serious sense of urgency is threaded within her words, "this particular sin is the strongest because it's what empowered humanity to strive and this is what he grew from. You think the many accomplishments in the modern world were achieved through genuine need? Humanity is driven by greed. You have to be the first people to do something or own something and this allowed Avarice to stay in slumber but get stronger as time passed on." Her voice starts to shake.

"What happened to him? How did he wake up?"

"Avarice wanted supreme control over all domains and the mystical powers that fuelled the earth. He travelled the globe, gaining power and murdering all those who stepped in his way."

"He sounds like a lovely man," I scoff.

"He stumbled upon a town hundreds of years ago. The small town of *Corvos Vallis* was laid to waste under his feet. He created monsters that killed the innocent and any who defied him he destroyed with a single glance. Fires tore through the town, cottages crumbled under his presence, rainstorms flooded the area. However, this town was the home of a very powerful oracle."

"An oracle?" I try not to sound too sceptical.

"Indeed. Avarice found out that this woman could foretell the future and he learnt that there was a prophecy."

"This story just gets more ridiculous as it goes on." I roll my eyes.

"Your scepticism only proves your inability to accept that you are destined for more," she scolds, sounding just like my mother when I have done something wrong.

"I'm just struggling to get my head around it, that's all. Please go on."

"The prophecy foretold that four women would accept their birth right of being the guardians and defenders of humanity against Avarice. The oracle tapped into the mystical arts and endowed each woman with mastery over one natural element; Earth, Water, Air and Fire"

"That's why Jessica called me a Guardian earlier."

Gwendolyn just ignores me and continues with her story.

"The four women faced off against Avarice in a vicious battle. They barely managed to defeat him. They each paid a terrible cost but they managed to scatter his essence into the abyss through the combination of their individual powers and mystical energies. His physical body remains cursed by the oracle to stay stagnant for the rest of time, trapped in a coffin deep underground. These women made a deal with the oracle to become the Guardians of the Abyss, named after their magnificent battle against Avarice and thus a new prophecy was created."

"More prophecies?"

"Well, this one includes you so you should listen...

'If Avarice be free once more,
May power be given to female four.

From land and sea and air and fire,
May they defeat the creature of desire.
These powered women shall flourish and rise,
To stop the demon that kills and lies.
From across the land they shall unite,
To end the evil's eternal night'"

There's a moment of silence as I try to process what she just told me.

"So I am one of the female four?" I whisper.

"It is your birth right."

"Do I have a choice in it?"

"To put it politely, no."

"Great."

"Throughout time Avarice managed to gather enough strength to escape from the Abyss, feeding on the greed from the world that once banished him, and allowed his spirit to search for his physical body. He still isn't strong enough to reclaim his solid form and instead must take over the body of a corruptible victim. He cannot sway those with a pure heart."

"He takes over the body? He must be in control of the Grim Reaper." I smile, though there is no joke, as I've just made my first link between this ancient fairy tale and my current situation.

"That is the truth. He currently inhabits the body of your so-called Reaper. I believe that he has possessed a couple of people now in order to attack you"

"So what does this have to do with me?" I question as I struggle to come up with the exact reason he would attack me. I hadn't even heard of him then.

"Every time the powers of the elements within four females are evoked, they unite and must defeat Avarice. You aren't the first set of

Guardians tasked with defeating him. Whenever he wakes up, the powers within four women blossom in order to fight him."

"So he did this to me? He gave me these powers?"

"No. Those powers were your destiny. Their purpose is for you to defend the very earth that you control."

"You said that we would unite. How are we meant to do that? Today is the first day that I met Jessica and I had already been attacked earlier on. Where were my magical sisters, then?"

"How do you think that Jessica found you?"

"Well, I doubt that she used the internet." I should really dial down my sarcasm before this lady unleashes some magical juju on me.

"When Avarice was first defeated by the Guardians, they each took a piece of metal from the coffin that his physical body was placed in. His body was enclosed in a tomb beneath the earth and the metal was crafted into four devices that would allow the Guardians to find each other throughout time."

"Oh my God…" My hand reaches up to my chest and firmly grasps my pendant.

"Indeed."

"My pendant is over a thousand years old?"

"It draws on the mystical energies that give you your powers and will always allow you to find your sisters."

"It was pointing towards Jessica! It opened earlier on and led me and Luke to the town square. I just thought Grim Reaper must have been doing it."

"Your sisters each have one. That is how Jessica found you and came to your aid," she explains.

"How did I get this? I don't remember being given it and I doubt this is something my parents would just allow me to have as a baby?"

"When the previous Guardian dies that pendant is taken into the earth and it rests here, in the Spirit world, until its presence is needed again. The pendant came to you when you were aged ten. It came to rest upon your body and the energies allowed for it to harmlessly integrate itself into your life, until the day it is needed, where it will act as a compass to guide you to your sisters."

"I have a camouflage pendant that gives me fake memories?" I raise my eyebrows in confusion.

"In essence, yes."

"This is all a little farfetched." I roll my eyes in disbelief.

"Believe what you may. But after all that you have endured, you should really open your mind."

"This is all a little bit too much story book for me, that's all. I'm just struggling to believe in all this ancient evil and things. Maybe Grim Reaper is just some crazy man who attacked me and I'm just in some horrifically bad dream right now." The words flow out of my mouth as if I am almost praying for it to be even a little true.

"How about I prove it?" she smirks. She raises her hands and the thick mist that surrounds us starts to filter away, as if someone just turned on a massive fan, and only drops of water remain hovering in the air. They dance and twirl in the light reflecting millions of little beams across the floor like a kaleidoscope. Gwendolyn clenches her hands and the raindrops gather together into one larger ball that she smooths out to make a large disc like shape. She waves her hand across the disc and the water spins viciously. A faint image appears in the middle that eventually becomes clearer. I crane my neck to see the image in full clarity.

The image shows a blonde child sitting in the middle of a grass-filled field playing with the long blades that intertwine with her fingers. She's wearing a little pink dress and her hair is pulled into tight pigtails that frame her little round face. She pulls the grass out in chunks but the blades never seem to disappear; only further wrapping around her little fingers. I look further into the murky image with a sense of familiarity.

The little girl sets off running back towards two figures in the distance as the grass becomes denser around her, the long stems of the nearby flowers growing in height and the whiter petals bloom to their full potential, yet she seems unaware of what's happening around her.

The image fades and the water disc crashes to the floor in a splash.

"Now do you see?" Gwendolyn breaks the silence.

"Who was that girl?" I ask in intrepid confusion.

"You have always had potential for greatness, my child." Her soothing words almost quell my fears.

"That was me," I state, "How did you do that?"

"The spirits have always been watching over you, my child. Every previous Guardian resides in this world and keeps a close eye on future generations. And now you need to return back to your friends. You have many more challenges that you need to conquer and heart-breaking dilemmas you need to face."

"I don't know if I can do this. I'm not strong enough." I weep, the tears slowly brewing in the corner of my eyes. I have no idea why I am crying yet all my emotions are just bubbling to the surface.

"Yes, you can, my child. After all, I never thought I could, and look at me now." She raises her hands as if to show off her beautiful frame but the water on the floor seems to follow the path of her gesture, lifting and hovering in the air as if frozen in time, "I am proud to call myself a previous water spirit of the Guardians."

The water moves towards me and rapidly swirls around my body, my vision becomes blurred through the torrent of water as I am cocooned within her makeshift waterfall. I desperately try to reach out for Gwendolyn but she is nowhere to be seen. I gasp, half expecting to be drowning, but find that I can effortlessly breathe.

Her voice calls out from the watery abyss.

"You need to find his body, child. He must never regain his true form."

"Where is it?" I yell, though the sound of my voice is drowned out by the crashing of the waves.

"*Corvos Vallis* is the ancient name for Ravens Valley. His body is…"

Her ethereal voice is cut off as a jet of freezing cold water is thrown against my face and I am physically ripped from this dreamlike world, the faint image of a woman fading into the blackness as I tumble back into reality.

Chapter 9

Jessica

I wonder which spirit she is meeting.

I stare at Evelyn's transparent body perched on the tree, staring vacantly into the distance with mist-filled eyes, and I recall the time I had my meeting with the spirits.

"I was only fourteen when my destiny was revealed to me," I whisper, although I only meant to think this and not say it out loud.

"What?" Luke calls out from behind me.

"Nothing. I just remember when this happened to me. I was only fourteen."

"What happened to you?" he asks.

"Pretty much the same as what's happening to her." I gesture to Evelyn. "I looked like that. I just didn't have anyone with me at the time."

"You said you had to go back to a place of magical energy or something."

"*Great place of mystical energy.* It means where I released a lot of my elemental magic." I turn away to avoid eye contact with him.

"We are sat here because Evelyn caused an earthquake here. What did you do?"

I really wish he would stop asking questions.

"Isn't it obvious?" I vaguely answer.

"Well, you can make fireballs," he jokes.

I laugh at his naivety. I'm glad she has someone like him in her life. She will need him to keep her grounded with the things that are going to happen. I turn to see him staring me down; apparently, he really wants to know what happened.

"Fine." I raise my hands in defeat. "When I was younger, and when my parents weren't at home, I was sitting downstairs. I was watching the television like every other night when something just changed. The fireplace started to crackle more than usual so I got up to extinguish it. As I reached out to put out the flames my arm caught alight."

Luke's eyes widen in horror as he registers what I just told him. He eagerly moves in towards me to learn more of the story.

"I panicked obviously. I started flailing my arms around and all I kept thinking was *stop, drop, and roll* but no matter what I did, the flames wouldn't go away. But the weird thing was that—"

"The flames were magic," Luke interrupts.

"No, Luke. They were just your regular flames. They just didn't burn me. They harmlessly just stayed on my skin." I decide to put on a little show for Luke and ignite my arm. I flick my hand forwards and thick orange flames dance along my skin, licking my arms as they travel up to my shoulders. Luke's eyes open wider than humanly possible as he debates stepping back or leaning in further. I let the flames caress my body and they move around my arms until I will them to extinguish themselves. They dwindle into small flickers before disappearing altogether in a puff of smoke.

"That is so amazing!" he laughs.

"Your best friend can move the earth. You would think that you are used to this by now."

"Never met a girl that can cook marshmallows without the bonfire!" He quotes Evelyn from earlier today. These two are extremely alike.

"That's a very inventive way of putting it," I laugh.

"I am a very inventive person. So what happened after you caught alight?"

"Well, I stopped panicking and just stared. I realised that I was fireproof and I just watched as the flames flickered on my hand. Sadly, although I was fireproof, my house was not and the furniture soon caught alight. The house went up in a matter of seconds." I look anywhere but Luke's face. I just want to avoid the looks he may give me.

"It wasn't your fault, Jess."

Okay, I really do not like being called Jess.

"People died, Luke. The fire didn't stop at my house. It spread along my street and turned into one of the biggest blazes that my hometown had ever seen."

"All that just because your arm caught alight." Luke raises his brows. He looks just like Evelyn when she does that, and I continue my story.

"I was so afraid when my house went up in flames that I tried to escape. I ran to my door but the fire blocked my way out. The roof creaked and started to collapse and I raised my arms to protect myself. Instead, when I lifted them jets of fire erupted from me. The force of them alone threw all the burning furniture away like a miniature explosion. Then the gas caught alight."

I let Luke fill in the blanks of what happened next.

"Everything blew up," he comments.

"Yes. I emerged from a burnt house without a single scratch to loads of people just staring at me. Fire fighters had risked their lives trying to save me, my parents were on the floor sobbing, and everyone thought that I had lost my life. But I was unharmed and four other people lost their lives instead." I blink away a tear in my eye.

"What happened after that? How did you become all ghostly?" He gestures to Evelyn.

"I went back a week later with the police to sort through the wreckage. As soon as I stepped through what used to be my door I felt the sudden surge of power. It hit me like a wave of pure energy and it threw me to the floor. I tapped into the mystical energies that gave me my powers and I slipped into the spirit world. The police just thought I was having a seizure or something. No one tried to touch me though, I think they just assumed that I had made some of the smoke rise from under the rubble, or maybe they just didn't believe that the sweet young girl had just gone see through. Maybe they didn't want to help me because I killed four people.

"Hey, that was not your fault." Luke reaches out and puts his hand on my arm to comfort me. I look down in confusion as most people just avoid touching me. I shrug his hand off me.

"I created the fire Luke. And then I made it one hundred times worse. There wouldn't have been people who died if it wasn't for me." I choke out the words.

"And think of all the people you have saved since then, since you became a protector."

"Guardian," I correct.

"Same thing. But you saved my best friend earlier today and that makes you a hero in my book." He smiles at me.

I blush. I haven't blushed since I was ten years old.

"That's a very sweet thing to say, Luke."

"I know." He cockily smiles.

I roll my eyes at him as I brush a lose hair off my face, tucking it behind my ear I start to sense that something is going wrong.

"Can you feel that?" I ask.

"Feel what?" Luke raises his eyebrows.

"Well, I will take that as a no, then." I move around on the spot, looking around curiously to try and sense where this deep feeling is coming from.

"What does it feel like?" Luke asks, looking around as well.

"Like a low rumble underneath me. It just feels bad."

"Wait." Luke hesitates. "I can feel it too."

"Seriously?" I turn around, looking for the source of this feeling.

"Nope!" He smirks at me.

"I will roast you alive," I threaten him, only half-joking. I focus on the feeling, trying to follow it to the source. It suddenly clicks in my head where the rumbling is coming from.

"It's Evelyn." I grin as I walk towards her, happy as I have just figured it out.

"Is she okay?" Luke instantly enters protective mode as he rushes to Evelyn's side.

"I think she is ready to leave. When I was ready to go I set a nearby tree on fire." I grimace at the memory. "Sometimes our powers get a little bit out of hand. We can't always control them when we are in the spirit world. We have no idea what we are causing back here on the mortal plane."

"You are really dangerous, aren't you?" Luke grins when he says this. He shows no sign of genuine fear towards me.

"Oh, yeah," I smirk.

"What exactly happens when you are in this dream place?"

"I will let her tell you. It's all up to her what she wants to share."

Luke just mumbles under his breath before crouching down in front of Evelyn.

"How can we wake her up?" he asks.

"She needs to do this naturally. That one was stronger." I reference to the rumble underneath us.

"Well, the last time she did this she destroyed the road," he states so matter-of-factly.

"Oh, well, that is just great."

I notice that the rumble is getting ever stronger. The small pebbles on the road start to bounce on the spot and roll away, like when you throw a stone into a pond, the stones ripple away from where we are standing.

"If you set fire to a tree when you were waking up, then think what Evelyn is going to do in a few minutes." Luke's mouth drops after he says this, as if shocked at his own revelation.

"She could tear the town apart."

After at least ten minutes of trying to rouse Evelyn, we have had no luck. She seems to have moved on from moving little stones to bigger stones now, causing the chunks of rocks that she dislodged earlier to now skid away from her as if being pushed by an invisible force.

"Luke, we need to wake her up."

"I am trying," he responds as he tries to throw something at her. He expects the little stone the pass through her like the hundreds of other things he has been throwing through her but this one hits her in the shoulder.

"She's becoming solid again!" he shouts. I head towards Evelyn and place my hands on her shoulders to find that I can feel her within my grasp.

"Well, wake her up then," Luke pesters.

"I can't. I have no idea what to do. You want me to burn her?"

"Don't you dare," he warns.

"I'm not being serious, Luke," I lie. If I need to, then I will; otherwise, blondie might tear apart the town.

"I just need to wake her up and I don't want her coming back with third degree burns," he scoffs.

I mumble under my breath and start pacing. It feels like I am standing on a vibration plate moments from erupting. The ground tremors beneath our feet as Evelyn twitches and shakes.

"I said I have no idea what to do!" I yell exasperatedly.

"How did you wake up?" Luke asks.

"You just wake up. My spirit wrapped me in vines that smothered me until I woke up." I grimace at the memory of feeling so confined.

"You had to be strangled to be woken up? That's kind of creepy." He frowns.

"No, Luke. The spirit I met was a previous Guardian of the earth and she transported me back to the physical world by cocooning me inside her abilities and then sending me home," I recall. "Evelyn just needs to talk to the spirits and learn what she can before she returns home." I absentmindedly roll my pendant around my hands as I talk.

"Evie does that when she talks as well." Luke nods to my pendant in my hand.

"Understandably. It was crafted thousands of years ago as a device that will bring us together."

"Is yours open?" Luke questions.

"It cracked when I set off on my journey to find Evelyn. It helped me find her."

"Can I see it?"

I debate handing over my pendant. I haven't taken it off since the day I found it. Well since the day it was *given* to me. I push my hair off my neck and onto my shoulder and reach back to unclasp my pendant. I stare at it momentarily, enjoying the familiarity of it in my hand, before I pass it over to an eager Luke. He initially rolls it around for a moment before tossing it between his hands.

"Luke!" I yell and yank it from him. "You need to be careful with it!" I rest my pendant on my flat palm and, despite having this for most of my life, I actually stop to take in its beauty. The pendant houses a ruby in the centre with thick silver framing around it with smaller swirls of silver interlinking around outside of the ruby. I re-clasp my pendant around my neck and let it fall back down behind my green blouse. Thank God I am wearing trousers because the temperature has become quite cold in the past hour but at least it isn't raining still.

"Sorry," Luke apologises.

"That's okay," I mumble as I make small talk. Despite how well Luke and I seemed to have clicked, it is still a little bit awkward to just stand here in the cold with Evelyn in another realm. The ground continues to shake but the tremors are becoming more sporadic and violent.

"We have to do something," Luke grumbles as he heads towards my car.

"We can't, she needs to do this herself," I yell at him.

"Well, I am not going to sit here and wait for something to go wrong."

"Luke, wait..." I shout at him as he emerges from my car holding a bottle of water that I left on my back seat. He walks over to Evelyn and opens the top before throwing the entire contents over Evelyn's face.

Her eyes whip open with such force the mist behind them startles me. Her face contorts momentarily with pain as the mist leaves and her clear blue eyes appear. Evelyn's clothes are soaked and her usually pale face is flushed red.

"What the hell, Luke?" Evelyn snipes and she raises her trembling hands to wipe her face.

"You weren't waking up, no matter what we did," he croaks.

"So you tried to drown me!" she yells, standing up from the fallen tree.

"In his defence, we did try lots of things. He even threw a pebble at you." I shrug.

"So that's why my shoulder hurts." She rolls her shoulders and sets off towards the car.

"Where are we going?" I call to her as she walks ahead.

"Get in the car and I'll tell you," she retorts as she opens the door and slides in, closely followed by Luke and I.

"So what happened?" Luke asks, turning his head around to see Evelyn in the back seat.

I set the car in gear and set off driving down the road, once again avoiding the chunks of misplaced concrete that Evelyn ripped out earlier. I swerve past the clumps of rock before we finally set off along a clear path back towards the town.

"So what happened?" Luke repeats.

"I met with a spirit and she told me what we need to do," Evelyn states so simply.

"And?" Luke pesters.

Evelyn details what happened when she entered the other realm including the history of Avarice, the origin of the Guardians and what we need to do next. Evelyn's face fills with fear when she tells Luke the story of Avarice and Luke just looks straight up confused. All the while she is scrolling through her phone and jotting down notes on a scrap piece of paper she found in my car.

"So where can we find Avarice's body?" asks Luke.

"Well Gwendolyn was just about to tell me before I was sent back. Prematurely I might add." She looks at Luke with a fierce gaze.

"I am not sorry for bringing you back into the regular world, Evie. I have no idea what you thought you were doing, but in the real world, you were about three minutes away from tearing a hole in the earth."

Evie blushes and looks out of the window her face full of shame. I tried to explain that it wasn't her fault and that she didn't know what she was doing but she looks so embarrassed. We continue driving down the road towards the centre of town. I stare out of the window, taking note of all the people in the town, all emerging from the indoors following the halting of the rainstorm. *Everyone* is blonde in this town. I tear my eyes from the identical townspeople and instead turn to face Evelyn. She is still solemnly looking out of the window.

"So do you really have a plan?" I ask.

"Yeah," she mumbles, still staring out into the meek town.

"You know, when I entered the other world, I set fire to a tree," I state ever-so-normally.

"Is this the part when I braid your hair and you paint my nails?" she sarcastically comments.

"You know what, Evelyn?" I start to lose my temper, "You play this mean girl act and you pretend to not give a damn about anything, but I see the way you look at Luke and you care for him so much, so you stop pretending that you don't care about anything and instead you focus on keeping that friend of yours safe." I gesture towards Luke who sinks back into his seat.

"You do not know me, Jessica, so you can stop pretending to be my new best friend," she grumbles.

"I am not here to replace Luke or anything. I am here because we have a birth right that needs to be finished. I just want you to lose this horrifically bad attitude and just suck it up," I yell a little too loudly.

"I never wanted this!" Evelyn gestures around as if to encompass the entire situation into one gesture. "I did not want to have powers or fight an ancient evil that will kill my friends in an instant," she starts to yell too.

"But it is happening…" I try to talk but Evelyn cuts me off. Rudely.

"Stop with the whole *destiny* mumbo-jumbo and just admit that you aren't strong enough to fight this demon yourself and that you need my help. Help that I do not want to give to you."

"Of course I need your help. But more than anything I want you to stop with the sarcastic comments and jibes all the time and just face this *mumbo-jumbo*, as you call it, head on otherwise we are all doomed. I will not let anyone else die at the hands of this man." I tighten my grip on the steering wheel and small wisps of smoke drift into the air.

"Jessica, calm down," Luke warns quietly in my ear.

"I'm fine," I lie. I need to close my eyes and focus on my breathing but the last thing I want to do is cause a car accident. I try to relax, but my breathing becomes hitched, and the smoke starts to become slightly thicker.

"You need to calm down," Evelyn also warns me.

"I am trying. Our powers are tied to our emotions and I'm pretty freaking emotional right now," I yell at Evelyn.

"Well, stop being emotional!" Luke shouts, before coughing from the thick smoke.

"Pull over now!" Evelyn shouts as she grabs the wheel and turns, causing the car to jerk in the road, and pulls into a layby where I quickly turn the car off. I push the door open and quickly jet into the open space, the cool air nice on my tingling hands, and I try to stop my staggered breath.

"What is going on?" Evelyn asks as she exits the car, "Do you always blow up when you get into an argument?"

"We were on a touchy subject." I pull my hands close to my chest and try to will the tiny flames that I just conjured away.

I can't tell her. Not yet.

"Well." Evelyn stands awkwardly, just looking at me, whilst Luke also exits the car. "You were right. I do have a bad attitude and I do care about people. I know I have a destiny to follow and I know that there are things I must do but I am allowed to be scared okay. I was a perfectly normal teenager a few days ago."

"Apart from the whole Mother Nature thing," Luke jests.

"Apart from that," she responds with a grin.

I shake the remaining smoke clear from my hands and turn to face them, hoping they can't see the tears that I tried to hold back.

"Was it because I said I didn't want to be a Guardian?" Evelyn quietly asks.

"No, it has nothing to do with that," I respond as I brush the hair off my face.

"Well, what then?" Luke pesters.

"Nothing. Can we please get going now?" I walk back towards the car and sit behind the driving wheel, noting the plastic is now bubbled and warped. I wait momentarily until Evelyn and Luke join me and we set off driving.

"So now what?" I ask, just to break the silence.

"We need to find where Avarice's original body is being stored," Evelyn answers as she continues to look in her phone.

"What are you looking for?" Luke sticks his head through the gap in the front seats and looks at Evelyn's phone.

"I'm trying to find the oldest buildings and settlements in Ravens Valley in order to see where they may have buried him," Evelyn announces as she continues to scroll through her phone.

"Are we going to see his body?" Luke groans in disgust.

"It's been thousands of years, Luke. I doubt he's flesh and blood," Evelyn responds.

"Actually, his body is preserved, ready for his spirit to finally return to it," I chime in, using the knowledge that I learnt years ago when I entered the spirit world.

"So let me get this straight. We are on the lookout for an ancient demon, whose spirit is currently wandering around the earth, waiting to become strong enough in order to find and enter his original body. We are expected to stop him before he can do this?" Luke looks so confused he might actually give himself a nosebleed. "When we eventually find and defeat him, his spirit will just go back to sleep until it is strong enough to wake up and repeat the entire process over again."

"Pretty much," I answer.

"Hardly seems worth it," Evelyn moans. I turn to her, locking onto her clear blue eyes, and raise my eyebrows as if to say *'what did we talk about earlier'*.

"Sorry. Always the pessimist," she jokes.

"So where exactly does his spirit go when we defeat him then?" Luke queries.

"It just…well… I don't really know," I struggle to answer because, truthfully, I have no idea what happens when he dies. I have always just assumed that he disappeared after he was destroyed because all the previous Guardians just weren't strong enough to finally defeat him once and for all. Assuming that you can actually kill a demon. This entire situation is so confusing. We just have to make sure he never manages to find his original body and enter it.

"Maybe he goes to—" Luke can't finish his sentence because Evelyn shrieks "Found it!" causing me to almost swerve off the road from her loud outburst.

"For God's sake, Evelyn, are you planning on causing us to crash?" I shout.

"I'm sorry, but I found it!" She grins happily.

"Found what?" Luke questions, once again sticking his head through the partition and looking at us.

"Where his body will be. I found the oldest landmark in the Valley." She's still grinning.

"And..." Luke gestures for her to continue.

Evelyn turns her phone towards Luke and he similarly grins. These two seriously look identical.

"Ravens Valley Church," Evelyn answers.

Chapter 10

Jessica

Despite how ridiculously boring this town is, it truly does have some beautiful landmarks.

The church, built from a sturdy grey stone, rises proudly into the sky. The magnificent tower rises to a staggering height and seemingly disappears into the low hanging clouds. The tower, which is decorated with dazzling rainbow coloured stain glass windows, captures the light and surrounds the grounds with a beautiful coloured glow. Directly at the base of the tower lies a large wooden doorway, wrought with iron rungs that lie across the wooden panels, giving the harsh illusion of entrapment, as if once you close the door you can never leave. The stones are a vastly different colour around the door, turning a dank black colour that fades into the natural grey, placing much more emphasis on the heavy door that seems to beckon us. The east side of the church is underpinned with a large mass of smooth tiles that stretch back far and steep down that similarly catch the light, due to the recent rainstorm, creating a glossy look that coats the high rising roof. The south wall holds a large clear window, once again surrounded by heavy iron rings that protrude from the stone and stretch across that window, encasing the window. This is probably an attempt to keep potential thieves from smashing the window and gaining entry but it only succeeds in looking like the bars that encase a prison cell. Standing high on the grass around the church is a wooden trellis which is decorated in beautiful roses that snake around the white wood-like ivy and climb high along the walls of the church. The red roses starkly contrast with the grey stone and truly draw the attention away from the architecture and instead make you focus on the bright red blooming flowers.

Luke hesitantly walks towards the door before placing his hands on the thick wood. He reaches down for the metal doorknocker, which is freakishly shaped into the face of a gargoyle who holds the hooped knocker in its mouth, and places his hand onto the low hanging metal hoop.

"You know, in the ancient times, they believed anyone with magical abilities, or those who associated with them, would be struck by lightning upon entering a church," Evelyn states from behind us.

"Are you kidding me?" Luke fearfully asks as he pulls his hand away from the knocker.

"No." She shrugs as if to say *'are you even surprised after everything that's happened?'*

"Don't panic, Luke. I'm sure we would have been struck down a long time ago if that were true." I glance over to Evelyn and give her a stern look.

"I did say ancient times. It's not like it happened recently," she grins.

"Or ever," I reiterate. I reach into my back pocket and pull out my phone. I scroll through my contacts and click on my most recently called person.

"Who are you calling?" Luke asks as I raise the phone to my ear.

"Someone who is very important," I answer.

The ringing stops and she answers with a soothing *hello.'*

"Who is she talking too?" Luke whispers to Evelyn.

"I have no idea," she answers as she moves closer to Luke.

I finish my phone call and place my phone back into my pocket.

"You will meet her in about ten minutes." I smile at Evelyn who still looks confused.

"Who?" She raises her eyebrows, exasperated at how cryptic I am being.

"Remember the conversation we were having earlier on?" I ask. "About previous Guardians and that most were dead?"

"Yes," Evelyn furrows her brow. She seems to finally click at what I am referring to.

"I also said that we weren't the only ones left. Guardians are a foursome remember, one for each element. We are part of the current four." I grin as I see the realisation on her face.

"About time," she whispers.

"You are about to meet the other Guardian."

The creak of the door opening echoes throughout the church. The three of us walk across the cold stone floor and into the small area just inside. Luke leafs through the dust covered pamphlets that have been discarded on the nearby table whilst Evelyn walks over to the smaller door that faces directly opposite to the main entrance.

"When was the last time someone came here?" I ask as the dust rises in the air, obviously disturbed by our appearance.

"Must have been a while. I actually haven't heard the church bells ring in years," Luke answers as he bats dust from his hands.

"An abandoned church. Fantastic!" I groan.

"This way," Evelyn orders as we walk towards the small blue door. She presses her hands on the wood and pushes to no avail.

"It's stuck." She pushes again.

"Allow me, ladies." Luke walks towards the door, eyes it up, and takes a step back. He rolls his shoulders before charging full speed towards the door. He hits the door, shoulder first, in an attempt to break the door open. Instead, he is harshly thrown back onto the floor in a lump as the door just rattles in its place.

"Our hero," Evelyn sarcastically comments as she helps Luke up from the floor.

"Stupid door," he mumbles as he pats the dust from his clothes and shakes the dust from his golden locks.

I walk to the door and place my hand on the metal joint on the right side. The metal, coated in rust, feels cold against my skin as I trail my finger across it. I feel the warmth inside of me and channel it down towards my hand where a small blue flame appears on the end of my extended finger. I push against the metal joint and watch as it starts to heat up. The metal soon enough starts to contort and bubble before snapping clean off. I repeat this on the other joint before retreating to stand with Luke and Evelyn.

"Now try it." I gesture towards Luke and then the door. He readies himself again before raising his leg and kicking the door with such might is falls down flat, releasing a flurry of dust in the process. We enter the new vast space as our eyes adjust to the darkness. Despite a large window, which should be more than enough to illuminate the room, the curtains that hang from the ceiling cover the glass and therefore smother any light that streams through the room.

"I got this." I raise my hands and conjure a fireball, momentarily giving us light, before I fling the fire at the hanging torches protruding from the wall. The nearest torch catches alight quickly, presumably burning some kindling that was left many years ago. I focus on the heat that I just created in the torch and I allow for it to spread through my body. I call out for the fire to move across the room, crackling as it leaps off the wall and dances across the space, as if with a mind of its own, and forming a perfect column of fire that spreads to the remaining torches. They quickly catch alight and I will the plume of fire to die out, leaving us with the torches on the walls as our main source of light.

"That was amazing!" Luke spurts out, his mouth open in pure admiration. "All *you* can do is grow fruit," he jokes as he elbows Evelyn, who looks a mix of annoyed and jealous.

"Do you want me to tear this entire building down?" She stares at Luke. "Because we both know that I could easily do that," she retorts as Luke mumbles an apology for his previous comment.

"I just thought we could use some light," I mumble.

"You could have opened the curtains," Evelyn answers as she walks forward into the large church.

At the far end of the room is a table located in a curved, semi-circular area, an *apse* I believe it is called. In ancient times, churches and buildings were modelled after a type of Roman buildings that had this as a main area. The chancel is the part of the church from which the service is conducted, being an elevated platform, about three steps up from the regular floor. Rows of wooden pews face this area, separated in half by a rich blue carpet that stretches down towards the platform. The stone ceiling has metal chandeliers that cascade down and precariously hang in the air, gently rocking in the breeze that we created with our entry.

Evelyn walks down the carpet and towards the apse. She climbs onto the platform and runs her hands along the table.

"What are you doing?" Luke asks as he heads over to join her.

"Trying to find a lever or something," she answers, as she crouches down and looks beneath the altar.

"For what?" I ask as I slowly walk towards them both, watching them search in the little coves in the walls.

"Because I doubt his body will be out in the open for everyone to see."

"True," Luke mumbles as Evelyn raises a valid point.

"Last year, in history class, we learnt all about the history of the town and that ancient catacombs ran underneath the outskirts of the town. Now, from what I found out from my quick internet search, the closest catacomb entrance was last documented to be near here, but that was over a hundred years ago," Evelyn enlightens us as she continues to look.

"You barely paid attention in history class, Evie," says Luke.

"Neither did you," retorts Evelyn.

"You two bicker like children, you know?"

They both turn to face each other before simultaneously replying, "Yes."

"Now the foundations of the church means that this area was built first, and then everything was constructed outwards, away from this altar," Evelyn states.

"As if they were building away from something," I answer.

"The entrance to the catacombs!" Luke grins.

We continue to look for something. Anything. Evelyn walks towards the wall, the ground creaking beneath her, as she riffles through a stack of books piled against the stone.

"Did you hear that?" Luke asks, stopping what he was doing.

"What?" Evelyn similarly freezes.

"The floor creaked when you walked over it."

"And..." I struggle to see the point Luke is trying to make.

"We are in a building made of stone, and the last time I checked, stone doesn't creak." He turns around retraces the steps that Evelyn just took. He walks over a small red rug and, as if on cue, the floor creaks beneath his weight. He crouches down and whips the rug off the floor to reveal a wooden hatched door padlocked to the stone ground.

"Luke, you are a genius," Evie gushes as she crouches next to him.

"Not just a pretty face," I smirk as Luke blushes at my comment. "How do you plan on getting down there?" I toy with the padlock.

"Just burn it off," Luke suggests.

"I have got this." Evelyn stands up and gestures for Luke to step back. She extends her hands and the ground starts to slightly tremor. The metal chandeliers swing in the air and dust cascades from the ceiling as the room starts to vibrate. The vibrations seem to localise directly underneath us as the wooden door bounces repeatedly as Evelyn clenches her hand. The tremors pulse for a second before a violent burst causes the door to rip clean from the metal lock and expel itself across the room allowing us to see clearly into the uncovered tunnel.

"Looks like locked doors aren't a problem for either of us," Evelyn smirks.

I walk over to one of the wooden torches hanging on the wall and yank it free from its restraints. I return to the trapdoor near the altar and wait for Luke to descend, passing him the torch once his head disappears from view. An orange glow emits from the dark hole, becoming dimmer as Luke retreats further away from us, his footsteps echoing down the tunnel.

"You can come down now!" Luke yells. "All clear!"

"He really didn't have to go first, you know. We can take care of ourselves," I mumble.

"Let him have his macho fun," Evelyn huffs as she lowers herself down the rackety wooden ladder. I quickly follow her, giving one last glance around the church to see if *she* is here yet. I whip out my phone and send a quick text.

"Gone down a hole. It's filthy. Come quick," I read aloud as I type before pressing send. I finish descending the ladder and jog after Luke and Evelyn, who have already disappeared out of my view. I follow the glow of the torch until I see them turning left around a corner.

"This place is disgusting," she mumbles, running her hand along the corridor wall.

The catacomb walls are made from stacked, yet loose, bricks piled at least seven feet in height. The ceiling, a concrete looking substance, is coated with water that drips and pools on the sandy floor, presumably the rain seeps through the ground outside the church and permeates deep into the catacombs. The drips of water splashing into the puddles it previously formed echoes throughout the vast tunnels creating a very claustrophobic feeling. I wrap my arms around myself, shivering from the cold.

"You okay?" Evelyn asks.

"I'm fine," I lie. Maybe it's related to my powers but I really do not like being in enclosed spaces. Probably because it's much harder to control a fire in a small space, or maybe it takes me back to the fire when I was younger. Being trapped in the small room as the house crumbled down around me. "I bet you like it down here," I mumble.

"Actually, I do. It's kind of calming to be away from everything else and so close to the earth." Evelyn breathes a sigh of relief, obviously revelling in the beauty of being underground.

"Just try not to cause a cave in," I joke.

"I'll try," she smiles. We continue to walk towards Luke, somehow managing to nearly lose him in the mass of interconnecting tunnels.

We could be wandering around here for hours.

We have been underground for at least thirty minutes and still no sign of… anything. The stone tunnels roll on for miles. The wet floor becomes more like sludge as we venture further into the dark abyss. The air is damp and the scent of mud and sand fill the air, the crackling of the torch being the only obvious sound, besides the crunching of our feet and the wind howling behind us. The tunnels seem to lead downwards, as if we are slowly descending deeper into the earth.

"Do you have any idea where we are going?" I ask Luke. After all, we seem to be following his direction.

"Nope!" He grins as he turns another corner.

"Do you have any idea how to get back if we are unsuccessful?"

"Yes. Every time we reached a crossroad, I always turned left. So, in order to get back we just have to do the exact opposite when we start to turn around."

"Okay, stop," Evelyn orders, "That's a good idea, Luke, but I have a better one."

She leans on the wall to her right and closes her eyes, her lips pursed as she breathes in and out, and starts to rub her hands. She crouches down and places her hands on the floor, digging her fingers into the wet sludge, and starts to breathe heavier.

"What are you doing?" Luke breaks the silence.

"I'm trying to sense for any disturbances in the earth in our area," she pants.

"What?" Luke asks, confused.

"Everything is pretty much a straight line down here, every corridor is interlinked. I am trying to find a break in that pattern. If it is connected to the earth then I can probably sense it."

"That's amazing," I mutter. It must be like when I sense nearby heat sources and I can detect how far away they are. Evelyn clenches her hand in the dirt before standing up tall. Her eyes, a normal clear blue, have become a deeper shade, almost grey. Within seconds, the colour visibly floods back into her eyes, like someone poured blue dye directly into her iris.

"About half a mile away, there is a large clearing." She wiped her hands on the wall, to clear them of the dirt, and set off in that direction. Whenever we come across a crossroad, she seemed to automatically know which direction to take.

Soon enough we enter a large space, the brick walls have become smoother and begin to circle out, creating a closed arena of sorts. The ceiling becomes tiled and rises high, creating a dome effect, and in the centre of the sand filled room lies a box, about seven foot in length and much slimmer in width, on a raised platform. Next to each corner of the box lies a column that raises from the floor to the roof, made of a marble like substance. The box itself seems to be made of stone, consisting of two parts that make the base and the lid. Along the side of the base are embedded gems and metallic swirls that twinkle through the gaps from the ivy that has tightly wrapped around the stone.

"It's beautiful," Luke mumbles as he reaches out to touch the gems, attempting to peel back the bound ivy, with no luck.

"Looks like this one for me," I state as I walk towards the box and place my hands on the plant. I create a ball of fire on my palm before I will it to spread and encompass my entire hand, like a burning glove, and press it firmly on the stone box. The ivy catches alight and the fire whips across the box, startling Luke and Evelyn, and the burning plants dance in the air before disappearing into a burning husk. The box, although slightly charred, is now clear.

"You know I could have just asked them to move," Evelyn grumbles.

"Let's focus on getting the lid off." I try to push the stone lid but it proves to be far too heavy. "Evelyn, can you manage that?"

"If you want me to cause a roof collapse, then I can gladly give it a go. I can control the earth, not stone, and the only way for me to crack this would be to cause a tremor to break the stone but I have no idea if this place could withstand the quake." She tucks her hands in her pockets.

"Well, we need to get this lid off and we need to do it soon. I think this is his coffin." I set about trying to push the coffin lid but it doesn't budge. We all take a section and try to lift on the count of three.

The lid doesn't move.

"There's no way we can do this," Luke dejectedly groans as he sinks to the floor in a huff.

"Maybe I could give it a go?" A voice from behind startles us.

Luke's jaw drops as he gazes at the beauty before us. Her glossy dark skin and thick bushels of curly ebony hair look beautiful in the glow of the torch. She stands tall, wearing cut-off jeans and a chequered shirt, she looks ready for both combat and the fashion runway. Her mud brown eyes flicker in the torch light and she stares us all down. I can tell why Luke is enamoured by this Amazonian beauty. She takes a hair band from her wrist and ties the mass of black hair off her shoulders and she breezes towards us.

"Who are you?" Evelyn asks. Luke just stares.

"My name is Amara." She sincerely smiles at me and I wink back.

"About time you got here." I jokingly give her a punch in the arm. She pretends to wince before leaning in for a hug. I welcome the familiarity.

"Parking was a nightmare," she jokes.

"Any help?" I ask, gesturing towards the coffin.

"Of course," she responds as she raises her hands. The wind becomes suddenly violent and the stagnant sand rips from the floor and flurries around us. Amara twirls her hands in a circular motion and the wind seems to follow. The sandstorm she has whipped up moves over the coffin before seemingly covering it completely, obscuring it from our view. The scraping sound of stone tears through the air as the lid appears to jut out of the sandstorm. The moment Amara puts her hands down the storm stops and the grains of sand fall harmlessly to the floor.

"That was amazing!" Luke guffaws.

"Oh God." Evelyn rolls her eyes at him.

"Ta-da!" Amara grins as she walks to towards the open coffin. We all join her, Luke moving quickly so he can stand next to Amara.

"Are all Guardians this pretty?" he mumbles. Amara just laughs and ruffles his hair.

"Guys!" Evelyn calls from over near the coffin.

"One second," Luke interrupts, "I take it you are the air Guardian, then."

"At you service." Amara bows jokingly.

"Guys!" Evelyn calls again.

"He was like this earlier. I think someone has a crush on people with powers." I laugh as I watch Luke stare into Amara's deep brown eyes.

"Guys!" Evelyn yells.

"What!" Luke responds in a similar tone. "We are trying to have a conversation with our newest member. You are being a little rude, Evie. You haven't even said hello yet," Luke scolds.

"I'm sorry I haven't exchanged pleasantries yet but there is something slightly more important that needs out attention."

"What?" Luke asks as he turns back towards me and Amara. The three of us walk over the Evelyn, who is leaning against one of the marble pillars at the base of the coffin. She points towards the open wedge that Amara just created by lifting the lid off.

"The coffin. It's empty," she whispers.

Chapter 11

Jessica

I have to physically pull Luke out of the way in order to look inside the coffin. My hand grasps firmly the rim of the cold casket and my eyes scan the empty insides. A thin, yet dust covered, purple silk sheet lies messily inside.

"Try not to panic," Amara whispers.

"What's the worst that can happen?" Luke wonders.

"What do we do now?" Evelyn asks.

All eyes fall on me. Three people so desperately looking for answers that I don't have, all look at me with a mix of expressions, ranging from hopefulness to confusion. I try to find my voice but I can't seem to form any words.

"Jessica?" Luke probes for a response.

I push my hair off my face and rub my eyes with the back of my hand. I try to gather my thoughts but they seem to be as lost as my voice right now. *Think, Jessica.*

"Okay," I croak. "We just need to rethink our strategy."

"Some strategy. Our plan went out of the window when we thought Avarice was still separated from his body," Evelyn quips.

"He might not be reunited yet. The Grim Reaper might have just taken it," Luke suggests. I admire his positive attitude in the face of danger.

"Who?" Amara asks, obviously needing to be clued-in with all of Luke and Evelyn's nicknames.

"He's this scary skeleton man who attacked Evelyn earlier on. We thought he was just a psycho but it makes more sense for him to be the body that Avarice possessed," Luke explains as Amara eagerly listens. Luke continues to explain what previously happened to Evelyn, from her many attacks throughout the day to entering the spirit world, as I try to think of our next plan of action.

"So Pandora was possessed," Amara states as she tries to mentally create a timeline. "Does she remember anything?"

"No. Just a blur apparently," Luke mumbles.

"Wait a second." I interrupt their conversation. "What time was Pandora possessed?"

"Early this afternoon. Why?" Evelyn responds.

"Because, in order for her to be possessed, Avarice must have been separated from his body. So he used Pandora as a vessel, then attacked you. He would then have had to leave her body in order to re-possess the Grim Reaper and come down here and free his body." I pace as I connect the dots in my head.

"There's no way his body would be strong enough for him now. He will need to get it out of here and bide his time somewhere else," Amara adds.

"What's to stop him from jumping straight into his original body? It's just been lying here, after all," Evelyn asks, confused.

"Because of that exact reason!" Amara excitedly states, "His body has been lying here for well over a hundred years. It's not going to be in fully working condition."

Evelyn stares at me and Amara, a confused look across her face, made sterner from the flickering orange torchlight.

"How do you know that he can't go straight back into his body?" she enquires, almost with an accusatory tone. "You seem to have a lot of answers."

"We all learnt different things when we entered the spirit world," Amara simply replies.

"What happened when you entered the ghost place?" Luke asks, enthralled. "Evelyn nearly cracked the world in two!" Luke exaggerates to bolster Evelyn's appearance.

"Did she really?" Amara raises her eyes in disbelief.

"No, I didn't." Evelyn shoves Luke aside jokingly.

"Well, my trip was pretty tame. I made my town a little windy, that's all." Amara shrugs off the question. We both know that's not what happened when she entered the spirit world but it is not my story to tell, its Amara's.

I have my own secret anyway. As soon as they find out what I'm hiding, nothing will be the same.

I turn to face Amara and she catches my eye. Her face looks just as normal as usual, but I can see, underneath it all the pain that she is trying to hide away. The pain that she feels for me.

"We need to go." I turn around and start walking towards the entrance to the tomb, kicking the dust underneath my feet, waiting for the others to follow. Amara soon joins me at the front, leaving Luke and Evelyn to take up the flank and walk behind.

"You need to tell them," Amara whispers into my ear as we take the first corner.

"Not yet." I keep walking. My eyes firmly planted on the sandy track we are following.

"You have to. They have a right to know," she persists.

"Amara, drop it," I warn.

"If you don't tell them, then…" Amara tries to issue a weak threat but I turn and swiftly cut her off. I grab her arm and drag her around the corner of the tunnel to our left, obscuring us from the view of the other two.

"Don't you dare threaten me, Amara! Not with this. I will tell them as soon as I am ready and not a second sooner," I growl at her. Her face is plastered with fear and I release her from my grasp.

"I have been your friend for years, ever since we found each other, and I would give my life to save yours and I know that you would do the same. I am well aware that you are struggling with your past, and what happened, but we need to do this together. I mean all of us, the Guardians, and that cannot happen until you tell the truth." Amara blinks away the tears as she keeps her voice to a minimum. I tuck my shaking hand into my pockets.

"I am so sorry," I whisper.

"I know. I will keep your secret for now but you will have to tell them."

"When I am ready." Evelyn and Luke walk around the corner and join us, confused as to why Amara's eyes are red and why we are standing so close.

"You guys okay?" Luke asks.

"Fine." Amara smiles as she turns and walks away, linking her arm with mine and dragging me with her down the long, dusty, tunnel. We let Luke and Evelyn pass us and walk ahead as me and Amara walk arm in arm as we silently think about what happened.

"Just one last thing." Amara leans in and whispers, "If you ever grab me like that again I will blow you half way across the ocean and leave you there."

I know full well that she is joking but part of me knows that she is capable of conjuring a wind storm that can do such a thing. That's what happened when she entered the spirit world, after all.

We follow the other two back down the passages, hopefully leaving the catacombs once and for all.

❋

Evelyn exits through the trapdoor first, followed by Luke and then Amara, leaving me to extinguish the flame and throw the torch back down the tunnel. I begin to climb the rungs of the ladder and emerge into the cold church, closing the wooden door behind me.

"Wait a second," Amara calls as she appears next to me. She reaches down, opens the trapdoor and takes a step back. Her hands rise into the air and she circles them, the air whistling around her as the dust begins to lift off the ground and follow the path of her hands. She violently thrusts down into the beginning of the tunnel and causes the loose wooden ladder to rip off the side of the trapdoor and be violently thrown into the darkness of the tunnels.

"Just making sure that no one else goes down there in a while," she smiles.

We all congregate in the centre of the church, with Luke sprawling on the nearby wooden seats, scrolling on his phone, and Evelyn paces around in a repetitive circle.

"So we need a new plan. But I need to go shopping for something for tonight," Evelyn mumbles as she heads towards the church door.

"What's happening tonight?" Amara enquires.

"I have a party to go to. Well, Luke and I do. I suppose we can all go, actually, as I'm sure Pandora would love all of the attention," Evelyn scoffs.

"Are you kidding me?" I yell, slightly louder than I meant to.

"Did I forget to mention the party? Whoops!" She shrugs her shoulders and once again starts to head for the door.

"You are not going to a party tonight. We have much more pressing issues to attend to." Amara's tone seems to match mine.

"Who do you think you are, my mother?" Evelyn raises her eyebrows and Luke joins her at her side.

"You think now is the time to be going to parties and socialising? When Avarice is moments away from attacking?" I am shocked at her disregard for the issues at hand.

"That's why I am still going tonight. I have spent all my life confused with my abilities, scared, paranoid and in a constant state of confusion. I had no idea what my powers were and where they came from and I had to balance being a normal teen and a freak of nature. So one of the few times in my life that I get to act like a regular teenage girl then I will jump at the chance."

Amara goes to open her mouth but Evelyn continues with her tirade.

"I know Avarice is out there, but you said so yourself that he isn't strong enough yet to get back into his body, and we have no leads as to where he is hiding so we will just have to wait. But there is nothing on this planet that will stop me from going tonight."

"Is a single party that important?" I ask, confused.

"I like to think of Pandora as the Avarice of my school." She looks proud that she made that reference, whilst Luke just nods in agreement.

"I really don't think you are grasping the severity of our situation Evelyn. He could attack any moment, and don't think that he will hesitate when it comes to murdering your school friends, because he will slaughter anyone in his path." I let the words seethe from me, trying to snap Evelyn into reality.

She raises her eyebrows and defiantly takes a step forward, "I don't think that you fully grasped what I was saying Jessica. I am going tonight, even if the world was ending, because I will not let my life revolve around being a Guardian. I didn't ask for this remember."

"We get you. None of us asked for this, but it's who we are." Amara shrugs understandingly at Evelyn's predicament, but I know that she gets the importance of who we are.

This girl is so insubordinate it's downright annoying.

Luke turns to face Evelyn, raising his hand and warmly placing it on her shoulder, "Maybe we shouldn't go tonight. They do have a point, I mean what if Avarice attacks the party and someone gets hurt? You would never forgive yourself if that happened."

"I won't let it happen okay, Luke! You may think that this is a stupid party, but to me it is so much more than that. It's showing all the people at school who think that I am worthless, or that I should be treated badly just because I am not part of their clique, that they have no power over me, and I will go tonight and prove every single one of them wrong," she announces so matter-of-factly.

I had no idea that she was having a rough time at school. She seems like the kind of girl who would be pretty popular to me. Luke is obviously the football player stereotype guy so I bet he is super popular.

"Well, if you are set in your ways, then I guess that we are coming with you." Amara smiles as she walks towards Evelyn.

I struggle to comprehend what is happening right now. "You aren't serious are you? It is a horrifically bad idea to go to a party when an ancient demon has just stolen his body and is about to cause havoc over the world," I yell. They really do not seem to understand how dangerous this whole situation is. I seem to be the only one thinking logically.

"It's one night, Jess, let's just suck it up and go. If anything happens, then we deal with it," Amara soothingly says, her tone always calming me when I get agitated. I can feel her words wash over me like a warm breeze, washing away the hesitations that I have.

"Nothing will go wrong," Evelyn promises as she places her hands on the heavy door handles and opens the thick wooden doors.

She spoke too soon.

Her body is thrown violently back into the church, flying through the air like a ragdoll, and crashing into the wooden pews with such force the wood splinters beneath her. Luke screams her name and rushes to help her, yet before he can even reach her body, he is similarly dragged into the air and thrown backwards straight into the tables covered in pamphlets and metal tins, littering the air with thin pieces of paper and his body smashes onto the table with a deafening thud.

Before my brain can even register what has just happened, I see the tall man, or Grim Reaper as they have named him, enter through the wooden doors, his arms raised in front of him with his hands lying limp at the wrist. He flicks his cold, dead, hands and the doors slam shut behind him. Amara is already summoning a heavy wind to repel him but he seems to be effortlessly walking through the gale force wind. Loose paper and stagnant dust is furiously whipped into the air and thunders around the Grim Reaper whilst I focus on channelling the heat inside me into my hands, engulfing them in white hot flames.

"Get back!" I yell to Amara, as I throw the first flame into the general direction of the Reaper. His dark suit chars under the heat, his skin blackens when exposed to the boiling temperature, but he simply pats out the flame as if it was nothing more than a mere matchstick flame. He flicks his hands again and Amara is pushed back along the stone floor, sliding as if it was made of ice.

This is one of the rare times in my life that I am afraid. Real, genuine fear that crawls over your body and paralyses you. The action continues around me as Luke crawls out from beneath the tables, his nose bleeding, and Evelyn appears from behind the stack of broken pews, with a vicious looking cut on her forehead, and they join the fray. I try to move but the feelings lay heavy on my body, trapping me within my own skin.

"Back off!" Evelyn yells as she thrust her arms forwards, causing a tremor to erupt underneath us and repelling the Grim Reaper back, the force of the earthquake cracking the floor underneath him and making him lose his footing.

"You'll bring this whole place down if you aren't careful, Evie!" Luke yells, grabbing a lose piece of wood nearby and swinging, with all his force, into the Reaper's face. The crack, making direct contact with the intended target, floors him as he spews thick black blood. His freakish body falls to the ground, willowy arms crashing to the floor, and his head lands with an uncomfortable sounding smack.

"What the hell..." Evelyn grumbles as she staggers towards me.

"I knew we should have started to track him." I choke the words out.

Luke stands over the body and begins to bring the wood down onto the Reaper's ghostly face, in a surprisingly violent attempt to finish him, only for one of the thin arms to quickly reach up and grab the wood mere inches before it comes into contact with his face. All we can do is gasp as we watch his long bony fingers curl around the wood and the normal brown colour beginning to change into a harder looking grey composite. He yanks the club from Luke and throws it towards us, clattering onto the floor, as we see it is now completely made of stone.

"Oh my God," Amara whispers as the Reaper rises from his position on the floor, not using his arms to lift himself, instead levitating into an upright position without a single scratch on him.

We all automatically flitter into battle positions, Amara conjuring wind above her, Evelyn calling on the earth for mud and vines to weave through the crack in the floor and grow around her. Luke grabs two pieces of metal, I think they used to be table legs, and I summon another fireball to match the one I already had. We get ready to pounce only to find that none of us can move.

We are trapped on the spot.

"What's going on?"

"Why can't I move?"

"Stay back, you freak."

All their words blur into one; a loud orchestra of fearful voices ring in my ears. The fear returns, bubbling inside of my gut like a warning to the rest of my body. Sweat forms on my forehead yet I can't move my body to wipe it. The only difference between me and a statue right now is the dazzling ball of fire that currently lingers on my hand, waiting for its order.

The Reaper strides over to us. His wax-like skin and cracked lips only adding to his horrific appearance. He eyes each of us up and down before taking an over exaggerated inhale, as if he is sucking all of the air out of the room and into himself. His head rolls back and his eyes close.

"What is he doing?" Luke quietly asks.

"If what I read in my books is true then they say Avarice could detect the weakness of his foes and use these to feed his hunger, and then play with them as he made the men head into battle. First he sustains himself and then he causes bloodshed." Amara's eyes fill with tears, a mixture from the stress of the situation and the fear of the unknown.

He walks towards Luke, looming over him, as Evelyn shouts threat after threat to get away from him 'or else' but he takes no notice. Instead, he croaks out the word "Love."

He steps sideways towards Evelyn, whose arms are still wrapped in vines awaiting her command, and leans in close and spits out the word "Insecurity." He pronounces each syllable as if they were hard to say.

The process is repeated with Amara, with the word "secrets," dripping from his mouth. Amara closes her eyes as not to look at him and he moves onto me.

I am not afraid. I am not afraid. I am not afraid. It's like I am trying to command myself to feel that way but the fear still traps me, coursing through my body like venom, and I tremble within my paralytic confines. He stares at me intently, his black and misty eyes raking over my flesh, and he spits the word "liar" into my face. I try to think of a plan.

"Call me that one more time," I coarsely order him. He leans in further, his cold breath rolling over my face, and repeats the same word.

"It's such a harsh word," I say as I force a smile onto my body. I just need him to take one step closer to me. "The only liar here seems to be you right now."

He does exactly as I want, moving intimately and threateningly close to me and I execute my plan.

I call for the flickering flame in my hand to violently explode, sending rays of hot fire in every direction, ensuring that the others were missed from the fire blaze, and causing the Reaper to stagger back in shock and blindness. This momentary lack of concentration seems to be enough to break his hold over us and our limbs begin to move again.

"Evelyn, send me your vines!" I yell and she quickly responds. The green vines flow through the air upon her command and I place my hands on the thick leaves and ignite them. The fire rips across the plant, a look of concern on Evelyn's face appears but I assure her I know what I am doing, and I call for the fire to burn hotter than ever. I ask Evelyn to wrap the vines around the Reaper, who is stirring from his shock induced accident and they wrap tightly around his thin body. The fire tackles his skin and, although he doesn't burn, his clothes begin to char under the heat.

"Amara, get him out of here," I order. She raises her hands and the doors whip open with a loud crash. Reaper's frail body is whisked into the air and violently thrown out into the open courtyard and far enough for myself and Evelyn to lose control over the fire and vines.

"We need to leave right now." Luke grabs our arms and pulls us through the door and immediately left towards the car park where my car resides.

"We can't just leave him here!" Evelyn yells. "He could hurt someone."

"He's going to have to recover somewhere. He is weakened and he needs to be strong enough to go back into his body. Right now we aren't going to defeat him," Amara calls back as she runs to her car parked just opposite mine. The fluorescent yellow, small car shines brightly behind her, her dark skin contrasting beautifully with the shiny metal, as she slinks behind the front wheel, taking Evelyn with her.

"Come back to mine," Luke yells towards the other car. "Evie knows the way."

The two of us enter my car and speed out of the parking area and straight onto the adjoining main road, flooring it so the church disappears out of the view of my mirror.

Chapter 12

Evelyn

I have lost at least one pint of blood.

Okay, well that is a little bit of an exaggeration, but the gash on my head is dripping viciously. Amara reaches into the back seat and rummages around for a clean white rag that I compress onto my wound.

"That is really going to hurt in the morning. We should stop at the hospital," Amara worriedly speaks.

"I'll be fine," I lie. My head really, really hurts. I try to blink away the drops of blood that have rolled down into my eyes and push harder to stem the bleeding. "I cannot believe that just happened."

"It's probably just a taster of what's to come," Amara mumbles under her breath. Her masked fear radiates throughout the car. She changes gear and speeds along the road, following the twists and turns of Jessica's car. I can vaguely see the shape of Luke in the passenger's seat and I seriously hope he is okay. Apparently, my worry is quite evident.

"He's fine, I'm sure of it," Amara soothes.

"He was bleeding too though and he doesn't like blood." I absentmindedly answer her as I wipe away the drying blood from my face. Now that the blood is going, it doesn't look too bad, more like a heavy graze across my right temple, so I'm sure I can come up with an excuse about it at the party.

Oh God – the party. I hope I wasn't too forceful.

"I am really sorry about how I acted earlier. I just really want to still be a regular teenage girl." I recline deeper into the leather seats of her modern fitted out car. "I just don't want my world to revolve around this."

"I understand. Just leave Jess to me, I will deal with her." She smiles.

"You two are pretty close. How long have you known each other?" I ask. They seem like best friends, effortlessly working off each other and combining their ideas to create great outcomes. They remind me of me and Luke, how well they react without needing to talk. Amara swallows and stares intently ahead.

"When our powers awoke we were both cast out. She was terrified and I was alone. When I entered the spirit world they told me where to look for her and I set off on my journey. I didn't find her for at least a few weeks."

"How did it happen, if you don't mind me asking?" I can see that it's a difficult question to answer but I need to know more. These are my prophesised sisters after all.

"I lived in Greece until I was thirteen. It is the most beautiful place in the world. My parents owned a little café just on the outskirts of a town centre and we had everything we ever needed, because we grew all our own fruits and vegetables, and we sourced everything else locally." She smiles at the memory. "When I hit my thirteenth birthday my parents sent me to live with my grandmother in New Orleans. I was so scared, and excited, at this new change and being so far away from everyone I knew. I arrived, met my gran, and lived with her for a few months and everything was going well." She wipes away a tear and takes a sharp left turn, mirroring Jessica in front of us. No wonder she is driving so bad – Luke is terrible at giving directions. He likes to wait until you nearly pass the turn-off to tell you should be heading that way.

"What happened after a few months?" I focus on learning more about her as something is clearly troubled in her past.

"I was walking home from a friend's house one night and a storm was brewing so I was hurrying home as quickly as I could. It was raining heavily and the thunder was so loud, safe to say I was terrified, when a car pulled up and offered me a ride home. He looked sincere enough, in his forties with grey hair and a little scruffy beard, wearing a pale brown suit. I remember him so vividly."

Oh no.

"So I got in the car, despite what they teach you at school, or what your grandmother always says about stranger danger, I still accepted a ride with him. The storm was getting so violent and I just wanted to be home and he was my best chance at safety." She forces a smile and blinks away her tears. She has obviously perfected a mask to hide her pain and misery.

"You sure you are okay to carry on?" I ask worriedly.

"Of course, it's actually nice to say these words out loud. I have kept them buried for far too long." She fakes a brave smile and continues with her story. "So we were driving home and he took the wrong turn. I tried to tell him where I needed to go but he kept driving, no matter how panicked I seemed to get. I kept thinking to myself to use my powers but I could barely summon a breeze, let alone anything stronger at that point, so I just sat there. He eventually stopped in an abandoned factory space and locked the doors. I was paralysed with fear and I just sat frozen in my seat."

"Amara, please," I beg for her to stop. I don't need to hear any more. She must have been so scared, my heart breaks just hearing the story.

"It doesn't end how you think it does, Evelyn. After he placed his hand on my mouth to silence my screams, I bit as hard as I could and kicked out. I hit the door lock switch and threw myself out of the car and just started to run. My lungs were screaming and my eyes were so full of tears that I didn't see him behind me until he threw me to the floor. I screamed and screamed but my voice just cracked under the fear. His entire body weight was on me when I started to feel weightless. My body effortlessly lifted from underneath him, as if his grip had no effect on me, and I hovered in the air for a few moments."

"You used your powers in a moment of great emotional stress," I quote Jessica back after what she said earlier to me. Well, if anyone one of us had a reason to be stressed when we used our powers then it would be her.

"I sure did. The wind from the storm whipped around me like the tendrils on an octopus. I could feel every single thing in the air for miles around as if they were touching my skin directly. I panicked, of course, and I started screaming. My voice, coupled with my fear, made the storm a thousand fold worse, buildings were tore from the ground and the rivers burst their banks."

Oh God. I quickly put the pieces of her story together and I think I know exactly which storm she is on about.

"It was the worst natural disaster that New Orleans has ever experienced, let alone America." I can see the tears fall from her face and I offer her a tissue from a packet stuffed between some old books and a ruffled jumper in the backseat.

"Your powers made the storm worse but you didn't cause it, Amara," I try to console her.

"Either way, I killed thousands of people." She speaks so abruptly, it's shocking.

"No matter how much you blame yourself, Amara, I know that you did not mean to hurt anyone and what happened was not your fault. Not only were you attacked, but you were also in the centre of an already existing storm. You have nothing to be sorry for." I am trying to make light of the situations but a deep nagging sensation in the back of my head keeps reminding me of the thousands of people that died during that storm. She was so young and even more inexperienced but that's no excuse. I am so torn about how to be feeling about this. Half of me wants to hug her and tell her that no one will hurt her again and the other half wants to think about the innocent people who lost their lives. "Think of all the lives you will be saving by just being here though, as a Guardian, because without you then Avarice would be at large and millions would be dead."

"It's pretty ironic that our powers are meant to save people." She seems to scoff at her statement and rolls the window down allowing a welcomed breeze to fill the stuffy car. "It's almost like a reminder. We have the power to save the world, but we can cause so much destruction as well."

"So how did you go into the spirit world?" I hopefully try to change the mood.

"I went back a few weeks later after the storm had passed to aid with the rescue but all I did was slip into a sleep and my body was hidden amongst all the debris. I entered the spirit world and all I saw was the look of fear across previous Guardians' faces. They all saw what happened and they were just so worried about how powerful I was. They soon calmed down, after they saw I was just an innocent, lost, little girl and they told me everything I needed to know, including Avarice's past and all about his possession ability."

It all becomes slightly clearer now. I think about how little I learnt in my spirit journey but at least the others are here to explain it. Jessica's car turns down the lane for Luke's house so I instruct Amara to follow them when I remember something from earlier.

"When Avarice attacked me this morning he gave me the most horrific pain in the world so I would go to the forest and try to let loose with my powers. When he cornered me, he just said the word 'earth' and then left. But he is much stronger now because when he looked at us he saw our faults. When he looked at you, he said…"

"Secrets. He was talking about my past," she groans at the memory of being so close to the Grim Reaper whilst I look out the front screen and see Luke and Jessica pull into his driveway.

"Who's messed up car is that out front?" she asks jokingly.

"Mine. Don't ask," I gruffly respond. "I have one final question, though."

"Fire away," she responds as we exit the car.

"When are we going to meet the current water Guardian?" I ask, confused as to why she isn't here yet.

"You need to talk to Jess about that. It's not my place to say really. Just wait for the right moment." She complexly avoids my question and she tries to avoid making eye contact with me. "We should go in. It's getting dark and the party starts soon, and if you are forcing me to go then I need to look my best." She winks and drags me towards the door.

Luke's home is a glow with the hustle and bustle of four very busy people. Jessica walks around the house rapidly ensuring all windows and back doors are firmly locked, peering out into the evening darkness for any potential sightings, before coming to the spare room to join me. Amara ferries large rustic looking books from her car into the house, totalling around fifteen books before she is finished, and stares contently at the large pile of books with a weird mix of anticipation and boredom. Luke quickly takes a shower in an attempt to freshen up and rid his face of any blood. I riffle through the wardrobe in the spare room as I try, in vain, to find suitable clothes for tonight.

"I'm sure that I have some things here that will fit you two," I call back to the two of them as they sit on the bed, watching in amusement as I struggle to find clothes in the back of the large wardrobe, most of my body disappearing into mounds of chiffon and plaid.

"Why do you have a closet full of clothes at Luke's house?" Jessica enquires as I emerge from the closet, my head wrapped in an old silk blouse that I struggle to get off.

"Because we have an arrangement," Luke answers as he walks into the spare room wearing only a towel wrapped around his waist, his hair still dripping wet, and the water glistening on his body. Amara looks on with a dopey smirk plastered on her face whereas Jessica impressively stares at Luke's muscular physique as he walks to the set of drawers and pulls out a pair of black jeans. I roll my eyes in disgust at the two shallow ladies on the bed eyeing up Luke. Jessica catches my disapproving look and laughs.

"Just appreciating the nice view, that's all."

I scoff in response and throw Luke a patterned shirt that he asked me to pick out earlier. I click my fingers to draw the attention of the girls off my best friend and back onto myself. "It's like you guys staring down my brother."

"You have a brother?" Amara asks, almost hopefully.

"No. Luke is the closest I have ever gotten to a male sibling." Luke grins in the corner as he puts on his jeans and throws the rolled up towel on the bed.

"Anyway," I try to change the topic, "Luke and I always have clothes at each other's houses so we never have to pack a bag when we sleep over," I rationally explain.

"You two are like a married couple," Jessica jokes.

"It just makes sense. We have been staying at each other's houses since we were children. So whenever we have a party to go to I keep my dresses here and then I can change my clothes as many times as I want so we don't worry about school the next day," I explain in more detail. I have never thought of it in any other way other than the fact that Luke and I are so close.

"Plus she hates having her dresses at her house just in case her mother sees them and starts to gain hope that she might wear them permanently." Luke laughs out loud at his comment and I reach over and throw a nearby pillow at him hitting him directly causing him to lose his footing and fall over with a thud. We all erupt into laughter as he stands up quickly, a foolish grin on his face. It seems weird that we are laughing like normal teenage friends yet moments ago we were being thrown around by an ancient evil.

"Here we go," I fish out two outfits from my wardrobes and hand them to the girls, who just look sceptically at me, at my choice of clothing.

"What?" I defiantly ask. "These are great outfits."

"If you insist," Jessica groans as she grabs one dress and exits the room to change. Amara however quickly thumbs through the wardrobe and selects a completely different choice of attire.

"I'll see if this one looks better," she states as she holds the new outfit. I place the lime green dress back into the closet defeated and wait for them to try on their clothes. I pull out my phone and switch the camera on, and point it to myself, so I can see myself reflected on the screen. I push my hair around so that my bangs successfully hide the graze across my forehead so that no one will see it tonight. After a few moments, Luke joins me on the bed, styling his hair in the vanity mirror leaning against the wall at the far end of the room, and I begin to half-heartedly scold him.

"Seriously, Luke. Did you have to come in here looking like an underwear model?"

"I can't help how I look, Evie. Plus the girls had no complaints." He smirks at me and I swat him with my hand. He feigns injury and throws himself down onto the bed. "When did this become our lives

Evie? It used to be schoolwork and football and classes and now its monsters and powers and ghosts." He breathes the words out as if in a dream.

"I have no idea. Part of me just wants to go back to the way it used to be."

"And the other part?" he persists.

"Always knew we were meant for more." I honestly answer him.

"You," he corrects. "You were meant for more. I am just here for the ride."

I lay down to join him and roll over so that I am propped up on my side, supported by my elbow, and Luke matches my position. We stare at each other's faces and I realise how much I need him right now.

"Luke, you are the most important person in my life. You are part of my family. There is no way I could do this without you because I am not strong enough. I would never let anything happen to you." I just let the words flood out as they come from deep inside of me. "I know we mess around and I joke about you a lot but I want you to know how much you mean to me. I really don't say this enough but you really are my best friend."

"Now, don't you go getting all soppy on me." He reaches over and pulls me into his arms, locking me in a much needed tight embrace. I relax and let all the stress from my body float away, leaving me totally calm.

"Are we interrupting something?" Jessica calls from the doorway, Luke and I sheepishly jump up and look at the girls in their party clothes.

I really hate to admit it but they look stunning.

Jessica stands elegantly in a classical dress with an edgy look to it. The black dress has a fitted bodice with a soft skirt that flares out at waist height. The bottom half dazzles with alternating red silk layers of underskirt and red flowers that frame the base of the black skirt, creating the more edgy look. Her fiery hair is pushed to the left side, pinned across with golden hairclips, where it tumbles effortlessly down past her shoulders. Her long legs lead to a pair of black open toed heels that she must have borrowed from Luke's mother.

Amara looks equally as beautiful in a sleeveless sheer black jumpsuit. The top half consists of two black straps that cross over at the chest and tie around the neck, falling down the backless outfit. Her hair is pulled back off her face, a headband pushing it back into a bunch that frames her dark face. The only splash of colour in this outfit is the bright red heels that she wears under the long jumpsuit leg that give her that well received burst of colour.

"Damn!" Luke exclaims.

"You look lovely," I correct, as I exit the room to get changed. I enter the open bathroom and try to fit into the dress that I collected. The agony of wearing something so colourful will be worth it when I arrive looking a thousand times better than Pandora thought I would. I fish into my pocket and quickly dial my mother and explain that I would be sleeping at Luke's tonight, and despite her reservations of sleeping at his on a school night, I assure her that everything is okay and she finally caves in. I finish the call with a simply 'love you' but it comes out more of a promise than a simple goodbye. With the dress now fitted, I set about fixing my hair in the mirror on the wall. I stare intently at my reflection.

I have pulled my hair into a mass of twists and curls, held in place by small pins, each decorated with a single white gem, leaving my bangs to fall down and hide my recent wound. The dress is a vibrant shade of pink that is both sleeveless and strapless. It fits snugly around the torso and chest before falling into layers of ruffles and chiffon. A large pink ribbon wraps around the waist and forms a large bow that rests on my hip.

"Now or never," I tell myself and I exit the bathroom.

All eyes turn on me. Jessica looks shocked, Amara looks surprised and Luke looks down right freaked out.

"That's the pinkest thing I have ever seen you wear in my life, Evie." He struggles to get his words out.

"Thanks… I guess."

"You look stunning!" Amara jumps up and runs to me, patting my dress with delicate hands.

"It's pretty," Jess similarly stands.

"It's pink," Luke repeats himself. They are all just kind of looking at me.

"If you have all finished staring, can we please leave now?" I ask as I attempt to get their stares off me as we exit Luke's house and ready ourselves to enter Hell itself.

Her house is just like her personality. Loud and in your face.

The large white mansion stands proudly amongst the vast green acres, spotlights shine brightly up the house, only further enhancing the sheer size of this gargantuan house. Pink and blue streamers are haphazardly strewn around the property, which is filled with the many teenage people I go to school with. Unsurprisingly the girls all hover in small swarms, each holding drinks and canapés that they have no intention of eating. The guys, however, are still in their pack mentality and are rushing around, throwing balls and clambering over each other. Fake shrill laughs and belches fill the air, the overpowering stench of perfume clogs my nose, and the loud thumping music booms aggressively, muffling most people's conversations. In the centre of Pandora's vast courtyard stands a raised platform on which hired performers are entertaining the vast mass of onlookers. Currently there are two fire breathers, spurting flames high into the dark sky, with two other people in the background spinning flaming batons.

"Amateurs," Jessica scoffs from behind me.

At the epicentre of the crowd stands the Queen Bee herself, wearing a very skimpy blue little satin dress, her hair pulled back into a tight ponytail highlighting her annoyingly perfect angular face.

"If this is just a regular party, then I would be terrified to see what she does for her birthday." Amara looks around in awe at the vast amount of effort put into such a small event. Pandora seems to be scanning the area, probably trying to soak up all the feelings of adoration, when she locks eyes with me. She whispers something to her little gaggle of friends and they all begin to walk over in perfect unison, Pandora at the helm, and the followers a step behind. They look akin to a small army marching into war.

"I am so glad you managed to come, Evelyn." Pandora shimmies towards me and air kisses to the side of me as she pulls my body into an unwelcomed hug. She is obviously pretending to be perfect in front of my new group of friends, having not yet assessed whether they are her friend or foes. "Who are your guests?"

"My…" I struggle to come up with a lie because I doubt 'Guardians' will swing with her.

"Cousins." Jessica steps in and politely greets Pandora, who just stands looking unapprovingly.

"The family resemblance is uncanny," she sarcastically smiles at us, eyeing up Jessica and Amara.

"Distant cousins," Luke calls out before he high fives and chest bumps his fellow football players nearby. "In town for a few days, right, girls?"

"Yes," both Amara and Jessica answer at the same time, identical smiles plastered on their faces.

"Well, the invite was only for you and Luke." She makes direct eye contact with me as if I was challenging her authority. *As if I care that much.*

"Now Pandora, that's no way to treat your guests, is it?" a soothing British accent calls out from amongst the crowd. Ethan pushes his way through the people and stands in front of me, two drinks in his hands, his dirty blond locks falling beautifully past his cheeks, looking very smart in a crisp white shirt and grey trousers.

"When did you get here?" Pandora asks, almost offended that he didn't speak to her first, but he seemingly ignores her.

"There you go," he extends his hands and offers me a plastic cup filled with a dubious looking liquid. I raise my eyebrows at the contents and he laughs and proclaims that it is only from the punchbowl. "You are looking as beautiful as ever tonight."

"Oh." *Oh... oh... is that all I could come out with? I seriously need to work on my flirting technique.*

"Don't forget the karaoke later Ethan We can do a duet if you want?" Pandora tries to be heard but no one is listening to her.

"You certainly do have a lot of attractive male friends, Evelyn," Amara laughs as she walks into the mass of football jocks who whistle while she is bombarded with offers to go and get her a drink. "Shall we go get a drink Jess?" She whisks her away into the crowd of people, with just enough for time for Jessica to shout out to 'yell if I need her.'

"Shall we go somewhere quieter? I can barely hear myself think," Ethan asks angelically.

"Yes, please," I respond as if I am begging. I am so embarrassing.

"Oh, never mind me. I'll just walk around on my own for a while until you two are finished having a chit chat." Luke angrily speaks before he walks away. Pandora huffs before heading in the same direction. It's just the two of us left and we begin to venture towards the large white patio doors. Once inside he continues to walk towards the grand staircase in the middle of the room.

"Where are we going?" I quietly ask. If he says the bedroom then I am heading straight for the door.

"I just thought we could watch the party from the balcony on the third floor. It's much quieter at the back of the house and we can even look at the stars." He quells my fears and takes my hand, his large palm enveloping my dainty fingers.

"That's a fantastic idea. Are we still on for Friday night?"

"Friday?" he confusedly asks, apparently forgetting that he invited me to see his friend's band play. My cheeks flush in embarrassment when I realise he was probably joking about the event.

I stutter as I try to jog his memory, "Your friends... their band...Friday night?" But his face remains as impassive as ever.

"Oh, of course! Sorry, I totally forgot. Yes we are still going ahead with that. You are so beautiful it messes with my head." He jokingly hits himself on the head and laughs at how bad his memory is. I continue to blush as we enter one of the large study rooms, shelves of books rise high, a large mahogany desk stands to my left and two artificial potted plants rest to my right. We walk over towards the balcony but before I can walk through the doorway and onto the stone balcony Ethan grabs my hand and spins me so I'm facing him front on.

"I am glad I got you on your own," he soothingly talks to me.

"And why is that?" I coyly answer him. He releases my hand and walks straight past me and out onto the balcony, his hands gripping the metal safety railing, his back towards me. For some reason I suddenly feel very self-conscious in my pink dress. "Ethan?"

His hands relax and he begins to slowly turn on the spot, the party lights illuminating half of his chiselled face until he is staring at me straight on.

"Because now I can kill you," he simply responds, despite my gasp, as his eyes completely glaze over with a thick white mist.

Chapter 13

Evelyn

Being punched in the stomach by a possessed football player really, really, hurt. Being thrown over a desk hurt a lot more.

I lift my head up and gaze at Ethan, standing before me, through tear filled eyes. His beautiful face contorted with a grimace of evil. Dreamy eyes now hide behind a pearly mist and his tanned skin now looks a sick shade of grey.

"Are you sure you are a Guardian?" he smirks as he throws me effortlessly through the air and directly into one of the hanging bookcases causing a cascade of hardback books to fall around me. I scramble on the floor in an attempt to put a few mere metres between myself and Avarice… or Ethan.

"You know, for an ancient villain, you really suck at torture. Throwing me into a bookcase is hardly world domination material," I sarcastically retort, gasping for breath between my words, as I rise from my spot on the floor. I am determined to keep him talking until I can get some sort of signal to Amara and Jessica.

"Your words are meaningless. Earth has always been the weakest element." He sneers at me as he brushes his hands down his clothes. He paces around the room with an intense look of discomfort on the normally beautiful face, his body moving stiffly as if it was unnatural for him.

"You sure about that? Keep hurting me and you will see how powerful I really I am." I stand valiantly although I am aware he can probably crush me with a single gesture. "If you think that I will hesitate when it comes to hurting you then you are mistaken.

"You would tear down a house full of your friends in an attempt to thwart me? You overestimate your power girl. The element of fire can burn on long after the Guardian has left, and the wind continues to howl even if there is no one controlling it. But the Earth Guardian... Alas your powers come from the very earth that you walk on and by manipulating this you cause more harm than good. Now that's not very kind of you." He grins as he says the last part. His words crawl under my skin like scuttling bugs made from lava. Hot waves crash over me, blood rushes to my face, and my hands tremble with a mix of power and fear.

"I don't need to crush this house to destroy you. We have met before and if I am correct I think I nearly killed you. Twice." I stand my ground whilst I think of what to do. I can't cause an earthquake because that would be too hard to explain. There is no earth around for me to manipulate, not even a real potted plant to explode, so I have to resort to brute strength.

"You had a forest to defend yourself. You have nothing here." He turns and gestures around the empty, and partially destroyed, room.

"You sure about that?" I decide to attack whist his back is turned. Allowing the adrenaline to fuel me, I run at full speed, or at least as fast as I can in these heels, and grab his extended arm. I twist it back on itself and pin him against the wall directly in front of us. I yank furiously upwards, and aim a kick towards the back of his knees, causing his body to crumple beneath me. Those self-defence lessons that my dad forced me to attend have seemingly paid off.

"Don't need to crush this house to make a point." I squeeze harder on his pinned arm, a stifled groan coming from his trapped body, as his other arm presses against the wall.

"I am over a thousand years old, I have destroyed cities and killed millions. I have been heralded as a god, a titan, a warrior and a myth. Do you really think that a stupid little girl can defeat me?" He grimaces as I apply more pressure to his twisted arm.

"Well this stupid little girl has just crippled a thousand year old demon. I don't really care about anything else."

"The acclaimed noble Guardian speaks in lies. There are things that you care for." He struggles against my grip for a moment before allowing his body to become relaxed. With a mere blink of the eye, he disappears from my grip, causing me to stagger forwards and fill the space he once occupied, and hear the sound of footsteps behind me.

"I conquered the globe once and I didn't exactly do that on foot. You have no idea of the powers that I possess child. But I know all about your weaknesses." I am expecting him to throw me into another wall, hit me, or at least fry me alive. Instead, he simply reaches down and picks up a piece of shattered glass from a framed painting that broke in our scuffle. He doesn't lunge at me, throw it, or even attempt to harm me. The shard is instead raised up and pressed against his neck.

Ethan's neck.

"Please," I whimper. I know that Ethan means nothing to him and he will slice through his skin like a knife through butter.

"I can just leave this body and gain another. Even yours." He pushes the glass further, a single drop of blood rolls down his pale neck and permeates the pristine white collar of Ethan's shirt.

Wait!" *Think Evelyn, think.* "You don't need to do this. You can do so much better."

He hesitates momentarily, the shard still digging into the ghostly flesh, before relaxing his hand slightly giving a few inches between the glass and his neck. His gaze never leaves my face, as if he is trying to locate something, most likely a hint of weakness.

"You don't want to return to your old body and the one you have been using is far too old to be of any use. So how about I make a deal with you?" I just need to keep him distracted.

"I am listening," he states flatly.

"You said so yourself, that you can take any body so why don't you take mine. Leave his body and take over a Guardian. Think of the power, you are a demon after all, so think about all that you can achieve if you could rip the world in two." I try to keep his eyes locked on my face as my hand, currently obscured by the edge of the table, rummages around in my small purse for my phone. "You would never have to fear the threat of the Guardians because you would be in possession of one. And if I am correct then the next lot of Guardians cannot be activated unless the previous ones all die or you somehow manage to revive yourself from death."

"I cannot die. I am immortal. My physical form is weak but my spirit can never die. It isn't long before I can reform myself"

"Exactly," I tell him, feeling my phone lie cold in my hand. Years of practice means that I can navigate around my phone without having to look at it. I quickly enter my call list and dial Amaras number, which we exchanged during our exploration of the catacombs, and start to call her. "You take my body, and leave my friends unharmed, and I will go willingly." I hear Amaras muffled voice through my purse as she questions where I am. I talk louder, just enough for her to hear me through the layers of material. "Do we have a deal? You take over my body and leave Ethan alone. We can make a solemn vow over there on the balcony, just above the pool and under the starry sky, and I will go willingly. You will not harm Jessica or Amara or Luke."

"You would do this for your friends?" He looks at me, puzzled.

"It's called having a heart. Do we have a deal or not?" I start to circle him and head towards the stone balcony overhanging the back pool. The party continues in the south corner of the garden, the flash of lights and hum of music carries into the distance, whilst the glow of the pool lights cast an eerie glow over us. The cool wind whips around us as we step onto the balcony and stand intimately close to each other. His glassy eyes stare me down as he takes my hand. This is *not* how I planned to have my first kiss with Ethan.

"If this fails, then you will not be leaving this house alive. This is going to hurt." He smiles sickeningly.

Now or never Evie!

"Just one last thing Avarice, if I can call you that, do you recall what you said earlier about Earth being the weakest element? You may be right about that. I can't get out of this small place without probably collapsing the building, I can't disappear on a whim like you can but there is one gift I do have. I have a fantastic brain and I don't get nearly enough credit for it. I know that you are only capable of what your host body can handle, hence why as the old man Grim Reaper you can't do much, but when you possessed the youthful Pandora you had access to all your abilities"

"What is your point girl? Your insolence bores me." His mouth curls into a snarl.

I pull my hands free from him and rest them on the stone balcony, feeling the cold stone against my burning skin. I really hope Amara is on her way.

"My point is that you possess people because you have spent most of your life as a spirit. Your real body was locked away until recently. So I strongly doubt and ancient demon can swim." His eyes widen in shock. "Just leave Ethan's body when you start to drown, he can swim back to the surface whilst you fly back into the Grim Reaper." I am taking a huge gamble here and I seriously hope it pays off, otherwise Ethan and I are both dead. Here goes.

I summon a tremor from the ground below and channel it up the side of the house silently, masking the violent shakes as the crack snakes up onto the stone balcony and spreads around the wall where the stone connects to the house. The balcony viciously shakes before chunks of rock shower into the air and we are both violently thrown off the now crumbling chunks of stone and head for the water, free falling through the air above the pool from the third floor.

A fall from this height would only take a matter of seconds yet it feels like we are falling for an eternity. A hundred questions whip around my already frazzled brain. What if he can fly? What if he doesn't leave Ethan's body? What if he can swim and holds me under the water?

The thoughts quickly leave my head when I slowly descend, still mid-air, until I am left suspended above the glittering pool as Ethan's body plummets past me and makes contact with the pristine water with a loud splash. I crane my neck and see Amara standing on the grass, her arms outstretched in my direction, with an extremely annoyed look on her face.

"You have no idea how glad I am to see you." I smile sincerely as I breathe a sigh of relief. Amara waves her hands and I feel by body being pulled toward her, the wind flowing around me and supporting me in the air, until I firmly plant my feet on solid ground. "I owe you one."

"Do you have any idea how stupid that was? What if I couldn't hear you through the phone and I wasn't here to help. You could have smacked into the water and been knocked unconscious," she sternly tells me off.

"I can swim," I justify myself as I slowly walk over to the edge of the pool where Ethan's body moves underneath the water. Both myself and Amara raise our arms and change our stances, ready to attack if Avarice climbs out of the water. A pale hand grips the stone edge of the pool, clawing at the small stones that rest there, before pulling the rest of the body out. Ethan rises out of the pool, looking surprisingly attractive, his hair flopped wet over his face.

"Ethan?" I hesitantly ask.

He slowly raises his chin, brushes the hair from his face, as his eyelids flutter open. Two brown eyes stare at me.

"Oh, thank God." I rush over and wrap my arms around him and squeeze him tightly into a hug.

"What the hell just happened?" His rich British accent cuts through the air as he remains frigid in my grasp.

"The balcony collapsed underneath you," Amara answers him, offering a distractingly dazzling smile, and taking his hand. "We should get you inside."

We enter in through the back door and navigate through the mass of rooms before entering the kitchen. Ethan leans against the counter as Amara fishes around for a towel to dry him with. I quiz him about the last thing he remembers but his face is the only answer I need – a look of pain and confusions firmly rests on his beautiful face.

"I was driving over here when I stopped because someone was standing in the middle of the road. I got out to see if he was okay and that's all I can remember."

"You must have drunk a little bit too much Ethan." Amara appears carrying a towel that she pats him down with. He takes it off her and rubs his hair dry.

"We need to go," Amara mouths towards me and I reply with a simple nod as we begin to leave the room.

"Ethan, I hope you feel a little bit better soon but I really have to go. I'll see you Friday." I stop for a moment and turn to face him and offer him a little test. "You do remember Friday, don't you? What time are we meeting?" I wait on bated breath for his answer.

"Seven-ish?" He looks confused as to why I am speaking so accusatorily.

"Perfect." I beam at him and quickly leave the room. We navigate through the crowds of people and struggle to locate Luke or Jessica. I fish my phone out of my purse and speed dial Luke.

"Hey," he answers, his voice cuts crisp through the loud music.

"Where are you and Jessica?"

"I know that tone of voice, Evie. What happened with Ethan?" he frantically asks.

I sigh. I spoke five words and he already starts to panic. "I am fine, I swear. Now where are you guys?"

"Hang on," he takes his mouth away from the phone and I can hear his muffled voice talking to someone. "Jess is over near the drinks table and I am at the front of the stage."

"See you in a moment." I kill the call and push through more people until I can see the raised stages area and Luke looking around, probably searching for me.

"Luke," I whistle and he locks eyes with me. He heads over, a little too quickly, and firmly takes my hands.

"What happened?" he sharply asks me before anything else.

"I'm fine. Ethan was Avarice the whole time," I answer him and his mouth drops in shock.

"Where is he now?" he worriedly asks me but I quietly assure him that when I sent his body falling into the pool that the only person who came out was Ethan. He continues to shower me with warnings about never going anywhere by myself again and how we need to travel as a group from now on. "So, where is he now?" he asks again.

"Ethan is in the kitchen drying off."

"I meant Avarice. If he left his body, and he is too weak to live on as a ghost or whatever, then he would have to take possession of somebody pretty soon."

"Oh." *Good point.*

"I can find out if he is possessing someone. I just need to get to—" Amara tries to talk but the music is abruptly cut off and Pandora's voice booms around the open area. She takes to the stage, her army of followers behind her.

"I would like to thank you all for coming tonight and spending the evening with me. Now it's time for me to give something back to all of you." The beat of a song rises from the speakers as Pandora begins to sing, her followers swaying to the beat with a mediocre dance routine, as she croaks down the microphone.

"She is so vapid," Amara moans.

"And untalented," I agree. We walk over to where Luke said he last saw Jessica to see her dancing with two boys from my school. She moves her body to the music fiercely, her loose red hair flies around her like flames and her dress hugs her body in a very flattering way. No wonder the boys find her irresistible. We head over to them and quickly shoo away the loitering men.

"I was having fun," Jessica protests. "I really don't know why you complain about school so much, Evelyn; these people are fantastic." She gestures towards the mass of gyrating people.

"I'm sure you wouldn't be saying that if you went here every day," I grumble.

"I miss school," Jessica groans as she walks away with us.

"Plan of action." Luke takes up the front of the group and details what happens now. "We go back to mine and assess the situation tomorrow. You two can sleep in the guesthouse at the end of the yard. My parents won't be back till late and they will leave super early tomorrow anyway for some medical conference in Hawaii." Luke gestures towards Jessica and Amara as he invites them to stay. Luke is so used to his parents being gone for large periods of time due to work, and being an only child he only has to take care of himself. "Let's leave."

"Going already?" A voice booms behind us as we head towards the driveway causing us to turn in surprise. I half expect Avarice to be standing a hundred foot tall and bearing down on us, but instead I see Pandora facing us from the stage, every pair of eyes in the audience locked onto us. "It's awfully rude to attend a party and not stay for the main event. After my fantastic performance, I think I should let someone else take the stage. Evelyn?"

All eyes switch solely to me. I shrink into myself and Pandora and her army have sick smiles wiped across their faces. There is no way I am going on stage and singing in front of all these people. I can't even sing.

"What's the matter, Evelyn? Cat got your tongue?" she persists.

"I'm good, thank you!" I yell from where I am standing, my voice cracks from embarrassment. "I told you that she was like Avarice in a mini skirt! Public humiliation is her way of asserting dominance," I whisper to the others.

"Just as I thought. Big enough to sneak off with the football captain but can't handle a little song. Tut tut." An eruption of whistles and mutterings spill from the audience with Pandora's words. Gossip already fills the air and I wish the earth would just swallow me whole. *I could probably do that.*

"I'll do it!" Amara cheerily answers from beside me. The whispers and mumbles turn from my love life to questions of who this new beauty is.

"The invitation wasn't for you, I'm afraid," Pandora splutters.

"That's okay. We are family after all." She gives me a wink and quickly ascends the stairs onto the stage. She ushers Pandora off before whispering to the band what song to play. The music fills the air as she boldly stands centre stage, all eyes on her. She opens her mouth and the most beautiful sound comes out that I have ever heard. She seems to not only have captivated me, but every member of the audience. The words spill from her mouth and pour across the audience like a fine mist spreading through everyone, mesmerising them.

At first I thought she was a good singer but the audience seem to be a little too invested in the performance. All eyes remain firmly locked onto her face, mouths slightly open, and their bodies remaining staticc.

"What's going on?" Luke asks, confused, struggling to tear his eyes away from the performance himself. "It's like everyone is a zombie."

"Not zombies. Their sole purpose is to watch her and listen." Jessica grins.

"How is she doing that?" I question.

"We were destined to work as a team to defeat Avarice so our powers grow stronger as we grow closer. When we first met each other our powers grew a lot and we developed so much more control over them," she explains as Amara rounds up her song. "Our powers amplify in ways you would never imagine. She is like a *Siren.*"

As Amara comes to a close, the air remains silent for a few moments, before a thunderous applause booms from the appreciative audience. She joyfully takes a bow before descending the stairs and joining us. Pandora has a permanent scowl locked onto her face as we leave, before unsuccessfully trying to draw attention back to her.

"And that is how it's done. If Avarice had possessed anyone, I would have just found out," Amara laughs as she walks with us away from the party.

Chapter 14

Evelyn

The sunlight streams through the gap in the curtains and rests on my face and just for a second I forget about everything.

There is no Avarice, no spirits, no powers and no Guardians. For a few mere moments, the world continues to spin as normal and I feel like a regular teenage girl. I want to wake up and get dressed, kiss my parents and my sister, head off to school and spend the day with Luke. We stumble through the day trying not to get into too much trouble until we drive back to his house and chill for a few hours, meaning I struggle with masses of homework and Luke tries in vain to beat his high score on some video game. We eat a delicious meal that his mother makes before I drive home, hop straight into bed and the day just repeats itself again and again for the next year until we leave for college. Those are the days, no matter how mundane they were, that I long for after all that has happened.

I was expecting to have the usual dream, stranded in the forest alone, but this time it is different. I'm not in the empty forest but instead I am in a vacated room. Damp mud slushes underneath me as I take a fearful step. The stone walls run high and disappear into the darkness yet white moonlight floods the room despite having no source for the light to enter. I run my hands across the stone walls and try to search for any signs of a way out but the smooth rock circles around perfectly with no cracks or imperfections.

The room is barely seven feet in diameter and I feel both alone and trapped at the same time. I scream for help but my voice just echoes around my small prison until it fades into nothingness. Willing myself to relax I allow my powers to stretch out far in search for any plant life but my attempt is fruitless as there are no signs of life, of any kind, within my locations. Kicking the water in frustration, it dawns on me that I'm not in a prison, but simply a *well*.

I'm stranded in the bottom of a well.

Screaming provides no relief nor does attempting to climb out of the well, but as time passes the moonlight fades and darkness descends, until it washes over me in a wave of pure fear. Stranded in the dark. Alone. *There's something in the darkness.*

Snapping back into reality, I wake with a jump. I sit bolt upright in the bed, a thin sheen of sweat on my body. I throw the sheets off my body and walk over to the window, lifting it up and allowing a welcomed breeze to fill the room. Despite how much I long for the days to be like they used to be. it creeps back into me that Avarice does exist, so do the spirits, my powers and being a Guardian. Like it or not it's real.

I walk around Luke's spare room, opening the wardrobe and hanging up the discarded dress from last night and selecting a simple pair of jeans and white woolly jumper. I walk across the carpet floor and knock lightly on Luke's door. I wait for his answer and enter the room.

"Good morning." He smiles as he applies the finishing touches to his hair, staring into the mirror, before turning and walking towards me and ushers me out of the room. We descend the stairs and into the kitchen where Amara and Jessica sit passively on the bar stools around the marble topped island sipping coffee. They greet Luke and me warmly as we pour ourselves some hot drinks and sit down alongside them.

No one talks for at least five minutes. Amara thumbs through a large, ancient looking book that is placed before her. Jessica has a town map open fully, covered with notes and scribbles that she has jotted down.

"So…" Luke breaks the silence.

"So…" The three of us echo.

"What's the plan?"

We all look at each other with uncertainty, no one willing to answer his question due to fear of embarrassment. Our last plan didn't exactly end well considering the body that we tried to stop Avarice from getting is now in his control. None of us know what to do anymore.

"There must be something that we can do," he persists.

"Luke, listen," Jessica calmly answers. "We are kind of at our crossroads here. We don't know what to do next because our last plan failed. Miserably. We can either go looking for Avarice but with no leads I strongly doubt that we will find him before he manages to enter his body or we wait until he regains control and then launch a full attack."

"That could be a suicide mission," Amara speaks up, her head faced down resting on her folded arms on the table.

"Or we can track him down now because he has just returned to the Grim Reaper's body, assuming that is where he has gone, and attack," Luke suggests. Hearing the word attack come from his mouth is an extremely uncomfortable thing to listen too. He is such a passive person, except when he is on the football field, but after everything that has happened, he is showing a whole new side of him that I never even knew. This aggressive personality and willingness to do whatever is needed maybe something that I need to adopt.

"We should start tracking him. He could be possessing anyone by now or, as I have stated many times already, he could be back in his body. Although tracking him may not be such a good idea considering we have no idea what his original body actually looks like," Jessica contradicts herself.

"Well, there must be something that we can do. We cannot just sit her and wait for someone else to be taken over, or killed." Luke continues to push the subject.

"Enough!" I yell, surprised at my volume. "I can't do this, Luke. I can't keep letting these plans fill our heads with false hope. I am scared, and I mean truly afraid, because I feel powerless. I can feel my powers evaporating and boiling away and I cannot do anything to stop it. The thought of going up against him again makes me feel so weak and so powerless. Our powers go stronger with our emotions yet my fear just dampens them. They are meant to boost when we are together but we are incomplete. There are meant to be four of us but you two are obviously keeping something from me." I continue to rant but I take note of the look that Amara and Jessica shoot to each other. "He is far too powerful for the three Guardians. Every time he wakes up, the Guardians destroy him and all he does is sleep until he is strong enough to wake up again, it's a never-ending loop that may be broken this time because we are not strong enough to destroy him. We are the first Guardians to ever fail their sole purpose of stopping him from finding his body and sending his spirit back to wherever it goes. We had one job and we screwed that up. We've already lost. I don't want to go up against him Luke because if he hurts you then I have no idea what I will do. You are walking round with a huge target on your back thanks to me and I will not let him harm you." I place my hand on Luke's arm sincerely, subconsciously reaching for his calming touch.

"We won't let that happen, Evelyn. Trust us," Amara states, never raising her head from the book that she is reading.

"Trust you? That is such a ridiculous thing to suggest. You are both hiding something from me and I cannot willingly follow you until you tell me what it is." I stubbornly stand my ground.

Once again they look at each other, casting stern glances, before facing me. "There are some things Evelyn that we can't tell you yet. They will cause more harm than good," Amara soothes. Jessica tries to avoid eye contact with me.

"You are awfully quiet, Jessica. Something to share?" I persist.

"Evie, drop it," Luke contributes, obviously sensing Jessica's abhorrence to answering the question.

The words continue to rip out of my mouth without even sparing a thought, like I am not even in control of what I am saying. "No I won't Luke. I cannot be expected to follow these girls into battle when they are hiding things from me. I barely know anything about the two of them."

"You know enough," Jessica mumbles, still not raising her head to look at me.

"I don't even know your surnames!" I yell. Despite having nearly died together it dawned on me, in the heat of the moment, that I didn't even know their full names.

"Jessica Wicker."

"Amara Dubois."

Luke raises his eyebrows when Amara states her surname but she quickly explains that she changed her surname to match her grandmother's when she first moved to New Orleans in an attempt to fit in.

"And the water element? What is her name?" Luke asks as he takes over from my previous role of interrogator.

"Her name is Raina." Jessica pushes a loose strand of hair from her face and neatly tucks it behind her ear. Her eyes glint as she moves when they catch the light, as if they are full of tears that are yet to pour down her face.

"Let me guess – Raina is waiting in the shadows for us to get into some deep trouble and then jump in and save us, just like you did." I gesture to Amara, whose head is currently buried in a pile of books, referring to when she saved us yesterday in the catacombs.

"You will meet her soon and that is the last time we will mention the subject, okay?" Jessica's eyes lock onto mine with a fierce, burning, intensity behind her rust coloured eyes.

"Guys," Amara interrupts, "I have found something." She points at one of the dust covered pages in an old looking green book. Fine writing fills the page with only a hand drawn sketch to separate the bulk text. The image is of a vase, a simple shape that starts out thin and fills out towards the bottom, with a curved lid resting on the top. There are various carvings etched onto the vase that I cannot see clearly, having smudged over the years.

"What is it?" Luke enquires, looking as confused as I do.

"I never really thought of it until I saw this." She dives into one of her many books and pulls out a coloured pamphlet detailing the artefact exhibition that took place in Ravens Valley a few years ago. She flicks through the pages before stopping on a page dedicated to an ancient exhibit, the vase, now shining bright gold, with the carvings much clearer. "I saw the vase in these books and I didn't really think it was important but I just realised that I saw it somewhere else before. This exhibit shows the same vase." She grins with pride from her discovery.

"I'm so confused. What does that have to do with Avarice?" Luke scratches his head.

"Because the supposedly lost vase, with ancient text dating back to the time of Avarice, miraculously shows up in Ravens Valley." Her smile practically beams.

"Let me see what I can search up." Luke whips out his smartphone and starts to search the internet about the current location of the vase.

"That doesn't necessarily mean anything though. All we know is that the vase is as old as he is. There are lots of ancient artefacts that date back to the time when he roamed the world." Jessica joins in with the disapproving looks.

"Alas," she points to the carvings on the vase, "these are Elder Futhark runes." She reaches over and grabs a loose scrap of paper and a pen before effortlessly scribing the runes down onto paper large enough for us all to see.

ᚠᚺᛗᚱᛗ ᛗᛁ ᛗᛗᛗᚻᛏᛉ ᛗᛗᛗᛏ ᚠᚻᛉᛈᛗᚱ
ᛉ ᛁᛪ ᚾ ᛉᚾᚠᛁᛁ ᛉ ᛗ ᛗ ᚲ

"All I see are scribbles," Luke answers, turning his head like a confused dog, before looking back at his phone. Amara continues to write underneath the runes, but this time in clear English.

"Where elements meet. Answers you shall seek." She reads aloud as she translates the runes across. She caps the pen and rests it on the paper, a smug look across her face.

"Since when could you translate ancient languages?" Jessica asks, looking as confused as Luke, apparently learning something new about her friend.

"Well," Amara begins, "when I went to live with my grandmother in New Orleans she was seeing a man who was an ancient languages teacher at one of the universities. He used to bring home books for me to read at night."

Jessica picks up one of the heavy books and hands it to me, the large weight pushes down onto me. "She actually thinks this is light reading," Jess scoffs.

"Well, lucky for us that I can translate because now we have a lead. A literal clue."

"I'm confused about something though. This vase obviously originates from the ancient times, Ravens Valley to be specific, and states that the elements meet. How did it know that we would be anywhere near each other? This vase couldn't possibly know that our pendants would lead us to one another," Jessica questions as Amara dives back into her books.

"Maybe its magic?" Luke suggests.

"Wouldn't surprise me." I roll my eyes.

"No way." Amaras eyes light up as I can see an idea form in her head. "It doesn't mean the elemental Guardians. It means the literal elements. Hand me that," she orders as she gestures for Jessica to hand her a folded map of Ravens Valley. She unfolds the paper until it takes up all the space on the table. Jessica, who had gathered the books from the table before the map was spread out, sets the heavy books down on the nearby counter with a loud thud.

"The natural elements." Amara points to the open map, which is coloured with grey lines and green fields. The map doesn't show any settlements, instead it shows the natural land and thin roads. "If I am correct then there should be four noticeable natural elements that the vase if referring to."

"That's an awfully big presumption. There have been hundreds of Guardians before us, are you telling me that not one of them found this clue before? The vase just happened to be around at the same time as Avarice. It could just be another prophecy that has absolutely no relation to the natural elements," Jessica sounds off in protest.

"Plus the world has changed over the years Amara. The natural elements that the vase was referencing might not even be here anymore, it's a pretty big chance to take." I agree with Jessica.

"That's pretty rich coming from you." She points towards me and although her words seem harsh they come out harmlessly, "you threw yourself off of a balcony with an ancient demon in the hopes that he wouldn't fly or teleport away, or at least that he wouldn't drown the hot guy he was possessing. You also hoped that I would be there in time to stop you smashing into the water and then run the risk of Avarice trying to drown you. Please trust me on this on," she pleads.

"She has a point Evie. You were pretty reckless and a hundred things could have gone wrong yesterday. Let's just run with this idea for a while." Luke warmly rubs my back as I raise my hands in defeat. It's worth a shot.

Amara smiles with glee as she realises that we are willing to see her plan through. She repeatedly smooths her hands over the map until it becomes creaseless and delves into her bag for some more materials. She withdraws two stacks of paper tied up with thin twine and sets them on the counter, eventually discarding the paper and keeping the twine, and pulls four gold push-pins. "So, if I am correct, the vase refers to the meeting of elements as a literal place. So if we can locate the ancient aforementioned landmarks then we can see if they meet. The first element is fire."

The four of us share confused looks as we gaze upon the map. Trying to find a natural landmark that represents the element of fire is slightly harder than we anticipated.

"Oh!" Luke exclaims with exuberance. "Beta Park Hot Springs!" He points to a greenery filled location with patches of wetland around it. "The water is heated from a natural spring under the earth. It's probably the hottest natural landmark in the town."

"You are a genius, Luke," Amara gushes as she pushes one of the pins into the location that Luke pointed out. "Now water."

Out of the corner of my eye I see Jessica nervously look away from the group, her eyes darting around the room as if she is looking for an exit. I bite my tongue choose to wait until later to quiz her about her consistent shadiness. She leans over and places her finger directly onto the large lake detailed on the map. "This seems to be the biggest body of water."

Amara repeats the process of attaching the pin as we try to find the location of the air element. I don't even have to think twice before I come out with an answer. "Right there." I point to the furthest part of the map. "Whistling Ridge. The way the rocks jut out causes the wind to whistle as it blows through. It can be heard miles away."

"And as for earth you can probably put the pin here." Luke circles an area on the map consisting of various grey lines. The rest of us look confused as to why he chose this area but he explains his reasoning. "It won't appear on this map but right here is the entrance to the caving system that runs along the base of the town. It's the oldest natural formation but most maps don't show subterranean levels."

We all simply stare, mouth wide open, eyes unblinking. Luke just grins like a cat.

"Seriously, how do you know these things?" I struggle to comprehend where this burst of knowledge has come from considering the most notable thing my best friend has ever done is being able to burp the entire alphabet.

"I am a very intelligent person you know. I went through a caving phase when I was younger." He brushes off the statement like it was nothing.

Amara, whilst we have been talking, has tied the pieces of twine around each pin. She ties a delicate knot around the water, pulls it straight and attaches it to the fire elements, repeating the process with the earth and air elements.

"How do you know which ones to tie the string around?" Jessica enquires.

"Because by doing it this way then all the points are exactly equidistant from each other and the first piece of twine will eventually converge with the other giving us a location."

Sure enough it does exactly that. The four pins lie in a perfect cross pattern and the twine follows a path until both pieces of string cross over.

"So the designated spot is," Amaras face contorts with confusion, "a muddy path?"

"Hang on a second." I push some of the papers around and grab a more updated version of the map and lie this over the pre-existing one. "The part when the lines cross is here." I circle the small location.

"Elkwood Manor."

"Looks like we have somewhere to go now. It wouldn't have appeared in the old map because it probably wasn't built then." Amara jumps up and grabs her coat before being stopped by Jessica.

"We have no idea what we are getting into Amara. There could be anything at this house."

"There could be answers."

"Or Avarice could be waiting," Jessica speaks quietly.

"Guys," I interrupt, "let's just think sensibly for a moment. We cannot just go running around some old house hoping to find a clue that an ancient vase, that we might have totally read wrong, is referring too. Think logically about this."

"I think it's a great idea," Luke smiles, his phone in his hand.

"And why is that?" Jessica stands, one hip popped to the side, her arms folded across her chest. I hadn't really noticed until now that they had already changed clothes, probably from a suitcase that they brought with them on their travels, after showering and getting ready in Luke's garden house. Jessica looks snug in a cream turtleneck and white trouser combo, with heels because apparently she needs to look even taller, and Amara looks ready for action in a sensible grey long sleeved jacket and matching coloured jeans. She contrasts the outfit with bright red boots that totally defeat the object of the stealthily coloured ensemble.

"It's a great idea because I am tracking the history of the vase and the most recent resting place of it is in one of the city council's oldest buildings, recently closed down due to renovations, rendering it completely empty and all artefacts safely encased." He reads from his phone.

"And does it mention the name of the place where the vase currently is?" Jessica rolls her hand to try to speed up his response.

"Elkwood Manor."

Amara fist pumps the air in realisation that her plan had worked all along. The writing on the vase, the meeting of the natural elements, the current location of the vase- it all links together. There's barely any time to stop her before she shoots out of the front door and jumps into her car, revving the engine loudly until we vacate our seats and leave the house to join her.

"Let's go find an ancient vase." Amara grins as the four of us speed off down the road. "That message is leading us somewhere."

Chapter 15

Evelyn

Amara turns out to be a surprisingly good liar. She calls the school and effortlessly spins some lie stating that she is my mother and that Luke and I would not be in school today due to coming down with a severe bout of food poisoning. The school seems to play along with the phone call and I have the sneaky suspicion that a lot of people would be calling in sick today, following last night's party. Pandora probably told her father to go easy on all the people who would be playing truant from school.

My train of thought is interrupted when I step into a large muddy puddle, sinking up to ankle depth, and thoroughly dirtying my shoe. I groan as I retract my foot and shake off the excess mud.

A throaty laugh erupts from Luke, standing beside me as he pushes his way through the foliage, before offering me his hand to help me cross a larger puddle. "You know, for someone who can control the earth, you really don't like being outdoors."

"I have no problem being outdoor Luke. I have a problem if I am not thoroughly prepared. I mean would it have killed you guys to warn me to wear a pair of waterproof boots?"

Amara giggles whilst Jessica turns to face me. "Are you even surprised? This house is in the middle of nowhere surrounded by grassy fields and meadows, and you are shocked that you had to walk in a little bit of mud."

"Well if I keep stepping in dirt I'm going to open a fissure and pull all of this filth away."

"Can you even do that?" Luke questions. He seems to have developed a new habit of questioning all the things that I can do. Or can't do. I haven't actually tried to open up the earth before, but considering all that has happened recently, it could prove a nifty trick. I brush away a stray branch before it rakes me across the face. I watch as Amara pulls thorns out of her arm where she has had a close run in with an angry bush, and Jessica tugs on her red hair that is trapped between two jutted tree branches,

"I've had enough of this. We have no idea where we are going. The directions led to a dirt track road and we have been walking on foot forever! It's just too thick to see anything," Jessica whines as she rips her hair free, rubbing her sore scalp.

"I think I can do something about this. Never tried it on this scale before though." I gesture for the others to step back before I close my eyes. I slowly part my lips and breathe in and out, feeling the cool air roll over my skin. I sense everything within my vicinity, feeling the pulse of life around me, humming with the life force of the earth. I open my eyes and it's like someone has flipped a rainbow switch. I can see the aura of the forest vibrating with energy. The trees glow with a neon green, the leaves dazzle with mixtures of brown and red. The vibrant hue of flowers residing in the bushes sparkle like diamonds as the sunlight reflects off them. The puddles on the floor, now mixtures of shades of blue, dance like someone has poured oil on them, all the colours mixing and moving around. I turn to face the others, expecting to see glowing people, but I only see humanoid shapes of glowing red. I can see one of the figures raises their hand and waves in front of my face, unsure which one of the group it is, but their wave leaves a trail in the sky, like a dark rainbow free floating in the air. Obviously, humanity doesn't throb with the vibrant life of nature, lacking the pulse of energy that the earth has to offer. I pull my focus back to the task at hand and turn back to face our blocked path. I allow the vibrations to run through me as I open my palms. As if someone turned the lights off ,I call for the aura around the bushes to go out. First the colours fade away, followed by the plants beginning to curl away and retreat. Not only do I drain the auras from the foliage around me but I also take the life force as well, literally pulling the heart out of the plants, until nothing but broken husks are left. I will the plants to die directly in front of us, creating a path, and allowing some of the dense woodland to be seen through more easily. With a simple wave of my hand, the smaller trees crumble around us, pulling their auras into myself as their black shells disintegrate into the wind. Accessing this new level of powers is frightening a first but I welcome the warmth derived from the coloured auras, allowing myself to be empowered by it. I blink away the rainbow effect, feeling the world fade away around me and blur back into the regular spectrum of colours. The area around us looks like a wasteland, with blackened trees and flattened ground. The surrounding areas now become fully visible, as the dense undergrowth has been thoroughly cleared, as if a fire has raged through.

"Whoa," Luke whispers as the ashes of the plants float around us.

"Never knew that you could do that," Jessica replies as she catches a black husk from a tree on her palm.

"Neither did I. Not really. Years ago, I discovered that I could pull the life force from plants after I stared at a potted plant for too long and it started to wilt. I did say I have never done it on such a big scale, though," I explain, almost ashamed of my destructive act, but I soak in the undeniable rush that this has given me.

"Well, I'm sure your death vision abilities will come in very handy," Luke laughs.

I give him one of my signature glares, both annoyed and amused by his ignorant bliss. "It only works on plants, Luke. I doubt that I could cause Avarice to wilt."

"It makes perfect sense Evelyn. Not only do we get stronger when we are around each other but we also gain strength from our elements. I get stronger when I absorb the energy from a fire. We can literally suck the force from something and allow it to replenish us."

"Imagine how strong I get when I stick my head out of the car window and into the breeze," Amara jokes as she clambers over a blackened log. "Right there." She points towards a large building in the distance. The large stone building rises high and wide in the centre of a meadow, with a cold looking, grey, slate roof that slopes off to a hard edge. A dark red chimney juts out of the furthest side. Ropes of ivy climb the front side of the manor and snake across towards the back of it, looking something akin to a green net firmly covering the manor. The four of us stare at the manor before Amara races towards it, her figure disappearing as she plunges into the high rising wheat that sways gently in the breeze.

"Amara wait!" Jessica yells as her friend fades into the blanket of wheat. The plants grow to about seven feet high, significantly taller than most of us. The rest of us walk towards the wall of wheat, leaving the blackened wasteland behind us. We plunge into the soft area allowing the warm wheat to snugly weave around us. I quickly grasp Luke's hand to make sure that we aren't separated. With visibility only reaching a few feet in front of us, I cling to him, using him as my anchor as I push through and walk towards the general direction of the manor. Jessica's calls for Amara echo around us, despite not being able to see either of them.

Luke and I eventually reach a small clearing, of which the manor stands directly centre, where we wait for the girls to join us.

"Try calling them," Luke suggests.

I pull out my phone and dial Amara's number, only to find that I do not have sufficient phone coverage.

"No service. No calls or internet," I groan. "Looks like we will have to use the old fashioned method."

"Which is?"

"Jessica!" I bellow at the top of my voice, startling Luke, causing him to jump and pull his hand from me, reminding me that we had been holding hands the entire time.

"Because screaming for each other is really going to work." He rolls his eyes. "Looks like we will just have to wait because it obviously hasn't worked."

"Evelyn?" A voice yells from the mass of wheat, quickly followed by Jessica plunging forward through the pale field, her flame red hair jetting around her in the breeze.

"You were saying?" I cockily smirk at Luke before heading to Jessica. "Where is Amara?"

"No idea. I couldn't find her and my phone has died."

"No coverage anyway."

"Well she knows where to find us. She will run into the manor at some point. I suggest that we go in and have a look around." Luke walks towards the large doors and, with a heavy push, swings the doors open.

For a house that is apparently undergoing renovations, it is surprisingly clean. The walls look like marble, smooth and pale, with red curtains that hang elegantly over large windows. Colours of green, red and purple fill the room, from the tables, carpets and cloths respectively. The only absence of colour in the manor is the stark white sheets that cover the furniture, protecting it from dust, but looking eerily like stereotypical childish ghost costumes scattered around the room. I'm half expecting one of these sheets to suddenly whip off a couch and fly around the room. The insides of this manor look like a luxurious version of hell thanks to the rich red carpets and large stone fireplace that rests on the far wall. The front door leads directly into the large open room, with small corridors that lead off into smaller rooms. The white walls are decorated with different sized mirrors that reflect the room back onto itself creating the illusion of a never-ending expanse.

"I bet the kitchen's that way." Luke points to one of the corridors before heading that way.

"Don't go too far, Luke," I warn before he enters a different room.

Jessica, like myself, eyes up the white covered furniture. She walks towards a large chair and whips the sheet off it and bats it with her hand.

"What are you doing?" I question.

"Look." She gestures to the air around her. "Dust came off when I hit it. Meaning that these sheets were placed a while ago. No one has been here in at least a few days."

She drops the sheet and paces around the room, peering under the remaining covered items. She appears to have not found anything of worth yet, until she reaches a tall case, similarly covered by a white sheet. She grins as she whips it off, revealing a glass casing on top of a wooden podium. Inside the glass stands the vase from Amara's books, a dark bronze colour, with the dark markings still etched into it.

"Bingo!" She smiles. "And you thought Amara was the only brainy one."

"I thought you were the stern one actually. Amara's just this weird font of all knowledge."

"You think I am stern?" She turns to face me.

"I mean she literally knows everything. Moving to live with her grandmother in New Orleans must have really turned her into a brain box."

"I'm not stern," she mumbles.

"I wonder if she was always super smart. She mentioned that she was raised in Greece. I bet she loved all of the mythology. I can imagine her now, sitting in the coliseums buried up to her nose in books"

"I get that I am a little focused and intense but I'm not stern," she continues to mumble.

"Maybe the whole Avarice thing shook her up and she dove into research."

"Stern is such a strong word. I prefer dedicated."

"Jessica. Let it go. You are just that kind of person. A natural leader and someone who keeps us all in check. It's not exactly a bad thing. I bet the fire element is always the leader in each group of Guardians." I raise my hands in defence.

She runs her hand along the glass, her eyes dart across the vase, as she mentally notes all the markings. "I wish Amara was here. She could translate some of the other things." She groans.

"I wish we had Wi-Fi. Just as useful," I joke. A loud clatter rings out from one of the corridors causing me and Jessica to head off in that direction. We come across Luke frantically cleaning up a mess on the floor, with metal plates and bowls scattered all around the stone floor.

"I was making a sandwich. I slipped." He sweeps up some of the spilt food and piles it back onto a plate. He pushes the rest of the mess underneath the fridge with his foot before chomping down on his reconstituted sandwich.

"Luke, no one has been here for a while. That food is probably gone off by now." I grimace as I watch him eat the food. "The fridge is working, though," he speaks through a mouthful of food.

"Why did you slip?" Jessica asks.

"Well, I thought I saw something. Probably just my reflection though." He takes another bite.

"God, you are just like a cat," Jessica laughs. It's a small laugh but to hear it come from her is a little bit of a surprise. She has been so sombre lately; well, actually, since I have met her she has been sombre, but today her morale has been significantly low. Nothing too noticeable to begin with, just glances and downhearted mumbles, as if she's just been given some very bad news. *Well* if there could be worse news than an ancient demon trying to kill us.

"You sound nice when you laugh," Luke talks as he takes another large bite of food.

"You say that as if you have never heard me laugh before." Jessica looks ashamed, almost apologetic about the fact she hasn't had a reason to giggle yet.

"Well, we have only known you a day," I glance at my watch to take in the time, "so we will forgive you for not showing us every emotion yet." I think about how hectic the last few days have been. "Although there will probably be time." I pace around the large kitchen, filled with smooth counter-tops and metal stools, before I stop near the large glass doors at the far end of the room. Thick white wood frames the crystal clear glass that gives us a clear look onto the expanse of land outside. Despite the house being surrounded by billowing wheat filled meadows the garden seems to consists of short grass that rolls on as far as the eye can see. The doors open onto a smaller courtyard, with the grass split into four equal segments, a gravel path running both straight through the centre and directly across, surrounded by a waist height stone wall. The centre of the wall breaks off to make way for a few steps that descend onto the rest of the garden, consisting of further fields of vibrant green grass. I push on the doors causing them to swing open and cool air to blow into the room. Jessica appears next to me, arms folded in front of her, a contemplative look on her face.

"It's weird that we even have time to see the beauty in some things. We are expected to devote our lives to the hunt yet we rarely stop to appreciate where we are or what we will see. When I was making my way down here I stopped at a little roadside café, and despite the fact that I am a fire controlling demon hunter, I just relaxed for a few moments and drank my coffee in front of a stunning view."

"It's easy to pretend to be normal sometimes isn't it?" I agree with her as I remember the exact feeling that she is talking about

"That was very deep, Jessica," Luke breaks the mood by speaking through a mouthful of food.

"I am more than making flames and being stern, you know." She shoots a wink towards Luke as he raises his hands in joke defeat.

I close the doors again, the chill becoming slightly unbearable before heading back towards the main room. Jessica and Luke follow behind me, both attempting unsuccessfully to call Amara on their phones, only to achieve the same result.

"I'm sure she's fine." Luke pats Jessica on the arm warmly.

"I hope so," I interrupt, "because she was the one with all the ideas. I have no idea what we are actually meant to be doing here. The vase is right there but now what?" I ask. Jessica just looks at me wide eyed. "Why don't we just split up and look around?"

"No!" Luke yells. "Do you not remember any of the horror films that we watch Evie? You never split up!"

"We aren't hiding from an axe-murderer, Luke. Just a demon." I try to justify my suggestion but I totally end up contradicting myself. "You two can go together then."

They try to argue but I send them off with a few stern words, watching them ascend the grand staircase and disappearing from view. I don't need someone with me holding my hand just to look around a house. I will be just fine.

For once in my life I wish I could say that without something bad happening.

My screams must have scared the birds away for miles.

I had only been in the main room for a few moments after Luke and Jessica went to explore. I wandered around aimlessly, taking note of the intricate exhibits that are stored underneath the protective cloths, ranging from crystal goblets to Viking weapons. A large axe had drawn my attention, after I had whipped off the white sheet and pressed my hands against the glass. The wood was at least a metre long, decorated with notches and scratches presumably from many battles, and tightly secured to a bronze axe head so sharp that it hurt looking at it. The hilt of the weapon was written with the same symbols that Amara had shown us earlier. The only symbols that I could recognise was the runic for *elements.* This axe probably played some vital part in our quest but obviously it's being kept a mystery from me just like everything else. Whilst my fingers draw lazy circles on the glass, I allow my mind to conspire, conjuring up paranoid thoughts like how little I actually know about what is going on. It seems awfully convenient that the vase with a hidden message on it was residing a few miles down the road from where I live. I had barely managed to wrap my head around who I was and that I had a destiny but there seems to be a lot of things that are even too farfetched for me to believe.

I push aside the negative thoughts and focus on the task at hand. Exploring. I wipe the smudges off the glass with my sleeve before walking over towards the stone fireplace. I pick up a nearby poker and push the burnt ashes around, etching random drawing into the soot until the sound of a door banging snaps me back into focus. I stand up quickly, leaving the poker on the top of the fireplace mantle, turning around to face the empty room, and heading towards the kitchen where the source of the bang came from. The sound of my heels clacking on the floor echoes around the ghostly quiet house.

"Luke!" I call out, hoping his cheery face will pop out from behind a door.

I push the kitchen door open only to see that the patio doors had been opened again. Placing the blame onto myself for not locking them earlier, I walk over and close them. I stare out into the garden, taking in the beauty, when something flutters in the distance. I squint my eyes and lean forward to get a better view, but the shape quickly darts behind a tree.

A cold shiver runs down my spine. The same shiver I get when Avarice is around.

I head back towards the main room, almost breaking into a jog, as I want to enter the warmth of the larger room. Once back inside, I can sense that is something different. Something has moved.

The wind whistles around me, a faint hiss filling the air, as I take delicate steps towards the fireplace. I struggle to swallow down the lump in my throat. *The poker has moved.* It has moved from resting on the mantelpiece to laying back on the floor. I wrap my trembling hands around the poker and see that the sharp end has crafted its way through the soot, similarly to my drawings earlier, to form what looks like a badly written word. I squint my eyes, turning my head to make out the scribble, when I see the word 'Hello'.

"Hello?" I repeat back to myself, questing where it came from.

"Hey!" a voice behind me calls out.

That's when I screamed.

I swung the poker around with enough force to break a window. Or someone's arm. I was half expecting to see a large ghoulish monster, with blood streaming from his eyeballs and skin as black as the abyss he crawled from, but as Luke would constantly remind me, my imagination may be running wild with me. Instead, I swing the poker down, full force, onto a young woman.

She gracefully moves out of the way, I stumble forward with the force of my attack, as she harmlessly giggles. As I stand and gather my bearings, pushing my hair out of my eyes and smoothing my clothes down, I see that she isn't as young as I first thought, appearing around fifteen years old. She has hair as black as coal, falling in loose curls down past her shoulders, framing her heart shaped face. Her petite figure, dressed in a loose white top that flutters down to thigh level and contrasting with the running shoes she is wearing on her feet. Her calm face houses bow arched lips, naturally a pale pink colour, and rosy flushed cheeks. Her dark eyebrows arch perfectly over green eyes. Despite being so young her eyes tell a thousand stories of pain and loss, all of which she tries to hide.

"Who are you?" I gasp.

"Is that how you greet most people? Attempting to cave their skulls in?" she retorts in an unusually calm voice.

"Well most people know that sneaking up on people is rude." I take a step forward, towering over her, not wanting to appear intimidating, but more of an attempt to hide the fact that my heart is beating like a mariachi band right now.

"Well, it's not like I didn't say hello," she retorts.

"That's a double negative you know," I quip. *Seriously Evelyn? Correcting someone's grammar has never been a good comeback!*

She chuckles, undeterred by my glare and words. "It's nice to know that the saviour of the planet passed her English exams." She nonchalantly slides past me and heads over to one of the red leather couches. She firmly plumps herself down and begins playing with her hair, never taking her eyes off me.

"What did you just say?" I question.

"The part about you being the saviour? Sorry, I know the preferred term is Guardian nowadays." She explains so calmly, as if she is recalling her shopping list, not the fact that supernatural heroes exist.

171

"I think that you have read too many storybooks little girl. You should go home," I warn.

"Or what?" she pushes. "You'll blow me away? Or will you shake this building down?"

I note that the only elements that she references are air and earth. I narrow my eyes and glare at her, her harmless smile comes across both cocky and entertaining, as she is obviously treating this like a game.

"What makes you think I won't burn this house down?" I play along with her little game, my hand still firmly grasping the fire poker. Her smile falters slightly, just for a second, before returning.

"Because you have none of the qualities that a fire Guardian has. You are more of a fire extinguisher than a fire wielder." She eyes me up and down.

I have had enough. "I don't know who you are kid but I think you should leave now. There are a few of us here that have some very important matters to deal with and I definitely do not have time to play along with your childish game." I stand my ground. I seriously hope that my younger sister never acts like this because I could not deal with this kind of behaviour all the time.

"So you've found the vase, but you have no idea what to do next."

My ears prick up and the corners of my mouth fall down. "What do you know about the vase?"

She turns on the couch, swinging her legs onto it and making herself comfortable. "That it holds a lot more than a few old words. It holds much more than that."

"You may think this is funny but you are seriously getting on my nerves now. I have had a very rough few hours and the last thing I need is a brat making it worse."

Her face drops and she sits bolt upright in her seat, "I am not a brat. I just wanted a little bit of fun. I get a little bit lonely sometimes. It's hard being the youngest. There are just so many I can get lost in the crowd." She quickly scans the room.

"What crowd?" I enquire.

"The Guardians of course." She gestures around her.

I turn on the spot, sensing a change in the atmosphere around me like static electricity clinging to my body, to see that the once empty room is now filled with people. The hundred mirrors that frame the walls are now filled with the images of women. In some kind of freakish illusion the women, all swarming around like moving pictures, as they watch me and the unnamed girl standing in the room. Despite the women not actually being present in the room, at least in person, but I can feel their presence all around me. Their warmth and strength flutters through the room.

"You can feel it can't you. It's like a thousand jolts tearing through your body."

"What is this?" This feeling is so unusual. A million butterflies are about to tear out of my stomach and carry me sky high.

The young girl steps up in line with me, beaming at the many faces that bear down on us. "They don't want to risk appearing in spirit form in case Avarice tracks them. It's safer for us all if they stay in their world and use mirrors as a conduit." She speaks so wisely.

"How do you know all this?" I beg.

She pushes her hair back and ties it into a loose ponytail with a band from her wrist. She turns to face me, her eyes determined and her brow furrowed, as the words pour from her mouth.

"My name is Raina. I am the water Guardian."

"LUKE" I scream. I want him here with me right now. I need to feel his arms around me. I want to feel his hand in mine as he tells me that everything will be okay. The sound of footsteps thud above me, confusing me as to why I can only hear them now after all this time, and Luke and Jessica appear, rushing down the stairs. His general presence already puts me at ease. He runs full speed towards me and embraces me in one of his bear hugs. I melt into his arms the only way that my best friend can make me.

"There was this girl and she…" I begin.

"I know, Evie, they are upstairs too. We were having a chat with a lovely little old lady. She was a previous fire Guardian hundreds of years ago," Luke answers.

"What girl?" Jessica interrupts.

"They were just staring at us. They wouldn't talk," I pour the words out.

"Seriously, what girl?" she persists.

I continue to grip Luke's hand as I explain to Jessica, who's being annoyingly persistent, about the bratty girl who appeared. The colour fades away from her face instantly and she turns her back away from us.

"She's the water element Jessica. Now that we are all here we could be strong enough to defeat Avarice," I suggest. She remains stoic and silent. One of the Spirits catches my eye, her ethereal grace draws my attention straight away.

"Gwendoline," I smile. The Spirit that I first met when I entered their world.

"Hello, my child." Her kind smile causes her to look like a beautiful painting hanging on the wall.

"Do you plan on telling us what's going on?" Luke persists. "I remember Evie saying how vague you were the last time you met."

"Of course. You have not only grown as a woman, Evelyn, but also as a Guardian. You are ready for answers." Luke releases my hand as I lean in towards the mirror and prepare myself to hear, hopefully, some answers.

"Avarice was a very powerful foe, but not as powerful as the elements that create the world that he walks upon. His soul is destined to wander the earthly plane, whilst his physical form stays trapped underground for all eternity, until he can gather enough strength to possess people," she begins. "He normally appears around the globe nearest to wherever the next Guardians are awoken. The previous set of Guardians were four women in a rural Chinese village. His soul appeared, possessing a beggar man, and after leaving the village desolate, he began to attack the Guardians. They managed to defeat his spirit and scatter his essence all over again."

"How long ago was that?" How long does it take for his essence to become strong enough to possess someone?" Luke ponders.

"The last time Guardians were awoken was in the year 1843. They defeated him and he has only recently gathered enough strength to possess the ghostly gentleman that attacked you so feverishly recently."

"Grim Reaper," I correct.

"So what are the odds that the next lot of Guardians happen to be in the same place his true body rests? It's awfully coincidental." Luke is like a dog with a bone when it comes to matters he wants answers on.

"That's because he has never had enough strength to awaken in Ravens Valley. This vase was blessed by a witch millennia ago to shield his hometown, Ravens Valley, from him so he could never find his true body. His soul would be left to wander the earth forever but never be able to become whole again. However, the current incarnation of Guardians isn't strong enough to ward him off. He detected where his true body lies and has managed to possess people within Ravens Valley. As soon as he enters his original body he will be strong enough to enact his plan."

"Which is?" I croak. My voice is hoarse from choking down my fears.

"He plans to draw on the energy of the vase, therefor the magic that also links with the spirit world, and be truly unstoppable. With that amount of power no one, Guardian or not, would be able to stop him."

The severity of her words weighs me down. My inner strength struggles to swim through a bog of harsh words and scary stories. Luke rubs my back, aiding me slightly, as he enquires more from Gwendoline.

"You mentioned that the current Guardians weren't strong enough to defeat him. What makes us so different?" I note that Jessica has quietly left the room. I want to call out for her, but Gwendoline begins talking.

"You are incomplete. The reason the water Guardian, Raina, appeared now, instead of joining you earlier is due to one reason."

"Which is?" I persist, driving for her to get to the point. Her eyes look past me and into the centre of the room.

"I died. Avarice killed me already. You have no water Guardian right now," Raina whispers.

The world comes crashing around me. Her words tear through me, filling me with dread. Luke gasps and Gwendoline closes her eyes solemnly. At first, I thought the blast of thunder was part of my imagination, a literal tearing open of my world, but Luke's quick reaction shows me that he heard it too. He steams toward the corridor leading to the patio doors and pushes them open, myself following straight behind him, and Jessica who appears from nowhere.

A slither of lighting streams down from the sky, a blinding arc of white light plunging into the earth, before disappearing instantly.

The three of us stare at the smoking ground as black and grey mist curls around the furthest end of the garden. We walk forward slightly, the gravel crunching beneath us. Where the lighting once struck now stands a figure, made of something akin to stone, reaching out towards us. We move closer, breaking into a jog until we are a few metres distance away. The stone statue is a young woman, with both arms reaching out as if she is yearning for something. Her perfectly detailed face, with high cheekbones and thick lips carved delicately into the stone strike familiarity with me. Her eyes, although vacant, look directly at me, as if we know each other.

Then it hits me. It's like a wave of realisation that knocks me directly over. I can see same look dawn on Jessica's face. There is a reason this statue looks so familiar to us. Her beautiful face, stylish clothes, both arms reaching out, suddenly cause us to all simultaneously whisper the name of the woman made of stone.

"Amara."

Chapter 16

Evelyn

Jessica reaches up and strokes stone Amara. Her pale hand gently rubs the perfectly sculpted cheek before she retracts, tucking her shaking hand into her pocket. Luke wanders around her, mouth agape, reaching up to tap Amara in various places. I cannot even find the strength to move, the emotions of today crushing me. Riding this emotional roller coaster, going from the high of finding clues, to the lows of the house actually providing no clues. I manage to push aside the issue of what to do next and instead focus on the fact that there isn't an active water element. If Avarice shows up now, with a fully-fledged attack, we are all toast.

Jessica walks towards me, visibly shaking, as she mumbles out a few words, "What do we do now?"

"Well, that depends on whether you are going to tell me the truth or not?" I dig my heels into the ground, fortifying my stance.

"About what?" She looks a mixture of confused and secretive. She is probably wondering what lie I am currently questioning.

"I am talking about the fact that the water element, Raina, is dead." Her face falls flat. "That's the lie I am wondering about."

She brushes a red hair away from her face, something she seems to do a lot when she is nervous, and opens her mouth only for stutters to come out. "Cut the lies Jessica or I swear I will leave this place and never look back. I do not care about the consequences."

"Evie," Luke attempts to calm me with a gentle touch but I tear my arm from his loose grasp.

"No Luke. This isn't the time to try and calm me down. Amara has become a gargoyle and Raina is dead. I cannot believe I just had an argument with a dead teenage ghost." I shiver the thought away. I barely managed to comprehend talking to a middle-aged ghost.

"Hey!" Jessica yells. "She has a name." She glares at me, the fire burning behind her eyes, as we engage in a fierce staring war. I will not back down. I am sick of all the lies.

"It's about time that the truth comes out of your mouth Jessica. I am sick of everything."

"Have you ever considered that the reason that Amara didn't tell you the truth is because we didn't think you could handle it? You haven't exactly led us to believe that you are the most mature of people." She rolls her eyes at me.

"Roll your eyes one more time Jessica and I swear I will tear them from your head," I warn.

"You are all talk Evelyn. I told you yesterday that you need to mature and you have to stop being such an immature brat! Actually you are a selfish, sarcastic, little witch who doesn't spare a thought for the people around her."

"How dare you! I am fighting a war that I asked to be no part of. You may think that I am being a bother in your life but trust me, the feeling is mutual." I allow my emotions to bubble to the surface, losing the shield that I spend so many years perfecting. I turn away, casting a glance at Luke, who just stares open-mouthed, as I walk back to the house.

"That's right. Walk away. You don't deserve to have these powers Evelyn. You are a disgrace to the word Guardian," she seethes.

That does it.

I turn around with enough force I rip up the ground beneath me. I set of running towards her, my arms outstretched, sending a wave of energy towards her. The ground beneath Jessica churns and bursts apart. She recoils over a clump of ground, being thrown past the stone Amara, whilst Luke narrowly dodges the spray of dirt and dislodged rock. "Evie, what are you doing?" he screams.

Jessica rolls over on the ground before standing up, her face contorted with anger. She flicks her wrist and jets of fire shoot from the cracks I just made in the floor. The searing heat from the fire burns my skin causing me to dive forward. I stare at her through my damp fringe, a sheen of sweat running over my body. "You aren't enemies, girls!" Luke yells.

The fire within me boils over, this flood of negative emotions becoming too much to contain. I clench my fists and call out for the ground beneath her to rupture. Before I can even cause any quaking, she spins around once, a trail of fire spreading around her, following her fingers, before she stops and aims her hands at me. "I am warning you Evelyn."

I release my fist and the earth tears apart. The cracking of the ground sounding akin to the burst of thunder. Jessica's circle of flames shoots forward, hitting me directly in the chest, whilst her body is thrown to the ground viciously. I pat the flames away, my skin heating up quickly. Now I am mad.

"Enough." Luke gets in-between us both, arms raised to warn us away. "What the hell is wrong with two? We are on the same team here! You can put away your petty squabbles for a while and focus on the more pressing issues. I cannot believe you used your powers on each other." My eyes remain fixed on Jessica, waiting for her make the first move.

"Bring it," she whispers.

I release a flood of pent up energy, the waves taking physical form, like waves in the air, and soaring straight towards her. Luke leans forward, getting caught in the blast, and is thrown back onto stone Amara. His head hits her rock form with a deafening thud and his body limps down. The anger immediately leaves me and worry floods over. I set off running towards him, Jessica mirroring my actions. I stop to his right side; his arms raised rubbing his head, as tears fall down my face. "I am so sorry Luke! I didn't mean to hurt you." I beg his forgiveness. He pulls his hands away from the back of his head and stares at them in shock. Red blood glistens in the light. The colour drains away from Jessica's face as my heart beats at an alarming rate. I run my hands over his body worryingly before he beats me away.

"Get him inside now," the voice from behind us orders. Raina joins us, lifting Luke from his slump, and wrapping his arms around me and Jessica, his body weight supported on us.

"What about Amara?" Jessica sheepishly asks. Raina casts her a glare and the two remain locked on each her for a few moments.

What's that all about?

Raina wraps her arms around the stone form of Amara and whispers a few inaudible words. Her form begins to flicker in the sunlight, like a mirage on a hot day, before she disappears without a trace, taking Amara with her.

The rest of us slink inside in silence.

Amara stands in the centre of the room like an expensive ornament. Luke sits with a bag of frozen peas firmly placed on the back of his head. Jessica stands next to the window, hands firmly folded across her chest, with a regretful look on her face. I lean against the fireplace, battling my feelings of resentment for Jessica and worry for Luke. I cannot believe that I hurt him. Raina walks into the room; the eyes of a hundred previous Guardians follow her. They soon switch from her to us, casting disdainful looks on us instead. Some old lady with grey hair wrapped messily in a top bun eyes me up and down before looking away. She was probably an earth Guardian. I just roll my eyes at her in response.

"I have no idea what that was about, nor do I care, but if you guys will continue to fight then we might as well walk to Avarice like pigs to a slaughter," Raina begins.

"That's ironic," I quip, "You were the one who played games with me earlier. I saw you hiding in the fields when I looked out of the window earlier. Don't say that we are acting badly." I look at her disapprovingly after all the lies that I found out today.

"That wasn't me in the trees earlier," Raina states, looking confused, before continuing, "I mean how stupid could you possibly be? It isn't enough that we have a demon hunting us, but you think it would be a clever idea to have a battle in the back garden. What possessed you?"

Jessica and I share a quick look before burying our heads. I feel like I am back at school and Raina is our headmistress, despite her young age, she carries this air of authority when she addresses us. "I am waiting," she persists.

"Maybe I can help with that?" a male voice in the arch of the door calls up. The four of us quickly snap our heads in that direction. A tall figure stands wearing an impeccable black suit. This strangely classically handsome man stares at us all, deep set hazel eyes watching us all intently. His straight nose rests above perfectly arched lips, and a shapely angular jawline gives him a strong look. His inky black hair perfectly rolls back in gentle waves, rising and falling like rolling coal before resting at jaw length. The muscular physique stands dominatingly in the doorway, obscuring the exit from view, before he takes slow steps into the room. "You two were being manipulated. Your anger was simply multiplied."

"And how do you know that?" Jessica challenges. *Where the hell did he come from?*

"Because I caused it."

Raina gasps, Luke leaps from his seat, and Jessica takes a defensive stance, arms raised to waist height, ready to conjure flames.

"Avarice," she chokes.

He flashes a dazzling white smile, perfectly lined teeth beam at us, and wrinkles his nose playfully. "In the flesh."

The glass tears at my skin as my body flies into a hanging mirror. The shards fall down beautifully around me as I stare at them through a red haze. Blood pours from my head, presumably the wound on my forehead being reopened, as I watch the havoc reap out before me. Jessica cannot even manage to weave a jet of fire before being flung through the air and into the ceiling, her limp body falling back down with a harsh thud. Luke bravely tries to swing at Avarice with a broken piece of chair, but the wood shatters harmlessly upon impact. Avarice turns around, a sick grin on his face, before simply flicking his forefinger, causing Luke to be thrown back into the hallway. Avarice's ability to move things without touching them is only the tip of the iceberg. He sets his sights on Raina, attempting to fling some debris at her from the floor, only for it to pass harmlessly through her like a ghost. I struggle to get to my feet, a pain in my gut almost blurring my vision, before lunging forward at him. I send a pulse towards him, shaking the manor, but throwing him off balance. Jessica, gathering what strength she has, grabs onto the exposed skin on his arm and sears his skin. Smoke curls away as her hand becomes white hot and Avarice's skin burns beneath her. He releases a guttural growl before tearing his arm away from her. Eyeing her up and down he mutters a few words before blowing on Jessica, causing ice to form across her exposed hands. She screams in pain, falling to the ground as she clutches her frozen blue hand, with Avarice towering above her. He raises his foot, ready to bring it down full force on her hand with full intent to shatter it. "And to think you call yourself a Guardian. You are a disgrace to the title." His deep voice booms around the room.

I can see that the previous Guardians are no longer occupying the mirrors, probably fleeing from the scene to preserve the spirit world. I don't blame them for abandoning us, I would most likely do the same. I grab a nearby shard of glass, careful to not slit my hand, and swing viciously across Avarice's back. Black blood spurts out from beneath the layers of clothes. He grimaces in pain, shrugging the glass from his skin before turning to face me.

My heart sinks. A lump the size of an apple forms in my throat. I never really thought about my death, but I never expected that an ancient demon would kill me. Imagine explaining that one to my parents. *Oh my parents.* I haven't even thought about them. I could not leave them this way!

I wait for him to strike a killing blow, only for it to never come. Jessica leaps off the ground, frozen hand clutched in the other, before yelling out. "I haven't finished with you yet." She raises her frozen hand, seemingly appearing to steam and thaw out, before red arcs of lightning erupts from her hand. The sparks fly across the room and hit Avarice directly in the chest, throwing his body across the room and directly out of the window facing onto the front lawn. "Are you okay?" she enquires as she runs to me, wiping the blood from my forehead with her sleeve.

"I'm fine." I brush her hand away. I'm not bitter about what was said earlier because neither of us was in total control. I am still far too wary of her due to the secrets she was keeping. "How could you not tell me there was no water Guardian?" I beg.

"Not the time right now. Later, I promise!" She sends another arc of lighting towards the window, blasting Avarice, who had just risen from his earlier attack. Watching Jessica's sudden boost in powers made me realise something that was mentioned earlier.

"Our powers are stronger when we are together," I mumble.

"What? Jessica shouts through the deafening blast of lightening. Avarice seems to be developing a kind of immunity from it now, batting away the burst with his hand as if they were nothing.

"Raina, a little help please!" I scream to the open room. I grasp Jessica's hand tightly. "I have a plan but you need to trust me okay?" I find it ironic that I am the one asking for trust now.

She casts me a pleading look before gripping my hand tighter. I call out for Raina one more time before I see her small frame materialise next to me. Avarice walks towards us, his menacing figure shadowing over us, whilst Jessica uses that lasts of her strength to blast him. "Take my hand Raina," I scream, feeling her hand tuck into mine I enact my plan.

Asking Raina to touch the statue of Amara I feel the jolts of power course through us like a million wasps trapped under our skin. I catch a glance of my reflection in the cracked shard of mirror on the wall. My eyes have totally glazed over and are glowing a vibrant red, similarly to the other girls, minus Amara. "You may break us Avarice, but you cannot break the link of the Guardians." I hear my voice boom out, as if tripled by the power of the three other girls.

Without a second thought myself, Raina and Jessica all raise a hand and unleash a torrent of pure energy towards Avarice. I feel the waves pulsate through my body, heating my flesh and boiling my blood. The unnatural warmth gathers in my hand and I hurl the energy at Avarice,

185

who recoils away from my burning blast. Raina and Jessica repeat my motions.

Layers of clothes burn off Avarice, his skin remaining intact, but his face growing more and more pained. "I'm losing my grip," Raina screams, the wind from the energy being released pulling out of my grip.

"Hold on" I try to shout but the words catch in my throat.

Raina's hand slips from mine and her ghostly body is thrown backwards, sliding along the floor before fading into nothingness. "I have a plan." Her voice echoes around the room. The immense conjoined power instantly leaves my body and I can feel the hollowness inside of me. Jessica, whose hair burns a fiery red and flickers around her, similarly loses the glow in her eyes and returns to normal. The air hangs around us, as the inside of the Manor remains trashed.

A single laugh breaks the silence.

Avarice bats his charred clothes, grinning, before standing directly in front of us. He raises his hand before quickly clenching his fist.

I wait to die…

Nothing.

Jessica and I share a quick glance before looking back at Avarice. His shocked expression turns to anger quickly as he tries to attack us. His arcs of lightning and blasts of darkness all completely avoid us; the blasts instead seem to hit what looks like an invisible wall in front of us. Every attempt to harm us fails, instead smacking and spreading along the invisible barrier.

"Didn't see that coming did you?" Raina chirps up, materialising next to me, spookily.

"What did you do?" Luke groans as he climbs out from beneath a pile of rubble. He has minor cuts on his face and I silently thank the spirits for keeping him safe. Even if they didn't I feel the need to thanks someone.

186

"I had the spirits re-enact the protection spell on the vase. I just made the radius a little bit bigger. You stay still and his magic won't hurt you." She grins.

He begins to laugh again, more manically this time, before snapping into seriousness. He walks straight up to the inviolable barrier, harmlessly tapping on it. He begins to speak although his words sound like he is talking underwater.

"Foolish girl. I killed you once and yet you still find a way to vex me. Your sad attempt to thwart me is futile. This barrier protects you from the magic that I have acquired over the years. It will not, however, protect you from my innate magic. I was born with a gift to cause humanity to submit to my will. I will make you submit to me."

"And how do you plan on doing that. We will never follow you." Jessica grits her teeth when addressing him.

"In your dreams, silly child. I am a demon. I am the thing nightmares are made from." He smiles a wicked smile.

Raina's face drops.

"Sweet dreams." He raises his hand. "Or not." Bringing his outstretched hands to his mouth he simply blows at us. Grey smoke curls out from his closed fist before dissipating in the air.

At first nothing happens. Then Jessica falls to the ground with a thud. Luke follows quickly. My heart rate speeds up, my eyelids weighing heavily. Before the blackness washes over me and my body falls down weightlessly, the world disappearing in front of me.

The last thing I saw was a sickening smile.

The beeping of my alarm clock wakes me up. I glance at the strange familiarity of my surroundings, the pink of my bedroom adding to the rays of sunlight streaming onto my bed. I whip off my covers and plant my feet on the floor, flexing and feeling the fur rug on my toes, before walking over to the curtains, quickly sliding them open.

It takes a second for my eyes to adjust, the red-hot sun softly burning against my face, before I peer out into the street below. The picturesque town, bathed in sunlight, continues as normal. The birds tweet in the sky, the wind blows calmly through the trees and the grass waves in the breeze. Rows of cars line up in the driveways casting a multi-coloured array of reflective patters from the sun.

It is just a normal day in Ravens Valley.

I walk towards my bedroom door, catching myself in the mirror. I glance at myself, noting that my clothes look impeccably neat, and my hair, now blood free, falls lusciously. I push open the door and call for my mother and father.

No response.

I slide down the stairs and enter the kitchen, radio playing out loud and the usual four bowls, ready for breakfast, are set out on the table. I shout out for my sister, and then the cat, before heading to look around in the other rooms. Something is seriously wrong here. My father always locks the back door before leaving for work but the latch slides freely when I turn the handle. I jog through the house, heels clacking on the solid floor, before lunging out of the front door. The cool breeze and warm sun make an eclectic mix.

"Hello?" I scream, wanting a response from anyone but silence fills the sky.

I wander up to my neighbour's door, politely knocking, before pushing the handle down and entering.

Nothing. *Where is everyone?*

Okay think Evelyn. What is the last thing that happened? Avarice attacked us and threatened to turn us into his followers. The remainder of his words slip from my mind.

I head through the town, finding the usual scene of shop doors open and footballs rolling on the ground, but still no people. "Hello!" I yell out again for someone, anyone, to answer me.

I am all alone.

I turn on the spot, frantically searching for a sign of anyone.

The last things that Avarice said, plague my memory. I try to recall his final sentence before I fell to the ground. Bingo! I hit the ground after he blew something at us. He was talking about having sweet dreams.

That's it! I am in a dream. Avarice has put me to sleep whilst he works around the protection spell on the vase. Right Evelyn, follow the stereotype, and pinch yourself to wake up. Simple.

Ouch! Too hard!

So that didn't work. Fantastic. Think back Evelyn.

So an ancient demon wouldn't just knock me into a slumber. He would do something much more spiteful and vindictive. He is the embodiment of greed after. He wants to take something from us.

Our morality.

This demon wants us to submit to his will and the only way to do that is by trapping us in our own nightmares.

Is my worst fear *really* being alone? I had no idea I was that self-dependant on people. All of sudden I feel very lonely.

No. I will not fall victim to this maniac. I hurt my best friend today when he was whispering in my ear so I cannot let myself fully submit to this evil. "Is this what you want Avarice? You want me to admit I'm scared and lonely and I want to follow you?" I scream at the open sky.

"Well, tough luck." I grit my teeth as I spit the words out. I have to get back and the only way to do that is to understand why this is my fear. The reason I am scared is because I have these powers. I stare down at my open palmed hands. I am trembling from anger.

"My powers are part of me. They make me who I am." I finally submit to the worry of my abilities. I am starting to sound like Jessica with all this power destiny mumbo jumbo.

"You ready Avarice?" I clench my jaw and grit my teeth. "I am coming for you." I send a threat out into the open empty world. I need to get back into the normal world, back to Luke and Jessica.

"I am not afraid anymore." I spread my hands out and call forth a tremor from underneath me. *I hope this works.* I will the shaking to spread further. Dust lifts off the ground and the trees shake down to their roots. Pulse after pulse of seismic energy tears the ground apart, chunks of rock and debris fling violently into the air. Buildings are flattened in plumes of dust and smoke as I cause the tremoring to rip this world apart. I unleash the full destructive capabilities of my powers.

This world crumbles beneath my palms as the darkness seeps out and consumes all.

"Luke. I am coming to you," I scream as the earth dissipates around me, taking me with it.

Chapter 17

Jessica

I've always loved my family's cabin near the lake. I was too young to have my powers then, so everything was normal. I rest my elbows on the wooden windowsill and stretch out, smelling the fresh air and water spray, before closing the shutters.

I have no idea how long I have been here now. It could have been hours. Or days. Time loses its purpose in this place. The seconds roll on for hours. I have walked around the lake at least three times and not once bumped into a passer-by or a tourist. The lake was always quiet but never this quiet.

The issue with this cabin is the shifting of the rooms. I woke up, laying lazily on the sofa, before jumping up out of fear. I wandered around for a while and yet every room I went into was different. I stepped out of my cabin main room and directly into my childhood bedroom.

I am trapped in between the best and worst places in my life.

I rest my hand on the mahogany table in the centre of the living room, of the cabin, whilst debating what to do. Firstly I walk around and firmly lock all the adjoining doors, just to make sure that I don't wander into my old kitchen or something, before resting on a wooden chair near the table. Think logically Jessica.

Avarice obviously trapped me in another world in order to achieve something. Judging by his use of the word 'nightmare' I take it that this isn't going to end very well. Maybe I should check under the bed?

I allow my mind to wander, hoping that an idea will come when I am distracted, but all I can focus on is Amara and Evelyn. I allowed Amara to get lost in the field and thanks to me, she was attacked and turned into a statue. I owe Evelyn a huge apology for attacking her – although it was not my fault entirely. Avarice manipulated our emotions and brought out the worst in us and we used our powers against us. We have probably broken a fundamental rule of being a Guardian; *'you should not attack fellow Guardians- even if they are a being a huge idiot'*.

Three knocks to the door behind me breaks my train of thought. My head whips around quickly to face the wooden door.

I should be elated that someone else is here, but instead I find myself getting out of my seat warily, and slowly advancing towards the door handle. I open my hand and conjure a small fireball that dances on my palm. Just ensuring that I still have my powers.

I wrap my hands around the solid iron and turn the lever.

The door swings open powerfully and knocks me down onto my back. I stand up in a fury to face the intruder only to find an empty doorframe. I lean out, eyes fixed firmly on the greenery outside, yet nothing catches my attention. I turn around and glare at the empty room.

Someone's here. "Show yourself!" I order.

"No need to be so bossy," a voice next to me calls out. A familiar voice.

"It can't be!" I cry out, emotions flooding to the surface. "How is this…?"

"How is it possible?" the voice answers. "Because you are in Hell, Jessica. That's where all ghosts go." She grins manically.

This can't be real. This can't be real. This can't be real. I repeat the words out loud but the voice continues to growl next to me. "Tut-tut, Jessica. Is that anyway to talk to me?"

"Go away!" I scream at the voice.

"You shouldn't treat your baby sister like this, Jessica. Isn't it enough that you killed me?"

I send a burning sphere of fire towards the direction of the voice but the flames simply extinguish themselves when they come into contact with the wall. She cannot be here. In a world full of Spirits I still can't tell myself that her ghost lingers on in this nightmare world. Not after what happened.

"No wonder no one trusts you, Jessie. You have kept me a secret from everyone. You made it seem like I didn't exist." Her voice cracks from behind me. I turn around to face her and I am greeted by my baby sister. Her face is still haunting me after all this time.

I try to get the words out but they come out a croak instead. "This is a nightmare. This is what he wants."

"You left me to die, Jessie. You abandoned me." Her words cut through me like a cold steel knife. I push through the agony and stumble to the table.

She appears in front of me, her pale face aghast and black hair whipping around like snakes. Her white dress flows off in unnatural directions as she hovers above the ground. I stare into her eyes and I am unsurprised to see that there is nothing behind them, instead pure emptiness.

"I didn't kill you. Stop," I cry, turning away from her.

"You may not have delivered the killing blow but you might have well as. You left me," she screams.

"That's not true!" I yell as I snap my head around and stare at her again. "I tried to help you. It was not my fault," I defend myself.

"Lies!" Her scream pierces my ears. The glass in the window shatters aggressively and falls down. I walk backwards, the shards crunching beneath my shoes, until my back hits the wall. "You abandoned me and I died because of you." She looms over me.

I stand my ground. I am sick of hearing these hurtful words come out of my sister's mouth. "You are not the girl I remember," I choke.

"Death changes a person," she spits.

"Enough!" I shout. "You want to hear the truth? Then I will tell you. This was not my fault." I walk forward, and to my surprise, she retreats. I begin to channel the fire that burns inside me, turning it into confidence. "I never abandoned you. In fact, you left me. I had begun my hunt for Avarice and you insisted on coming along."

"I was my destiny as much as yours!" she seethes.

"You were too young! You should have not involved yourself in this world. We had only stopped for a break in a meadow for less than an hour when you ran off. I tried to find you but I couldn't."

"You forgot about me." Her harsh words take on a lower tone, more of regret.

"I looked for hours. And when I found you it was too late. You were standing in the centre of a field clutching a single rose. I screamed out for you to stop but you sniffed it." Tears fall down from my face. "I raced to you but you had already hit the ground. Your face was blue and your eyes were so…" I cannot even finish the sentence, the memory is too painful.

"Dead?" she angrily suggests.

"Empty," I correct. "It wasn't a rose that you sniffed. It was deadly Belladonna augmented by Avarice. He made the poison a thousand fold more lethal, even for a single inhalation. He attacked you to make me weak."

"You forgot about me after that."

"No!" I scream loudly. "I would never forget about you. I just turned that pain into my work. The reason I am like I am is because I lost you! I could never, ever, face the loss of a loved one again so I focused on the hunt instead. I channelled losing you into being a stronger person. They call me stern but I have to be practical and stay in control so no one gets hurt." I justify my actions but she simply waves me off with a gesture. "How dare you think that I would leave you?" I run over to one of the doors along the far side wall. I pull on the door handle, turning the lock at the same time, and throw myself into a new room.

The smell of fresh linen fills the air. I stare blankly at my childhood bedroom, running my hand over the soft comforter on the bed. What is Avarice playing at? Taking me back to the house I grew up in. The place where everything went wrong. I burned this house to cinders when my powers were activated.

The knocking on the door begins again. "Go away!" I scream, the ferociousness coming out in my tone. If Avarice wants me to hide away, then he is getting what he wants.

The knocking becomes more persistent until I can no longer ignore it. I summon a fireball in my hand and advance towards the door. I prepare myself to enter the cabin and burn the place to the ground. That girl out there is not my sister and, despite any memories I may have, I can no longer watch the place I love tarnished by her ghostly presence. I will burn this place to cinders like I have done many times before. I face the door and with a mighty kick I force it off at its hinges, facing my fears. I fling the ball of scorching flames directly towards the presence standing in front of me.

Oh God.

It's Evelyn.

She narrowly manages to dodge the burning ball as she throws herself to the ground. Her halo of blonde hair flows around her, the tips being singed from the intense heat, as she takes cover. "What the…?" she manages to squeal out.

"Evelyn!" I yell as I jet out towards her, checking her for any burns. She ungracefully clambers up, grasping at the nearby table, before facing me. Her right eyebrow cocks up, giving me her signature look, and showing her emotions plain and clearly. "I didn't see you."

"I gathered." She pats the dust from her clothes.

"How on earth did you get here?" I quiz. I thought I was alone.

She smiles a knowing smile. "I was trapped in a world like this. I thought it was a dream at first but then I realised that we are trapped in a world of our own fears." She looks around, noting the blue glistening lake outside the window. "Are you afraid of water?"

"No."

"It makes sense. Being a fire Guardian you know."

"Evelyn I am not afraid of water."

"Maybe if you go for a swim we can conquer your fear and pop back into reality."

"Evelyn!" I yell, stopping her rambling words. "I am not afraid of water and I am a perfectly competent swimmer."

She looks at me, confused. "Well what then? Are you afraid of beautiful wooden cabins in the middle of paradise?" she sarcastically comments.

I bite my lip and avoid eye contact with her. I don't really want her to know that this is my worst fear.

"I will find out eventually," she flatly says.

I sigh, thinking of how to put this into words. "A few years ago I lost my sister." Her face drops. Heavy silence fills the room. "Avarice murdered her."

"Oh. Jessica, I am so sorry." she begins but I raise my hand and stop her.

"I understand you are just being polite but you didn't know her Evelyn. It wasn't your fault she died so you have no reason to apologise, do you? I don't want your pity," I snap.

"It wasn't pity. I have a sister, Jessica, and if I lost her, I don't know how I would go on. I think you are being very brave." She warmly takes my arm.

"Thanks. We have a destiny to fulfil and that cannot stop just because I lost someone. Just think, we only need to defeat him once and then it will be years before he is strong enough to form again. We will probably be dead."

"And he will be the next lot of Guardians' problem," she justifies. "So is this where her death happened? Is that why we are here?" She gestures around to the cabin.

"No, Evelyn. This is my favourite memory. Yet every door I go through takes be back into my childhood home. That's my worst memory." I look around, feeling very lonely again, despite Evelyn's presence.

"Well, the only way to get out is for you to conquer your fear. When you start to do that, I can break us out of here. Literally."

"Easier said than done. What was your worst fear?" I look to her for answers.

Evelyn looks away ashamedly. She picks at her cuticle before looking back at me. "I was afraid of being alone. I was worried that my powers would tear everyone away from me," she mumbles her words out.

"Well," I take a step forward and take her hands in mine, "That will never happen okay. You will never be alone. A team remember." I allow my warmth to spread over her, reassuring her. She may be a rude, ungrateful, girl but now it is so clear. She is just so afraid of everyone leaving her so she pushes them away herself. She squirms to my touch but I can see the relief in her eyes.

"Well, let's get you out of here. We have to face your fear. Open up to me and let it all go."

I hesitate to tell her, worrying that this secret will forever turn her against me. I stutter the words out. "Evelyn. There is something you should know. It's about my sister."

"What about her?" she calmly asks.

I begin to tell her, but an icy wind creeps up my back. I turn around, feeling my blood run cold, and face my sister, looking as pale and ghostly as ever. I did not want Evelyn to find out like this. I wanted to open up to her and tell her the truth. My sister hovers in the air for a moment before gliding forward and making her presence known to Evelyn.

Frost forms on the windows, scratching and cracking under the icy pressure, whilst the look on Evelyn's face turns into pure horror. I can see any trust she had for me quickly disappear, and fear take its place. She tries to open her mouth but only gasps come out. Her hands tremble next to her pale body and her legs begin to shake. "Evelyn I am so sorry." I begin. "She's my sister. Avarice killed her and now she haunts my nightmares."

The words slip out of Evelyn's mouth, a quiet whisper so silent I barely heard it.

"Raina is your sister. The dead, fourth Guardian is your sister."

"I was meant to protect my sister, and instead she died. She said something right earlier which was that her death was due to my negligence. Avarice would never have been able to kill her if I had taken better care. Thanks to that it's my fault that we aren't strong enough to defeat him.

My sister developed her powers at an unnaturally young age. We both had matching pendants, which we assumed our parents gave to us, but in actuality, they were the first steps into being a Guardian. She manipulated the ripples of a pond we were playing in and my parents were terrified. I had yet to develop mine, despite being older, and they had no idea what was going on. That's why we moved houses so many times – people would ask questions about the freak occurrences that happened when my sister was near water. A few years later, she lost control of her powers at a pool party for one of her friends. Torrents of water poured and flooded the nearby houses. Our mother and father were so shaken they packed up and forced us to move but Raina sneaked out and returned to the neighbour's house to see the damage and that's when she was taken into the Spirit world. They explained to her that she was the youngest emerging Guardian, at the age of thirteen, and that they will keep an eye out for her.

They weren't watching the day she died. Hundreds of Guardians tracing back through time and not one of them could have saved her. Their golden rule is to use their vast powers to manipulate the events of the natural world in subtle ways and to never directly interfere. The act of entering the Spirit world was considered more than enough help and anything after that was our job to figure out. These rules were set into motion by the first ever Guardians, aptly named the First. These four woman, the progenitors to the Guardian line, ensured that they would not sway the battle in the way of good and make sure that it was fair and the forces of good would prevail naturally. I learnt all this during my visit to the Spirit world so I fully understand why Evelyn gets angry due to the cryptic nature of her meeting.

The spirits forcibly took me into their world one night, whilst I was sleeping, to console me for the loss of my sister. They explained that they could not take physical form and aid Raina due to the cardinal rule of not interfering. At the age I was, when I lost her, I just became so emotionally inverted. I kept myself to myself and followed my destiny. Travelling the world, abandoning my parents without a single word, managed to make dealing with my grief easier.

I was crossing through a rustic town one day when I was attacked. Driving through the scorching desert, the sunlight heating up my car beyond belief, meant I had to stop off for a drink in a local tavern when I noticed something in the distance. At first, I thought it was a mirage but I think the bolt of lightning that tore my wheels to shreds gave it away. Avarice, in possession of a village elder, wreaked havoc through the town and completely annihilated it. His recent success at killing my sister meant he finally had enough power to possess people again, speeding up his process of gaining strength gradually by years. Hundreds of innocent locals were slaughtered in the name of this demon. I would have been dead as well if not for Amara. I tried to protect some of the locals from his wrath but I couldn't do enough, the weight of my sister's demise dragged me down into ineptitude. Avarice was seconds away from delivering the killing blow, finding me hidden underneath the rubble of a downed building, shielding some locals. Amara fought him off long enough for me to run to my car and wait for her to join me. Since that day, she became the sister that I needed.

I only ever lied to ensure that we would focus on the task at hand, I didn't want my personal history to effect the tasks at hand. I didn't want the death of my sister to be the root cause of any failure that may happen. I can imagine it now… *'It's your fault your sister died and thanks to you Avarice will destroy everything."'*

The look on Evelyn's face proves to me that my lies only succeeded in ruining any relationships I could have. I didn't want Evelyn to find out this way. To be honest I never wanted her to find out at all. But now the truth is out and Evelyn knows all the lies I have told.

Raina hovers in the air her ghostly appearance terrifying Evelyn down to her core, her trembling body a huge giveaway. "How could you keep this a secret from me?"

"She is my sister, Evelyn. I didn't want her name dragged up every time. You may have just found out that there is no fourth Guardian and we are down a water element, but at the end of the day, I was the one who had to bury my sister. Not you. No one else has a right to complain about her not being here," I bluntly respond.

"You are right." She raises her hands in defence, taking my statement to heart and surprisingly agreeing with me. "I just wish you would have told me from the beginning. I'd have like to have known exactly where we stood in regards to fighting the ancient killing demon."

"Well its three versus one. I'm sure we will be fine," I joke. We are probably toast. We will be the first Guardians in history to fail their one task. Eras of Guardians arose to their task and managed to defeat him before he regained his true body. We already failed at that part.

"Well in order to actually start that fight we need to return to our world. Or our bodies. Maybe we are just trapped in our own heads?" She tries to get her brain around the current situation but she just looks incredibly confused. "So let's face your fear and get back. Have you noticed that your sister hasn't spoken once since I have been here? She is a figment of your imagination Jessica, you are in control."

I turn to face Raina, who's still hovering in the air, and stare into her pale gaunt face. I stand my ground, firmly digging my heels into the floor, before I open my mouth and force the words out. *Remember Jessica- you are in control!*

"Raina. I am sorry about what happened, and no one regrets it more than I do. But I need to let the past go. There are things that need my full attention and in order to do that I have to let go of the grief that I am carrying around. You have to let me move on. Please do not think, not even for a second, that I do not love you." I reach out to take her ghostly hand but my hand passes straight through her. "You will always be in my heart and I will never, ever, stop thinking about you."

Silence hangs in the air. I share a quick glance with Evelyn.

"Is she broken?" Evelyn whispers, leaning in.

Raina zooms in, her stark features becoming uncomfortable close, as she remains silent.

That doesn't last for long.

A single, high-pitched, scream erupts rom her mouth. Evelyn and I drop down and clutch our ears, trying to protect them from the onslaught of sound. "Raina stop!" Evelyn screams above the screeching tone.

Raina's ghost picks Evelyn up by the waist and effortlessly flings her into the wall at the back of the cabin. Her body slides down and rests on the floor, a disoriented look on her face. I try to reach for her but Raina blocks my path. "You think you can simply forget about me? I will never stop haunting your memories," she screams.

"She isn't real Jessica. Trust me!" Evelyn shouts above the sound of Raina's wails.

"I will make you pay for this Jessie. I will burn you away just like you burnt me." Raina spits the words out before moving over to the lit fireplace. She reaches in and catches a handful of flickering flames, allowing them to dance on her skin harmlessly.

"Jessica she isn't real. She is a figment of your imagination." Evelyn's voice pales into the background.

"I…" I begin to form words but my sister crudely cuts me off, flinging a nearby wooden chair in my direction. I roll out of the way, allowing it to crash behind me, before I face off against her again. Before I can even talk to her, she lobs the ball of flames onto the curtains hanging against the window. They catch flame instantaneously and the white-hot flames ascend up towards the ceiling. The temperature of the room begins to increase to boiling heat but I simply shrug this off. Evelyn begins to pant and sweat in the heat.

"You will burn with me, Jessie." She twistedly smiles.

The flames crawl along the floor, reaching out to me, before trapping us both in a fiery circle. Red-hot flames dance in the air as my sister and I become suspended in a plume of fire. Evelyn becomes obscured by the jet of flames, my attention solely focused on my sister.

"Raina, listen to me. I will never forget you, but I cannot let you continue to affect me the way you have done. You will remain in my heart until the day I die, but until then I have a lot of work to do. I have to save the world." I push the words out, summoning the strength from the fire that surround me.

"You will burn," she threatens. The flames leap out of the column and begin to crawl up my arm. The ticklish sensation, lethal to anyone else, only serves as an annoyance.

"No Raina. I will not burn. I will never burn." I extend my arms and will the fire to leave my body. The flames disappear with a puff.

"Evelyn now!" I scream, using my powers to open a gap in the plume of flames, which I leap through and rush over to grab Evelyn's extended hand. The world around us begins to shake and the flames are whipped away into the growing darkness.

"I love you Raina. Remember that." The words leave my mouth before the darkness takes over me and Evelyn, whisking us away.

Chapter 18

Jessica

We hit the ground with a painful thump.

Evelyn squeals as her body lands in an ungraceful position on a pile of loose wood. I rub the back of my head, blinking away the black spots around my eyes, as I banged my skull against the dank, white wall. I reach out and offer her a helping hand, which she accepts, and pull ourselves upright. Our eyes strain in the darkness as we take in our new surroundings.

A thick blanket of dust lies over every surface like filthy snow, coating the stacks of papers piled up along the walls and cascading all the way to the foot of some dank wooden stairs. Chunks of wallpaper cling lifelessly to the walls, some falling off and pooling on the floor messily. Tables thickly encrusted with dried up mould, lie haphazardly on their side with many broken chairs strewn around them. Dust covered mirrors obscure anything from view whilst the smell of mildew, stale air, and a fog thick with dust fills the air. Shafts of moonlight pour through the gaps in the boarded up windows, creating illuminated paths that only serve to enhance the filth in the air. Along the hallway facing us, thickly lined with a white fungous growth, stand several doors, all covered with a thin layer of grime that has lain there for years. One of the doors creaks open, moving only an inch at a time, scratching slowly at the floor. Evelyn slowly steps forward and pushes on the wood only for her hand to crash right through the slimy door. We peer inside and see a further room covered with a thick coating of dust and more tables plastered with mould. We step back tentatively, leaving the filthy room. I narrowly avoid a dark hole underneath my feet, where a floorboard used to lay but has now snapped, weak from the weight of the grime above it. Cobwebs hang from the ceiling like grey clouds that brush our faces as we walk deeper down the hall. A frozen shiver runs down my spine as all my instincts tell me to run.

"Where are we?" I ask as I spit the dust from my mouth.

"I think," Evelyn begins as she wipes her sleeve on the grimy wall. Clumps of dirt fall off and reveal a tattered poster underneath, some kind of animal in a humorous pose wearing a football jacket. "I think we are at my school. This is our mascot." She points to the animal poster.

"Wow. Your school is disgusting," I groan as I pull my heel from a sticky heap of mess on the floor.

"It doesn't normally look like this you know. Something's wrong."

"Seriously?" I sarcastically retort as I regain my balance after nearly falling over a pile of rotten books. "If this is someone's mind they are seriously messed up."

"Well, as powerful as Avarice is, I doubt he can put a spirit to sleep so I think that rules out Raina. Not to mention Amara is a statue right now so we have no idea if she can even have nightmares so that just leaves Luke." She looks around frantically. Hearing Evelyn calling my sister a spirt is strangely satisfying, as if there are no more secrets between us.

"So does that mean Luke is afraid of dirt?"

"No." She shoots me a look. "Something else is going on here. We need to find him."

"Just take your time, Evelyn; it doesn't look like it's the safest place in the world." I once again jump over a hole in the floor, the weight of the rotting floorboards creaking underneath me. This place gives me the creeps.

"We don't have the time. We have no idea what Avarice is doing in the real world right now whilst we are stuck inside Luke's head."

"Calm down okay." I place my hand on hers and squeeze, mirroring what I have seen Luke do sometime when she gets stressed, "I'm sure the magic of the vase is still protecting our bodies whilst we are here. Let's just focus on getting to him safely. Now, can you get a reading on him or something?" The tense grip trick seems to work. I know I am not Luke, and I doubt our relationship will ever be as close as theirs, despite us being prophesised sisters, but this seemingly small act completely soothes her.

Evelyn steps into a beam of moonlight and closes her eyes. Her lips part slightly and a small exhale escapes, her breath wisping out in the cold air. She raises her hands delicately and waves them across the dusty air before stopping still, pointing towards another hallway, before darting away in another direction. "I can't really pick anything up here, it's like there is something dampening my powers, but the only plant life I can sense is coming from that way." She gestures towards the darkness.

We walk down the dank hallway, the blackness slowly creeping in on us, as the moonlight becomes blocked out by the boarded up windows. I open my hand flat and summon a small ball of fire that rolls around carelessly, flickering in the wind, and provides sufficient light to brighten the way. I can already feel the force pushing against us, like someone squeezing my powers straight out of me, crushing them from the inside out.

"Nice to know that you double as a flashlight." Evelyn subtly grins.

"Keep walking," I joke as I playfully jab her in the back, ignoring the feeling inside of me. "Wait a second…" I pause on the spot and tuck my hair behind my ear, freeing it to hear more clearly. "Can you hear that?"

Evelyn similarly pause and cranes her neck, a confused look on her face. "Hear what?" she mumbles.

A faint sound coming from down the corridor blends in with the whistling of the wind. The soft, hitched, sound croons slowly. "It sounds like someone sobbing."

"Trust me, if you went to my school, you'd sob too." She looks distastefully around. For such a smart girl she seems to really hate her school.

We continue to plod forward through the darkness, the only source of light now comes from my flickering ball of orange flames, until we meet a dead end. The grimy brick walls run alongside us, before turning and meeting around a thick wooden door that blocks our path. Moonlight pours in through the cracks in the door, yet no matter how hard we exert our strength and try to open it, it remains firmly bolted in place. Evelyn tries pushing, kicking, and ramming the wood before giving up with a huff of defeat.

"Want me to burn it down?" I ask her as I make my flame grow bigger, fighting through the oppressive force.

Evelyn places her hands flat against the door, running her fingers across the wood, before whispering, "Let's try something more subtle." She spreads her hands flat and waits for a few seconds, before bringing her shoulders and arms back, then violently thrusting them forward. The air ripples around her and the ground shakes beneath us. Waves of seismic energy pulsate from her hands and bombard the door, which rips from its hinges and gets thrown far into the distance. She turns and smiles before walking through the door, leaving me aghast.

"You call that subtle," I mumble as I follow her through.

I thought that the abandoned school was creepy but this place takes it to a whole new level.

Rows upon rows of gravestones line an eerie, grey, graveyard. Some recent looking ones still retain their dull presence whereas the others take on a more cracked and decaying appearance. All of the mould covered, crumbling gravestones contain detailed engravings, sincere messages dedicated to the dead. Withered trees, which I assume is what Evelyn could sense, all grow around the stones, heavy roots wrap around the stones and crush them leaving chunks of scattered rock, as the branches from the trees all reach out for one another like black bony fingers. A tall black fence, topped with sharp spikes, surrounds the graveyard creating an eerie similarity to a prison cell. The stench of mulch and stone fills the dry air; clumps of weeds weigh our shoes down, as we navigate around the tombs of the dead. A gravel path weaves around through the catacomb of graves, snaking through the thick dead grass like a predator, before disappearing into a mass of black weeds. The same chill runs down my back from earlier and I just want to get out of this place.

I reach down and grab Evelyn's hand when I finally locate the sound of the ominous sobbing.

A figure, wrapped in a tattered black jacket, hunches over a grave at the far end of the yard. Evelyn's hands tremble inside of my grip as we walk over to the figure. We slowly encroach on him and stand intrepidly next to him. The crack of a twig beneath my foot draws his attention to us, and he slowly turns his head and faces us. The colour drains from Evelyn's face when she locks eyes on who he is.

Luke lay slumped against the gravestone, half of his face covered in shadow, and the other bathed in moonlight, almost a white as the moon itself. His eyes hang dull and large, with huge purple circles resting beneath them, the normal dazzling blue irises now as colourless as glass. His skin, a sickly ashy tone, shows the dramatic absence of colour, which seemingly faded a long time ago, His football jacket now covers his frail figure, looking like skin wrapped around bone, as all of his previous muscle has wasted away, leaving a husk of the man we knew.

"Luke," Evelyn whispers his name as she leans in close, her body trembling with fear. "It's me, Evelyn."

"No." His voice comes out a weak croak, "My Evelyn is dead."

His body moves sluggishly away from the stone, slumping on the black grass instead, as the moonlight bathes the gravestone showing the perfectly detailed engraved message.

'Here lies the body and soul of Evelyn Harp'
'Rest in Peace.'

❈

It's all so clear now. Luke's worst fear is a world in which he and Evelyn aren't together. My heart physically hurts for him. He is so worried that his whole world will crumble and decay around him if Evelyn was to disappear.

"I promise, Luke, I will never leave you. This isn't me." Evelyn gestures over towards the gravestone. She shivers when her eyes come into contact with it, I can hardly blame her because it's not every day you see your own grave.

"You are a ghost. You have been sent to torment me forever." His words seep out of his cracked lips.

"No!" she yells, cupping his icy hands and pulling them close. "Luke, please, you have to listen to me."

"You left me all alone," he whimpers and Evelyn pulls him into an unnaturally tight embrace, yearning for the physical contact, whilst I just stare passively. It must be horrific to truly believe that your best friend, your entire world, is dead.

I can sympathise with him. I know *exactly* how he feels.

"Luke, I can prove it." She releases his bony fingers and instead grabs a dead flower from a bouquet nearby. She brings the black, rotten, petals to her mouth and takes a deep breath in. Luke watches, half dazed, as she softly blows out, breathing life into the dead flower. The colour changes as her powers wisp across it, subtly at first, before the entire flower now blooms a pale white, the petals uncurling with the reinvigoration of new life. She hands the flower to Luke, who sparingly accepts it, before giving him a gentle smile.

He crushes the flower between his skeletal fingers. His eyes remain sorrowful and heavy, staring at Evelyn as if she was just a memory.

"Well that didn't work," I add, under my breath. "Try something more drastic."

"Like what?"

"I don't know. I could zap him. Or maybe you could just cause that magic earthquake that you have been doing so well and pull us all back into reality?" Despite the force sapping my powers from me, I am sure I could summon the strength for at least one bolt of lightning.

"I only pulled us from world to world after we conquered our fears. I don't want to tear Luke out of here when he is like this just in case it becomes permanent. I don't want my best friend to be a walking skeleton forever."

"Well think of something or the next step is a few jolts to the nervous system," I harmlessly warn her, I wouldn't intentionally hurt Luke, but we need to get back to the real world very quickly and we have no time to waste. Evelyn's reluctance to do the necessary could be our downfall. Amara and I have trained all our lives to kill Avarice.

Can Evelyn really take a life?

"God, I hope this works," she groans before leaning in, gripping Luke by the arms, and pulls his lips to hers. They meet in a weird mix of warmth, on Evelyn's side, and cold, on Luke's side. She releases her grip on him, and moves in closer, gently placing her hand on the back of his head, before eventually letting go completely and stepping away. They just stare at each other.

"What on earth was that for Evelyn?" I cringe at the display. These two are far too close to kiss. It just seems unnatural.

"He is still a teenage boy. I thought the power of hormones may help us. Not to mention when we were kids we grew up reading fairy tales where kisses wake people up." She shrugs.

"That just gross Evelyn. And this isn't a fairy-tale."

"We have magical powers, hunt demons, and talk to ghosts," she states confidently.

"Touché," I mumble. She has a fair point.

Luke continues to stare at us, unmoving. At first it was unrecognisable, but it looks like a small flush of colour has appeared on his grey cheeks.

"Luke," she says his name slowly, and extends her hand for him to take it. "Come home."

"I have no home," he mumbles. Evelyn and I gasp in annoyance over how that kiss didn't work.

"That's it, I'm zapping him." I feel the energy pulse in my hand as I summon the electricity within. Red sparks wiz across the air around me.

"No!" Evelyn yells. "We have no idea what hurting him in this world does to his real body. You could end up lobotomizing him!"

Luke, now completely ignoring us, walks towards the other side of the graveyard. The wet ground squelches beneath his feet. "Where are you going?" Evelyn calls after him.

He ends up facing the door that we walked through earlier, the other side being the abandoned school, and he reaches for the door handle. He pushes gently and the door creaks open to reveal pure darkness. The school on the other side has dissipated and instead a black void has taken its place. The stark absence of anything only causes the fear inside of me to grow. He goes to take a step before Evelyn pulls him back harshly.

"Do not go through there!" She warns him, panic coursing through her voice.

"It's the only way to get rid of my pain."

"No, Luke." I join in Evelyn's frantic pleads. "If you go through that door, then Avarice wins. You will belong to him. You'll be nothing more than a zombie."

He brushes our words off and takes another step. The door rattles vigorously on its hinges and the blackness sweeps out, like a thick smoke curling across the floor. The tendrils of darkness rise up and beckon Luke to walk towards them like a gothic siren call. The wind whips aggressively around us, and Luke's body begins to be pulled into the darkness.

"No!" Evelyn screams as she grips his hand, anchoring him in place. The sheer force of the wind lifts his frail body from the ground, and he dangles weightlessly in the air. "Jessica! Help!" Her sharp words draw my eyes away from the abyss and onto Luke. I grab his other hand, the weight of myself and Evelyn being enough to keep him from being pulled into the darkness.

The wind blows stronger.

"I'm losing him!" she screams above the tempest.

"Hang on!" I shout, before letting go of one hand, keeping Luke tethered to my left hand, and I shoot a jet of red flames towards the abyss. I will them to, instead of burning away, to rise and stay in place, creating a wall of fire that blocks the door. The wind dies down, and Luke falls harshly to the ground, due to the sudden decrease in the force pulling him. The smoke, cut off due to my flames, dissipates into the air.

"That won't last for long." I focus my attention on maintaining the wall of fire, using it as a shield against the enchanting pull of the door.

Evelyn drops down to Luke on the floor and further pleads with him. I cannot make out their words, the crackle of the flames being too loud. I can feel something on the other side pushing back against my flames. A force that doesn't want to be trapped.

"Evelyn, hurry!" I yell, the darkness begins to pour through the gaps in my flames. A thin sheen of sweat form on my face, the intensity of my powers draining my body. I will the flames to burn hotter, preventing the black smoke from seeping out, but my attempts begin to falter. "Evelyn something is pushing back. I can't hold it any longer."

The darkness rips through my fire, extinguishing the flames, and throwing me back.

"Jessica!" Evelyn cries out, struggling to choose whether to stay by Luke or come help me.

I put her mind at rest. "I am fine." I stand up, brushing off the dirt and ignoring the pain in my back. The black smoke continues to pour out of the door and crawl along the floor towards us.

"That's it. I'm getting us out of here." I head over to Luke, whose feet are now hidden by the thick smoke, which slowly crawls up his body like a boa constrictor. "He will be fine," I tell Evelyn, although I literally have no idea if he will.

I stand above Luke, call forth the electricity inside of me, and gather a ball of red sparks in my hand. Evelyn's protests fall upon deaf ears as I plunge the glowing ball down onto Luke's body.

He convulses violently for a second before falling limp. Volts of electricity course through his body, under my control, as I will them not to cause any harm, but instead pulsate around and draw him out of his mentally induced funk. I struggle to swallow a thick lump in my throat.

"Luke!" Evelyn cries as he stops moving.

Please work.

His eyes slowly open and he stares blankly at us. His dry lips part and a few words slip out.

"That was rude."

Evelyn cries in gratitude and throws herself onto his body for a hug. I just sigh in relief that I didn't kill him. Before the hugging can continue, I aid Evelyn in pulling his frail body out of the encroaching smoke.

"Now would be a good time for a reality breaking earthquake," I ask Evelyn as we face the growing black smoke. It rises high off the ground and looms over us, its presence striking up a deep hollow fear inside of me. Evelyn summons an earthquake around us, the ground trembling with a force so deep it can tear open worlds. The smoke plunges forwards at us, wrapping around our bodies like an unwelcomed blanket and begins to firmly cocoon us.

The two contrasting events, the possessing smoke in the dream world and the shattering of this reality, fight a heavy battle. The smoke cannot fully take us due to this world becoming weaker by the second. I scream out as the smoke begins to clog my lungs.

"One last push, Evelyn. Take us home," I choke as I implore her to channel all her strength and pull us back into reality. She screams in pure anguish.

The tremors crack this world in two as we are yanked from it, tumbling through the hazy darkness.

Chapter 19

Jessica

A bright light floods the room with a welcomed warmth.

I groan as I stretch out from my lying position, rolling onto my front, before standing up sluggishly. My eyes dart around the room, taking in the familiarity of the surrounding area, before a soft mumbling behind me causes me to turn. The source of the blinding light nowhere to be seen.

Evelyn, her hair slightly dishevelled, emerges from behind a couch and joins me in standing up, batting her clothes down.

"Are we still in a dream?" She rubs her eyes with the back of her hands.

The contrasting pale walls and vibrant red curtains could only belong to one place. We are back in Elkwood Manor. "Nope, looks like home. Well, whatever you want to call this place."

"Then where is—"

Before she can even finish her question, a voice pipes up, "Right here." Luke waves from the ground behind Amara's statue. He uses her body, to my distaste, as a frame to grab and lift his body weight. He smiles at us before standing beside me.

"Did you just use my best friend as a helping hand to stand up?" I tut.

He blushes and looks away, presumably embarrassed that he probably just grabbed Amara inappropriately.

"Where is he?" Evelyn interrupts as her voice cuts through the air. We glance around, searching for Avarice, expecting him to be waiting on the other side of the protective barrier.

"Are we even sure this vase is still shielding us?" I ask. I walk towards the cold metal and place my hand on it. I feel the power emanating from it, like a silent hum of pure energy. It courses through my body like a wave of harmless electricity. "Don't answer that. My sister swore it would protect us."

"What?" Luke looks at me in confusion. Evelyn and I share a quick glance before looking back at him.

"Shall I tell him?" I wonder.

"He does have a right to know," she justifies.

"Know what?" he cries in confusion.

"He isn't a Guardian technically. It doesn't massively affect him."

"Jessica! He was trapped in a dream world with us. He has as much right as anyone to know! He is willing to risk his life for us. It's only fair to let him in on the secret." Evelyn folds her arms in defence to my objection.

"What secret?" His cries become more shrill and needy.

"Luke. The fourth Guardian is Raina."

"That's not much of a secret." He tilts his head like a dog.

"She's my sister."

"Oh."

"She's dead."

"Oh." His face drops.

He goes to open his mouth but nothing comes out.

"You don't need to say anything. I don't want a pitiful apology or anything. Let's just take that information in, move on. We have bigger issues."

"Like how we almost lost Luke to the darkness just then?" Evelyn mumbles as she bites her nails. Luke just looks away.

"I tried to fight back. It's like the sadness just took over. Those weren't my words coming out. I don't remember much though."

"Thank God," Evelyn whispers.

"I remember you kissing me." He grins childishly.

Evelyn blushes and buries her head in her hands. She groans embarrassedly and walks away from us.

"C'mon Evie! Don't act like you didn't love it!" he calls after her, laughing as he talks.

"Stop!" she cries out. Their interaction makes me laugh, but I also long for Amara to be here. I stare at her stone figure.

Luke catches up with her, and plasters soft kisses all over her cheeks, as she tries to push him off her. They end up tumbling to the floor in floods of laughter.

"Did I not just say that we have pressing issues? You two are like children," I scold.

They both stand and apologise, continuing to elbow one another when they think I am not looking.

"We narrowly escaped being turned into *his* minions a few moments ago. We severely underestimated his power." I pace around the room, trying to juggle the thoughts in my head.

"Jessica," Luke interrupts, "I don't think it was a few moments ago," he calls out from over near the window, peering out into the distance.

I strut to the large curtains and whip them open forcefully. The moonlight floods into the room and bathes us all in a silver glow. "Oh my God. We have been asleep for centuries." Luke frantically runs his hands over his body, before settling on his pocket and pulling out his phone. He swipes the screen and sighs in relief. "It's just later in the day, that's all."

"My parents are going to worry," Evelyn mumbles. Luke just taps his screen a few times before popping his phone back into his pocket.

"I just texted them saying that you are staying at mine whilst my parents are out of town. I know the signal sucks, but it will probably send as soon as we get a little bit of coverage. So, now what?"

"I have no idea," Evelyn states.

"Me neither," I agree.

"Lucky for you, I do." Raina calls out from behind us. "You never had any bright ideas sis." She winks at me before walking to the front of the group. "Right, the Guardians are working on some magic juju that will help break Amara free from the stone curse and then the three," she looks at Luke, "Well, four, of you have to go out and face him. You need to face your birth right."

"He will annihilate us," Evelyn coldly replies.

"Then you will be the only Guardians in history to ever fail at your sole task. I mean seriously girls?" she mocks us. "All you have to do is hurt him badly enough that he separates from his body. By the time he regains control again he will be the next set of Guardians' problem and you will be sat all cosy in your retirement home!" She smiles at the image before plopping down on the couch.

"And how do you expect us to do that? We are one woman down," I state.

"Thanks for calling me a woman, Jessie." She throws another wink in my direction. "I can't help. It's against the rules, sadly."

"Stupid rules," Evelyn mumbles as she picks at her fingernails.

"I didn't make them." Raina raises her hands jokingly. "This battle has to be won fair and square with no intervention from either party's spirits. I mean, can you imagine if Avarice brought an army of evil spirits with him?"

We shudder at the thought. We are already losing this battle, we don't need a million demonic ghosts on his side.

"You need to act quickly though. The vase was damaged during the fight. It won't shield us all for much longer. You should seize the advantage and attack first. Strike whilst the iron is hot...or something like that."

I quickly glance at the vase, noting a single crack rising up from base to tip. "We need to think this through."

"We may not have the time," Luke says, before pushing past me and walking towards Raina. He goes to touch her but his hand passes through her, unsurprisingly, but her body seems somewhat off. Her body now appears more see through, flickering in the moonlight like an old cassette tape.

"Oh" She looks down at her transparent body. "The spirit world is anchored to the vase. We are using it to stay locked onto the physical world. That's why we can communicate right now."

"And if it breaks will future Guardians still be able to enter the Spirit world?" Evelyn asks.

"I'm not sure. But if this vase breaks then there is nothing protecting us. Avarice could be strong enough to tear the barriers between worlds apart. He could cross over into the spirit world and destroy us all." She ominously warns, turning her head away from us as she continues to flicker.

"Well then we need to stop him before that happens then, don't we?" Evelyn steps forward, placing her hand on my shoulder for support. "But we need Amara to do that."

"I'll see what I can do." She disappears into the air with a quiet sigh.

At first a single crack appeared, followed by more, that snake up the stone base. Chunks of rock slowly fall from the stone Amara, leaving casts of her body across the carpet, as her clothes reveal themselves.

After five minutes, half of her body is completely freed. Her legs, both clear of stone, stand rigid in the same position.

"This is taking too long." Evelyn steps up and places her hands on Amaras chest. She breathes out and sends a pulse across her body. Waves of vibrations roll across her stone body, sending the remaining chunks falling to the ground.

"Evelyn! That could have killed her," I call out in fear.

"So could've zapping Luke. We both placed trust in each other and it worked." She looks up at Amara. "Well I hope it has."

Amara, not looking as normal as usual, stands frozen on the spot. Her eyes open in fear, remain a grey colour.

"Evelyn, try something for me?" I ask her.

"What?" She looks at me impassively.

"Remember in Luke's dream, you breathed life into that little flower?"

"Yes. But that was only a dead flower."

"Please," I beg, hoping that she takes my hint and gives it a go. She sighs in defeat and walks closer to Amara. A quick inhale, followed by a harsh exhale, is all she delivers. "You aren't even trying."

She rolls her eyes before taking another breath. She blows a lot more slowly this time, opening her eyes at the same time, as her power wisps from her mouth.

The colours pulses back into Amaras eyes.

"You did it!" I shriek in happiness as Amara falls down from her standing position, coughing up small amounts of powdered rock.

"I cannot believe that just happened. I breathed life into a person." Evelyn whispers in shock. Luke wraps an arm around her comfortingly.

"Try being turned to stone. That really does surprise you," Amara jokes. "So, do I need filling in?"

"You have missed so much," Luke laughs before he details what happened over the past few hours.

"I did not passionately kiss you!" Evelyn jumps up to defend herself.

"Calm down. If you wanted another kiss all you had to do is ask," he jokingly mocks her.

"I will turn you into a daisy Luke. I am warning you."

He simply blows her a kiss in return.

"You heard what Raina said; we have a war to get ready for. We attack first. Give him no time to respond." Amara stands up, ready to head towards the door before Evelyn stops her.

"We cannot just launch a full powered attack. We need to lure him here where he is away from anyone. We cannot risk him killing a civilian because we chose to attack him in the middle of the town centre. Bring him here and we have him secluded." Evelyn's wise words cause Amara to agree. "And what about Luke? He could get hurt."

Luke walks quickly over towards one of the sheet covered cases. He whips the cloth off in a flurry, revealing the detailed axe from earlier, before lifting his foot high. He rams it forward with enough force to shatter the glass into a hundred pieces. He reaches in; avoiding the sharp ridges of the glass, and grasps the axe firmly in his hand. Eying up the craftsmanship, he tosses it heavily between both hands, testing the weight, before resting it at his side. "Don't worry about me. I can take care of myself."

"Against an evil demon with multiple unknown powers," Evelyn scoffs, although I can sense she is only being protective.

Amara pats him on the back sportingly. "He is in a human body. I assume he can still be hurt. I think I got a good punch to his nose when he attacked me earlier." She cracks her knuckles.

I want to press her further, ask her exactly what happened, but I don't want to rush her. She will share any information when she deems it necessary. I cross over towards her, sitting on the pale sofa next to her, and place a hand on her knee comfortingly. Her dark eyes fix on mine and a soft smile is offered. After a warming moment, her eyes quickly divert towards the axe that Luke holds in his hands. "Can I see that for a second?" She points to the handle, eyes squinting as if she is trying to make something out. Luke hands her the axe willingly.

"These symbols. I know what they translate to."

"I could make out the word *elements*. That's all though." Evelyn shrugs.

Amara smiles and nods in agreement. She furrows her brow and begins to translate the rest of the runic symbols. "Destroy the elements. Plunder with force. Raise the Cult of Avarice." Her smile disappears into a glum looking frown.

"Did that just say cult? As in evil worshipers?" Luke frantically asks.

Amara hands the axe back to him, subconsciously wiping her hands on her trousers, as if to wipe the feeling of it off her skin. "I had heard rumours but I never thought they were true. When I was travelling years ago I heard whispers that there were cults that formed to worship the primordial demons, including Avarice."

"Hang on, there are more demons than Avarice?" Luke shrieks.

"They all died out years ago. I think Avarice managed to survive by feeding on the greed of humanity," I inform him, remembering all the long, yet boring, chats I have had with Amara over the years.

"They are just normal cults though," Amara continues. "Human beings, who blindly followed the demons, were imbued with superhuman gifts. Together they promised to wreak as much havoc as Avarice himself, and convert any survivors to joining their fanatical ranks. The older Guardians spoke of fighting these people but they have not been seen for millennia. I just assumed they were wiped from existence."

Luke paces the room. I watch his grip tighten on the handle of the axe. His knuckles turn white with the pressure, the blood draining away as he enters deep thought. "This axe isn't millions of years old, meaning that some of his followers must have survived in order to make it and use it as a weapon against you guys." He gestures towards me, Amara, and Evelyn. "If we come across these guys, or they make themselves known, then we deal with them." He speaks coldly. Evelyn frowns at him, shocked at how these words have come from her beloved Luke's mouth.

"They are just people Luke," she persists.

"Do you think, given the chance, that they would hesitate to kill you?" His words strike hot. A burning sensation inside of me that just screams 'self-preservation'.

"I am not killing regular people Luke," she states flatly.

"Then it looks like I will have to keep an eye out for you on the battlefield then. I won't let them hurt you."

Evelyn rolls her eyes at the comment, turning away to pick at her fingernails. She mumbles some words under her breath. I can make out her saying how much Luke has changed. He just continues to pace around.

"We are talking about a cult of people that probably died out guys. No need to get irate," Amara tries to calm the situation. "Plus, we have to face the big guy first!"

Evelyn leans forward, brushing her hair behind her ear, and craning her neck towards the garden. Her fingers tighten on the edge of the seat, her knuckles protruding. "There is someone coming. Walking across the back courtyard." Her face snaps towards us, before slipping out of the momentary daze, blinking away the intense stare that probably hurt her eyes. "Sorry, I was in sensory mode. I could feel a disturbance in the field outside."

223

"If I ever get lost, remind me to call you," Amara laughs, completely avoiding what Evelyn just said.

"How many?" I ask flatly.

"Just the one," she responds.

We stand up, all facing the hallway that leads to the exit into the garden.

None of us go to move or make the first step.

"So this is it?" Luke asks.

"Looks like it," Evelyn mumbles.

"You guys ready for a fight?" Amara asks.

I turn to face her, offering a soft smile. "Always."

We walk through the dark corridor, through the glass doors, and into the cold night air. I grip Amaras hand tightly in mine, seeing comfort in the familiar touch. I throw a glance towards Evelyn who catches my eye and sheds a slight smile, and a soft nod, as a sign of courage.

Luke just looks scared as he twirls the axe in his hands like a baton.

We step onto the grass, the soft, slightly wet, ground squelching beneath us as we advance across the field. A single figure stands in the distance, a tall man in a black suit. His sickening smile beams across the distance, his eyes fixed intently on us, burning through us like hot pokers.

"Why do you face me when you are incomplete?" His deep voice booms across the field.

"Because we aren't scared of you," Amara responds confidently, although I feel her hand trembling in mine. "You have no hold on us."

"Oh is that so?" He cockily laughs and walks closer towards us. His strong jaw and intense eyes makes me understand how some people may fall willingly towards him, without the need of magical intervention. "The fact that you stand before me shows you conquered your fears. Quite admirable how you continue to stand beside each other considering the depths of your lies." He looks directly towards me.

I choke down the lump in my throat and summon the strength to talk to him. "I trust these people unconditionally."

"A foolish mistake," he spits. "Humanity has an innate ability for deception."

Luke takes a small valiant step forward, Evelyn reaching out for him as he steps in front of her. "That's where you are wrong. You know nothing about us, you are nothing but a demon after all."

Avarice smiles, brushes an inky black strand of hair away from his face, and tucks his hands into his trouser pockets. "You assume I am oblivious to the world, child, yet you never thought to question my mortality. I was there at the dawn of humanity. Demons prowled the earth long before you even discovered fire."

Out of the corner of my eye, I can see that Evelyn has clenched her fists, ready for something to happen. Before she has chance to launch a surprise attack, Luke pipes up again.

"How do you manage to keep coming back?" He turns around to face us, and noting our stern glares, simply cocks his head. "I just wanted to know, that's all."

"A fine question. You see, after humanity became discordant, and the need for control, both of people and possessions, I discovered that I could feed on this energy and turn others to my side. Back then, I was only a minor demon, until I summoned the courage to face the one true entity. The only thing in this world that is guaranteed."

"Taxes?" Luke questions. *If Avarice doesn't hit him I will, he has no self-control.*

Avarice remains stone faced, the joke wasted on him. "No. Death." He untucks his hands and cracks his knuckles, the sound causing Amara to flinch. "I made a deal with death to be a true immortal. I no longer wished to be a simple demon. I wanted to be *the* demon. From the moment of my conception, I was ridiculed for being a demon with no credible strength. I made sure I changed that."

"Are we meant to feel pity for you?" Evelyn scoffs, "And since when is Death a person?" before Avarice can answer she speaks again. "Actually, never mind. Stupid question considering the surrealness of what is happening right now."

"My spirit, along with those who made the same bargain, can never be destroyed. My physical body can be damaged, and the two can become separated, but I will never truly die. All I have to do is bide my time and wait for my essence to become strong enough to regain my ability to possess people, and then I begin the hunt for my body." His crisp voice courses through my body.

"How come I have never heard of any other like you? Demons who still prowl the earth?" Amara enquires, thirsty for the knowledge he can provide.

The moonlight casts a silver glow across him, almost soothingly, but his twisted features overpower all feelings of calmness. "You have heard of others like myself you foolish child. I was one of seven demonic entities, our origins date back further than your tiny mind can even comprehend. We were not born with names, instead we adopted the titles which you people so aptly gave us. My siblings and I ruled your world with an iron fist, mercilessly slaughtering anyone who faced us, manipulating them to our own advantage, and drawing out the worst in people. We each had a specific skill set" He laughs to himself as he talks about his powers. "I had a knack for finding people's secrets and making people yearn for more. I could harness the never-ending thirst that humanity had for control, and use it to exert my will. It was you who named me deadly after all." He grins.

"You are a human embodiment of greed. Your siblings are the other deadly sins. "Amara answers him, "Where are they now? How come only you have Guardians tasked with killing you?"

His eyes burn with a fire so hot even I can sense it. "That's because my gift came with a price. Death himself stated that I would only stay truly immortal if I was the only one. I bided my time and waited until the others grew lazy, fawning over the respect that humanity gave them, and when they were least expecting it, I stole the gift of immortality from them. I slaughtered my family with my bare hand and returned the gifts to Death, who as promised, made me the sole immortal being in all the cosmos. You may think that it was hard to kill my siblings, but I didn't even blink when I wiped their blood from my hands. I started with my eldest brother, *Superbia,* first. He thought he could take me down, but he was always an arrogant oaf."

"Superbia translates to pride," Amara clarifies for the rest of us. "You killed the other demons until you were the sole survivor."

"Exactly child. I reigned supreme as the ruler of humanity until four blasted women, imbued with abilities given to them by a witch, found the loophole to my gift from Death and split me from my essence, and trapped my physical form deep within the earth I walked upon."

Luke narrows his eyes, the betrayal of Avarice, though unsurprising to us, harrowing Luke to the core. "For an all-powerful super demon you spend most of your time asleep."

He smirks, eyeing us up and down distastefully. "Well that's all down to the infernal interfering of the same Guardians who separated my forms. They made sure that I was never able to find my true body by using the magic from a vase to keep it hidden from my senses. But thanks to the current incarnation of Guardians being incomplete I was able to sense my body, possess a lowly beggar man, and travel all the way here to reclaim what was once mine." He speaks with a patronising tone, as if we should be unsurprised at this display of power.

Luke steps back in line with us, taking Evelyn's hand as a silent sign of support. "I just have one question," Luke begins, "Why not stay in the body of someone you possessed? You have travelled the earth for thousands of years, being beaten and resurrected in a vicious circle with the Guardians, when you could have just stuck with one body and raised hell from there."

Evelyn elbows Luke in the side, "Don't give him ideas Luke."

Avarice smirks, cocking his head to the side and looks towards Evelyn, his eyes boring into her. "A good question. As demonstrated when I had a run in with the earth Guardian at that gathering yesterday, I take on the hindrances that a human body has. No mortal being can house the abilities that I have. They would burn up in moments. Instead I have to subject myself to using minimal power whilst inside a host and search for my real body, where I can use my powers freely."

"But you are the physical form of pure greed, searching for human control. Why do you even need a true form? You are powerful enough as it is."

"I want to corrupt and ruin humanity but to do that I need a true form. My essence just isn't strong enough to absorb the greed that humanity seeps out, but this body can. Although by the looks of it, I can kill you people, no matter what form I am in," he scoffs at us.

Luke nervously rolls the axe around in his hands when Avarice talks about killing us.

"You better think again," A female voice calls from behind us.

Raina strides across the field, a determined look wiped across her face, before settling next to us. "It looks like you will be facing the four Guardians after all." She shoots him a sickly sweet smile.

"Raina, what are you playing at?" I warn her, my heart beating at an alarming rate. Worry courses through my body, the fear of her being here overpowering me.

"I will not let you do this alone. I will face the wrath of the spirits when I return but for now, I'm sure we can kick some demonic ass."

"You cannot directly meddle with the current Guardians. You can only advise," Amara states, panic flooding her voice. She understands as much as I do that there are some rules that cannot be broken. Raina instead just smiles at us. "I have found the strength to stand beside you. Let's put it to use."

"Enough!" Avarice bellows. "I am sick of all the questions and family reunions. Didn't I kill you already?" he growls at Raina.

"I guess it didn't stick," she retorts.

"Maybe not. But these will." He raises his hands, slowly clenching his fingers until his fists, still pointing upwards, begin to haze with power.

A cracking sound fills the air. We all turn our heads to look at the manor where we see the windows begin to vibrate with intense force. The glass rattles within its frame, arcs of cracks course like veins across the surfaces before shattering into millions of pieces. Like a swarm of bees, they course through the air, glinting in the moonlight above us, before hovering around Avarice. He brings his arms down and begins to weave his long fingers into a mixture of patterns. The glass mirrors his movements and begins to take shape.

Hulking humanoid figures stand beside him, like glass warriors, with long pointy pieces of glass jutting out threateningly into the air. Their long arms stretch all the way to the ground, resting next to two equally sharp legs. Instead of having a face they have two incredibly long slithers of glass that point outwards, looking eerily similar to devils horns.

"Let's see if you can handle me, as well as my Shards." He begins to maniacally laugh.

"It's now or never guys," Raina calls out. She catches my eyes and gives me a calming smile, quelling the adrenaline pulsing through my body.

Heavy gusts of wind whip around us violently, sending leaves whipping into the sky. Amara begins to lift off the ground, hovering weightlessly in the air, the wind wrapping around her like support cables. Her hands sway in the breeze, her hair dancing around her, and she summons plumes of wind that tear down from the sky. Evelyn, taking Amara's lead, drops down on one knee, before plunging one hand into the ground. She begins to hum with power as she causes large roots to snake out from underneath us, rising high around us like tendrils. Cracks begin to appear on the ground, chunks of earth spewing out like blood, spreading out like ripples towards Avarice. Luke readies his axe, his broad muscular frame looking as imposing as one of the Shards. He brings the axe back, ready to swing it down onto something with unmatched strength.

Raina too drops down and spreads her hands on the floor. She slowly rises, dragging droplets of water out with her, pulling the fluid from the depths of the earth, suspending it around her. The drops dazzle in the moonlight as they begin to whip around her viscously like a hurricane. She becomes blurred from my visions, the violent swishing of the water shielding her from sight. I call out for my flames to appear, channelling any emotion that I can muster.

I begin to feel it all. Losing my sister, finding the other Guardians, abandoning my parents, the fear of this battle. I allow all the emotions to crash down onto me like a wave of pure strength. I force the feelings into the heat of my fire, turning it from its normal orange flame to a searing blue whilst sparks leap off of my body as arcs of lightinng fizzle around me.

The four of us race forward, Avarice mirroring our movement, his Shards creating thunderous booms as they leap across the field towards us.

All hell breaks loose as we meet with a ferocious crash.

Chapter 20
Jessica

The sound of glass shattering was buried by the overwhelming roar from Avarice's mouth. A single, bellowing, primal roar erupted from his throat, a signal for his army of Shards to advance on us. They slashed across the ground, uprooting chunks of grass as they plunged their long dagger-like arms into the earth. They run like a stampede of rhinos, a collective group of pure blunt force, coupled with the deadly sharp edge of a million pieces of glass.

Under the icy chill of the mist that spread over the field, a violent clash of magic meeting glass rips its way across the swirling muddy green ground. The Shards scream in pain, or make a noise akin to screaming, and they clutch their grievous wounds and fall to the ground, but the waves continue to push forward. Amara plucks some of the glass warriors from the ground and flings them into the sky as she moves across the field like a dancer. Her agile body leaps across the ground, the wind whipping around her, weaving patterns in the sky, as she crushes the Shards that cross her path. A single hand gesture tears the glass monsters piece by piece and leaves them laying cluttered on the ground.

The moon shines down on Evelyn as she crawls across the ground with the ferocity of a panther. With every plunge of her hand into the soft ground, geysers of dirt and rock spew out and hover in the air around her. She twists her arms into uncomfortable looking positions, causing the loose rocks around her to zoom forward and entrap the

Shards. Looking something like a sandstorm, the gravel and dirt spins at a high velocity around the Shards, tearing the glass and shattering it into smaller pieces. The dirt slices with its microscopic edges, mimicking tiny blades, and becomes just as deadly as the glass that makes the monsters.

Raina, still wrapped in the ball of water that moves at an unparalleled speed, tears her way across the ground, sending waves of water that washes over the Shards with enough force to crush them. The sound of gushing water fills the air as her hurricane plunges through masses of glass monsters. I spend half of the time keeping an eye on her. I am not sure a ghost can be hurt in a fight, but my elder sister mentality comes into fruition and I cannot bear the thought of her being injured in any form.

Evelyn continues to move across the field, and when faced with one particularly hulking Shard, she raises her arms in defence, creating a large root that shoots from a fissure in the ground. The Shard slashes at the brown root, scattering chunks across the ground, but Evelyn ensures the root continues to bloom and interlock around the glass. It crushes the Shard like it was nothing.

Luke, although he possesses no powers, manages to hold his own. After narrowly avoiding the sharp edge of a Shard's swor- like arm, leaping away in the nick of time, he becomes cornered by two of them. Before Evelyn can get to him, or the Shards can slice him apart, he swings the axe with such force it shatters them into millions of pieces with a single swipe. He continues to lay siege through the battlefield, screaming out loud as he races forward.

I send out jets of blue flame that scorch the monsters surrounding me, thrusting jets of steam into the cold air. I push wave after wave of smouldering heat towards the Shards, melting them where they stand, but more seem to advance on me. No matter how many I burn away there seems to be a never-ending onslaught.

One particular Shard stands right in front of me, squaring off as its hulking body bears down on me. "Go on then!" I scream at the glass creature, egging it on to deliver the killing blow. I will not go down without a fight.

"Jess! Get down!" I hear someone scream behind me. I drop to the floor, listening to the voice, as a single shockwave pulses through the air and hits the Shard directly in the centre. The glass shatters, sending splinters of debris flying into the floor like tiny knives. I turn to look behind me and see Evelyn standing above me, arm outstretched as the air waves around her, vibrating with a vigorous force.

"Thanks for that. I owe you one." I take the outstretched hand that she offers me and pull myself up to my feet.

"I'll take you up on that if we survive the battle." She smiles at me, before running off to face another herd of glass monsters.

Where is he getting all this glass from?

"There is no point fighting all these monsters if Avarice is just going to keep sending them, we have to take him out first." I duck to avoid the swipe from a Shard's arm whilst Evelyn rips open the ground, the fissure swallowing up the monsters whole. "Do you trust me?"

"Do I have a choice?" She groans, knowing that I have a plan.

"Oh c'mon, Evie. Learn to live a little. Stop being so stern." I wink at her, calling her by her nickname and playing on the irony of our earlier conversations. She blushes and a small smile appears in the corner of her mouth.

"Hit me with your best shot, Jessie." She turns on the spot and the two of us race towards Avarice.

The moonlight beats down onto the dank field as the onslaught continues. Gusts of wind and the sound of cracking glass floods from both sides of the field, each team furiously trying to gain an advantage. The sweet smell of decaying plant matter and the water from Raina's localised hurricane, mingled with the night breeze, fills the air. Evelyn and I set our sights on Avarice, standing at the back of the field, barking orders at the Shards.

"Give me some kindling," I yell at Evelyn, asking for her to give me something that I can use to set aflame.

As we continue to run forward, Evelyn waves her hands around and the ground cracks open. I leap across one of the fissures, narrowly avoiding losing my shoes, as two large root-like tendrils shoot high out of the floor. I summon flames in either of my hands and launch them towards the flammable material.

The two roots, now aflame, continue to tear through the ground as we march forwards, snaking around like a burning serpent. Evelyn wills the burning chunks of plant to slam down on top of Avarice, but he effortlessly slides out of the way, the black burning husk landing on the ground with a deafening thud.

"You think a little piece of burning wood could possibly harm me?" He spits the words out.

"No, but this might," Evelyn retorts as she brings the other large root down with equal force. The trunk hits the ground and catches Avarice's leg. He falls to the ground, the bottom of his trousers catching aflame, as he crawls across the wet ground.

"Foolish girl. I will watch your rotten body burn to cinders!" He screams as he throws his arm forward. Two large arcs of blinding white lightening shoot out of his hand directly towards Evelyn. Her quick reaction time allows her to lift her hands up, pulling a chunk of dislodged rock from the ground, shielding her from the white-hot blast.

Before I can move to protect her, the second blast hits her in the gut, throwing her back a few yards.

"No!" I scream, racing towards her smoking body. She pats her singing stomach, before doubling over in pain. She tries to stand but her weak legs collapse beneath her. I race beside her and take her weight onto mine, allowing her body to fall limp in my arms. "I'm fine," she gasps, struggling to get the words out.

"Relax, Evie, I got this." I lower her body to the ground, noting that there seems to be some blood forming around the clothes on her stomach. Stepping forward I summon two balls of blue flames that I fling towards Avarice's body.

He rolls out of the way, grabbing two pieces of glass that lay on the ground, before rising and swinging them at me, slicing off a few strands of my hair. I jump back, avoiding the slicing motion of the dangerously sharp glass. He brings his arms down in quick succession, I barely manage to avoid the deadly impaling from the glass. We continue to have a makeshift sparring session for a few moments.

"For an all-powerful demon, you seem to hate using your powers. What's with the glass attack?" I breathe as I duck underneath another bombardment of swipes.

"I do not care how you die you foolish child. As long as you stay dead." He brings the glass down with enough force it shatters when it hits the ground.

The deafening sound of an explosion behind me throws me off balance. I turn and see Amara and Raina sending torrents of rain and wind at the mass of Shards, who explode when they come into contact with the hurricane.

"Jess, look out!" Evelyn screams from beside me. Whilst I was watching the onslaught behind me, Avarice had scrambled to his feet and lunged towards me. I side step, his hands almost grasping me. I roll out of the way, as his hands make contact with the soft ground. The grass begins to lose all colour, paling in the moonlight, before a thick grey stone replaces the blades of grass.

"That's a pretty awesome Medusa touch you have there." I note as I watch his power pulsate across the floor before coming to a stop. He stands up on the newly converted ground.

"I have met Medusa. She was an overrated sow." He spits.

Evelyn gets to her feet, staggering around a few times before addressing Avarice. "Actually, I am big fan of hers. She was always my favourite Ancient Greek figure. Maybe it was the stone gaze thing?" She flicks her wrist and the new stone ground crumbles. The earth cracks apart and Avarice loses his footing. He sprawls across the floor, crawling away to avoid the tremors.

The use of her powers exhausts Evelyn, her hair dampened to her forehead with sweat, and her skin taking a sickly green hue.

"There is a reason we were given these powers. The Guardians were gifted elemental mastery but we could have been given any powers." I loom over his crouched body. "Your weakness is the four natural elements." I summon the fire from within and will it to swirl around my body.

"All demons have a weakness to the elements. We are abominations of nature, so nature fights back." He seethes. Arcs of white lightening fizzle around his body before he sends another beam towards me and Evelyn. I summon the lightning from inside of myself, its dazzling red colour leaping across the air until it meets with Avarice's powerful blast.

The two streams of lighting battle for dominance in the air, sending shockwaves and burst of light into the black sky. I push more power into my blasts.

Black dots appear in front of my eyes, sweat drips down my face, and I can feel my powers beginning to falter. A soft hand rests on my shoulder. I turn to face Evelyn, a determined look on her face, as she matches my pose and raises her hands. Waves of seismic energy and tremors erupt from her, all pulsating towards Avarice, as he tries to fight the two of us off. He begins to stagger back, the combined effort from the both of us becoming slightly overwhelming, pushing him further away, as his lighting begins to flicker erratically.

"I will decimate you all. I have fought hundreds of Guardians," he bellows over the crackle of the lighting.

"And yet you have never won. Aren't you sick of the circle never ending?" Evelyn retorts as she sends a larger pulse towards him, throwing him off balance.

His body flings through the sky as Evelyn and I stagger backwards, drained from the overuse of our powers.

Evelyn, still clutching her bleeding stomach, advances towards Avarice, who's smoking body lay across the ground.

"Earlier on, when we were talking about demons, you said *we*. I thought you were the last one," she questions. I note that as she asks him the questions, her eyes are instead focused on the battlefield. She darts around, looking for Luke, praying he is okay.

Avarice wipes the blood from his mouth, a small cut on his plump lips, before grinning. "You possess intellect child, an admirable quality. When I was at the apex of my powers, years ago, a group of loyal fanatics formed, creating a cult in my image. They begged that I spare their lives in return for their unwavering support. I granted their freedom and to this day they still roam the earth."

"So you have a cult of psychos. Big deal" I scoff.

"You underestimate my followers. When I was faced with the task of destroying my family, I couldn't bear to take the life of my youngest sister. Her power knows no bounds, but my love for her prevented her demise. I gave my followers the ability to cloak her from Death's presence, and therefore he never knew she existed."

Evelyn and I share a frightful glance. "Maybe she is the embodiment of the sin *sloth*. She could be sat in a burger bar eating fries for all eternity," she fearfully jokes.

"She never made herself known, so no Guardians were formed to harm her. Quite clever actually." He groans in annoyance.

"So we hunt down your cult, and then your sister. As I said earlier, no big deal," I quip.

A scream from behind distracts us. We turn to see Amara clutching her arm, blood spewing down her dark skin. She stumbles to the ground as Luke and Raina leap to defend her.

"Stay here," Evelyn orders, waving her hand, causing the grass to rapidly grow and cocoon around him until Avarice is firmly wrapped in the greenery.

"Will that hold him?" I ask.

"No idea," she answers as we run over to Amara. Luke swings the axe and destroys the towering Shard, before standing aggressively and warning off any of the glass creatures. The ground behind us begins to crack, the grass that binds Avarice tearing and snapping at the roots. Evelyn sees to the gash on Amaras arm, tearing a strip of cloth from her shirt, before tightly tying it around her bicep, stemming the bleed.

"I tried to use my siren song on one of them. It didn't work and that *thing* nearly severed my arm off." She speaks through gritted teeth as Evelyn tends to her wound.

Luke stands guard whilst our attention is diverted, keeping a close eye on the creatures that move through the mist. "We could really use your death vision right about now Evelyn." His gaze never falters away from the surrounding battlefield.

Evelyn tears another strip of cloth from her clothes and rests it in her mouth while her hands are busy. "They are inorganic creatures Luke. I can't suck the life out of them," she mumbles, before taking the cloth out and tying it around Amara's bleeding arm. "That should be enough to stop the bleeding."

Amara breathes in relief and rubs her pained arm, thanking Evelyn before questioning her. "How do you know to do all this?" She gestures towards the tourniquet.

"Luke's mother is a doctor, I used to follow her around when I was younger, and I guess I picked some techniques up."

Raina rushes towards me, taking my hand. She soothes me with a simply hug before turning to Evelyn. The mist settles around us, the wind whistling softly. The hulking glass monsters stand silently around us, circling us and firmly trapping us. Their menacing faces glint in the moonlight sending beams of white lights shooting into the sky. If these creatures weren't made by an evil psychopath, then they would be stunning pieces of art.

"You need to trust me okay, Evelyn. I have an idea." Raina takes Evelyn's hand as well. "You need to channel us."

The five of us stand side by side, staring into the thick mist that has descended onto the grass field. A roar tears across the battlefield as Avarice tears free from his organic cocoon.

He pulls the chunks of plant matter from his body, now covered in dirt, a menacing look smeared on his face. His stereotypical good-looking features become contorted with madness. Dangerously dark eyes, which have locked onto us, glow with pure fury that burns like a raging fire.

"I will kill each and every one of you with my bare hands. I will laugh as I watch the life drain from your eyes." He spits.

"Enough talking. We end this now, so get ready to take a nap." Raina smirks.

"Not this time," he fires back. "I will finally end the cycle, and when I slaughter you all, there will be no one to stop me."

Luke scoffs at Avarice. "There will always be Guardians to stop you."

"And yet you aren't a Guardian." He eyes Luke up and down. "You are a pawn in their game. No Guardians will emerge when I slaughter you four because I will end your line. The Guardian legacy will end with you."

Raina grabs my hand, interlinking our fingers in a tight grip. I repeat the gesture with Evelyn, who's standing beside me, who in turn takes Amara's hand.

"Evelyn, listen up," Raina orders, "You have to do everything I say, or else we all die."

"No pressure, then," Evelyn quips.

"You need to channel us, feed off of the energy that we are all emitting. You take it, absorb it, and send it towards Avarice."

Evelyn begins to shake. "Why do you think I have that kind of power?"

"Because you are the earth Guardian. You can control the ground that we walk on, and Ravens Valley is the birthplace of Avarice and the other demons. The earth is literally teaming with untapped magical energy that no other Guardian has ever touched because we never knew where he originated from. Tap into that magic, and use it to your advantage. We are going to finish this once and for all. There won't need to be any more Guardians after we are through with him."

Avarice begins to stalk towards us, his army of Shards a few steps behind him, both arms outstretched as electricity begins to buzz around him. He sends arcs of high voltage lightening speeding towards us, only for it to hit an invisible barrier, and bounce harmlessly off.

"I can't hold this forever," Amara groans, as she deflects another bolt of lightning. The invisible barrier that comes from Amara appears to be a very skilful use of her wind manipulating powers.

"Now or never Evie," Luke calls out.

Evelyn closes her eyes and slightly parts her lips, soft breaths coming out. Her hands begin to shake, as her body hums with power.

The ground vibrates with a low energetic throb that spreads across the field. Her eyes whip open, startling me, as they now glow a brilliant white, whilst her hair whips violently around her. "I am the Guardian of the earth. I bind you where you stand." She lifts her head, looking down her nose at Avarice. Her voice sounds like multiple people talking at once, booming across the field.

He goes to take a step forward, but his legs cannot lift from the ground. He begins to yell and scream in anger as he tries to tear his feet from the ground but they are stuck firmly.

Evelyn clenches down on my hand, allowing the warmth and energy to spread through us. All four of us, now invigorated with new life, lift from the ground, hovering delicately in the air.

"I am the water Guardian. I will draw the life from your veins." Raina booms, as she focuses on Avarice. He begins to gasp and splutter, falling to the ground, clawing viscously at his throat as he begins to turn a dank grey colour.

"I am the fire Guardian. I will snuff out your flame." I send wave after wave of burning energy towards him, smothering his body with a scolding heat that encompasses his cowering body.

Lastly, Amara speaks up, looking the most fearsome of us all. Her dark skin glints in the moonlight, her ebony curls billowing around her. "I am the air Guardian. I will separate your entire being."

With her free hand, she thrusts it high into the sky, summoning a violent windstorm that blows around us. The clouds above turn a shade of grey and purple, blasts of thunder and lightning fill the dark night, before a she gathers the wind around her. With a single gesture, she sends a strong pulse towards Avarice.

"I will kill you all!" he screams as his blood boils and his skin husks away.

The force of the wind smashes into him and tears his essence and body apart. He disappears into the sky with a final screech. His army of

Shards just stand and watch powerlessly as their leader tears violently in two.

❋

The four of us land back on the ground, the glowing colour fading away, and the mystical energy leaves our bodies.

"You guys were amazing!" Luke shrieks, his voice beaming with pride, after watching the display.

"We need to act quickly. We have no idea how long it takes before he will reform. We need to destroy him once and for all," I call out to the others. I order Luke to keep an eye out for the Shards, ensuring if any of them go to take a step he will quickly dismantle them. "Raina, go inside and get me the vase." She gives me a confused look before disappearing into the moonlight.

"Trust me girls, I have an idea." I take the vase that Raina offers me, after she appears in a wisp of smoke, before prying open the lid. I peer into the emptiness. "The issue with Avarice is that he always has the chance to reform because his essence is just left to linger around. We need to finally trap him. Ensure his essence and body cannot ever meet again. Amara, I need you to search through the air and gather his essence, and put it in here."

Amara sets to doing that, whilst I turn to Evelyn. "We need to hide this somewhere once he is trapped, prevent the risk of anyone ever opening it."

Evelyn scans the area, before settling on something in the distance. She squints in an attempt to make the object out more clearly. "Right there." She points to a small stone object jutting out of the ground.

"What is that?" I ask as we begin to walk towards it, Luke continuing to keep an eye out for the Shards that stand precariously around Avarice's crumpled body. Raina stays put with him in case the horde try to attack.

The object turns out to be a circular set up of rocks, all precariously perched upon each other, until they reach waist height. I peer into the centre of the stone circle to see that it descends deep into the ground, plunging deeply into the earth below us, darkness obscuring our view.

"How on earth did you know there was a well here Evelyn?" I ask, confused.

"I had a dream about it. Well, actually, I had a dream where I was inside of it. I just assumed it was the spirits sending me another message," she mumbles. "'Where elements meet, answers you shall seek'. It means the well right here. Everything has led to this moment-the writing on the vase, the place where natural elements meet. This well is where he is destined to die!"

"Maybe." I frown. They normally aren't that forthright with their messages. This is what the vase meant: we had to come here.

My train of thought is interrupted by Amara appearing behind me. She greets us, before peering down into the dark abyss. "You want me to throw his essence down there?"

"No, if you have gathered his essence from the air, then put it in the vase. The Guardians use this as a mystical anchor to tether their world to ours. Trapping his essence will leave him trapped forever." She does as instructed. The wind whips around us, the grey clouds circling around us, before funnelling into the vase in my hands. It rattles with great force, as if something is trying to get out.

I close the lid, trapping the force inside.

"What now," Evelyn asks. I hold the vase close to my chest, feeling the warmth coming from it.

"We need to make sure it can't be opened, at least for a long time, and then hide it." An idea springs to mind but the others may not like it.

"Do you trust me?" I ask Evelyn and Amara.

They both answer in unison with a *yes*, although Evelyn looks at me suspiciously.

"Give me your pendants." I extend my hand. They look at me blankly.

"Why?" Once again, they repeat in unison.

"Firstly, we will not be needing them anymore now that Avarice has potentially gone forever. Secondly, these pendants are made from the same material that his coffin is partially made from. It's an impenetrable metal that can only be cracked with a serious amount of magic," I explain.

"Well, for your sake, I hope we never have to use them again." Evelyn grumbles as she unclasps her pendant and places it in my hand. She pats the area where it used to be, obviously missing the feeling. Amara similarly hands me hers.

"Raina!" I call out across the field, before shouting for her pendant. She disappears from where she was standing, before reappearing directly in front of me. "I need your pendant"

She looks sheepishly away, avoiding eye contact with us. She used to do that when she was concealing the truth from our parents. "I don't have it anymore. When I died, it disappeared. I assumed the Spirits took it back."

I roll my eyes in annoyance towards the Spirits. They have a knack for getting in the way – or providing a lack of help when needed. "Well then, I guess three pendants will have to do."

A deep, ominous, voice booms across the field, as if coming from all directions. "You will not keep me trapped forever. There is no force on earth that can keep me trapped forever and when I find a way out I will return to my body. Not only will you suffer at my hands, but you will face the wrath of my sister. She will sense my entrapment and find you."

"For once in your eternal life, shut up!" I yell as I rip my pendant clean from my neck. I place it in my cupped hands along with the others. I summon a scorching heat from deep inside of me, blue flames flicker around my hands, as I begin to boil the metal. Immune from the searing heat that curdles the metal, I cup the scolding liquid in my hands, before pouring it over the closed lid of the vase. The metal runs down, completely covering the joint where the lid meets the vase, and effectively sealing it. With the permanent closure of the lid, Avarice's booming voice disappears.

"And now we hide it," I state, as I hitch the heavy artefact over the stone wall and watch it tumble into the darkness.

The four of us stare in into the darkness, holding our breath as we wait for something to begin. To our surprise, nothing happens. Our plan actually worked.

"Girls!" Luke screams from across the field. We turn around to see, in the misty distance, the Shards beginning to vibrate aggressively. Their shiny exterior glints in the moonlight as they begin to seize and shake.

"Luke, get back!" Evelyn screams as we all set off running full speed towards him.

The Shards begin to shriek and emit gut wrenching roars before exploding, sending sharp blades of glass in every direction.

Amara summons strong gale force winds that blow the dagger like glass shards away from us, but more continue to stream through the sky like bullets. Evelyn throws her hands into the air and the earth follows as the grass rapidly grows and weaves into the sky, effectively creating an organic shield around both of us. She continues to scream Luke's name, but every attempt to run to him is thwarted by quick flying shards of glass.

"We're okay!" Amara yells, flinging the blades away with gusts of wind before they reach anyone. After a few more whizz past us they seem to dwindle out. Evelyn wills the earth to fall down before we race towards the others.

A searing pain tears up my arm causing me to fall to the floor. Evelyn turns around and catches me. The pain floods my hand, tears erupt from my eyes, as I clutch my burning hand. I am not used to the sensation of something burning my skin, making this sensation so much more painful. I can see Raina similarly falling down to the floor in front of me.

I look down at my left hand, palm faced down, to see a red scald appearing on my skin. A shape begins to burn its way across my hand, branding myself with an interlinking pattern of crosses and crescents. I note that Raina has a similar pattern on her skin too.

"It's the Spirits," she chokes out through the pain. "They are mad that I helped you. They are screaming that I shouldn't have interfered. I am sorry!" She screams into the air around her, before being forcibly pulled back into the spirit world, disappearing in an angry, red-looking puff of smoke.

"Evie," Luke whispers from behind us, but she silences him with a wave of her hand.

Amara takes my hand, whilst Evelyn rubs my shoulders. I tell them I am okay and stand up, I tuck my hand into my pocket, ignoring the brand, whilst my mind spirals of into a worry about Raina.

"Evie," Luke softly calls out again.

"What!" she sharply responds as the three of us turn around to face him.

No.

Luke stands in front of us, the axe loosely hanging from his limp fingers. His face has taken on a sickly white hue, his hands and arms trembling softly, as he goes to take a step forward. His shirt, a fresh grey one that he placed on earlier, is now drenched with dark red blood, pouring down from the top.

A large shard of glass juts out from the centre of his chest. One exploding shard of glass found its target.

"No!" Evelyn screams as she rushes towards him.

He falls to the ground with a thud.

What do we do? Tears fill my eyes as I struggle to form any words.

"Somebody help him!" Evelyn screams, taking her jacket off before pulling the shard from his chest and pressing her jacket onto the bleeding wound. I run forward and throw myself near his head, placing my hands underneath his soft hair, supporting him. Amara leaps down and places her hands above his chest, mirroring Evelyn, so that she can take over her role.

Evelyn places her bloodied hands on Luke's face, whilst Amara tries to stop the bleeding.

"Please… do not leave me," Evelyn cries out, her tears flowing from her face. "Do something!" she screams into the night sky, imploring the Spirits to do something.

"Evie… I…" Luke splutters some words out, blood seeping from his mouth.

"Don't talk. Everything will be okay." She chokes the words out.

My heart races as fear floods around my body. I watch as Evelyn clutches Luke's pale face. Tears fall down Amara's face as the two of us watch helplessly.

He lifts a weary hand and brushes a stray hair off her face.

"Don't leave me alone," Evelyn whispers as more tears pour down.

His hand falls from her face, his head falling back limp, as the colour drains away from his eyes.

Chapter 21

Jessica

Luke's lifeless body hangs in the air for a moment before lowering softly onto the cream couch. Amara weaves the air around him, bringing him inside from the cold, and letting him lay peacefully. Her hands shake as she places him down not wanting to harm his body in any way.

Evelyn just stands close by, her face stagnant and showing no emotion, never leaving his side at any point. She lowers herself so she is sitting on the floor, directly next to his head, eyes fixed firmly on his face.

The moonlight that streams in through the window casts a serene glow across his face. His arched lips and strong jaw look beautiful, as if carved from marble. Evelyn reaches over and softly strokes his hair, pushing the stray strands down, and smoothing out his waves. His ruffled clothing, blood drenched, is covered by a white sheet that I whip off one of the artefacts. I don't want Evelyn staring at all this blood.

"Evelyn," Amara begins to talk, but quickly stops, struggling to find anything to say.

The tears still hang in Evelyn's eyes, twinkling when the moonlight catches her. Purple circles have already formed underneath them.

"This shouldn't have happened. He was never a part of this," she whispers, her hoarse voice catching on some of the words. "This was our fight."

"Not only did he save our lives, he also saved the world, Evelyn," I try to comfort her.

"His family will be waiting for him." She cuts me off, stifling a sob. "His mother will be home soon and she will start to worry. He never even said goodbye." She begins to tear up again.

Amara drops down to the floor and wraps her arms around Evelyn, gently soothing her.

"I can't do this anymore," she responds flatly.

"You no longer need to, my child." A voice calls out. A tall woman walks towards us, standing in the centre of the room. "You have all fulfilled your purpose." Her long hair falls and pools around her feet. Her sheer blue dress, a thick green belt tied round the waist, and long draping sleeves looks like something straight out of the renaissance era.

"Gwendoline." Her voice hitches again. Evelyn stands up, still not leaving Luke's side, and embraces her with a warm hug. "This should have never happened."

Gwendoline reciprocates the hug, wrapping Evelyn in her long arms. "I know my child. His sacrifice was valiant."

"It was unnecessary," I state. Gwendoline gives me a soft, knowing, look. The aura that surrounds her reminds me of Raina. This woman is a spirit.

Evelyn begins to pace around, keeping an eye on Luke's body. "He only wanted to help."

"And he did, my child. In more ways than you will ever know. His sacrifice will not be in vain. You have all sacrificed more than enough during this battle, so please allow us to do this favour for you."

"What favour?" Evelyn asks panicked.

"Allow us to let his body and soul ascend into the next plane of existence. His sacrifice in life warrants a true reward in death." She raises her hands and silver smoke begins to weave around the couch. The wisps of smoke gather around Luke's body, cocooning him until he becomes obscured from our view. When the mist clears, his body has disappeared.

"No!" Evelyn yells at Gwendoline. "He needed a proper burial."

"Hang on a second," Amara takes her hand, "How would we explain this to anyone Evelyn? It's probably better for him to go this way."

"I cannot believe this is happening," she gasps as she sits down on the sofa, her hands covering her face.

Amara sits next to her, whilst Gwendoline just stands elegantly in the middle of the room.

"Where is my sister?" I ask, a slight annoyance to my tone. My heart goes out to Evelyn, I know what she is going through right now, but I want to know what happened to my sister when she was just ripped from our world.

"Your sister has been taken back into the spirit world. She broke a fundamental rule when she interfered with the battle."

"She is a member of the current incarnation of Guardians. She was fulfilling her duty," I argue Raina's defence.

"When she died she became a Spirit. She no longer had the right to intervene." Her calm tone infuriates me.

"So you branded us?" I show her the scar on my hand.

Her eyes fall down to my burn. "Some of the older Spirits have harsher methods when dealing with rule breakers."

I am about to throw a ball of fire directly towards this woman. She may be Evelyn's Spirit guide but the way she talks about my sister makes me want to hit her, ancient ghost or not.

"Believe me when I say no true harm will come to her. She is now a Spirit and we protect our own."

"Funny way of showing it," I mumble under my breath as I take a seat next to Evelyn.

The silence lingers in the air for a moment, before Evelyn speaks up.

"Get out," she orders. The rest of us all turn to look at her in surprise of her harsh tone. "I don't want to look at you right now."

"Evelyn, please…" Gwendoline begins, before she is silenced with a rude gesture from Evelyn.

"I never wanted to be a part of this. Instead, I had this prophecy forced upon me, and Luke couldn't bear the thought of me being on my own out there. He followed us on this journey, although he had no obligation to do so, and instead he died right in front of me." Her words come out coldly. "I want to go out there an annihilate Avarice. The man who took his life. I can't do that though because he's gone forever."

"Evelyn, be careful what path you go down next," Gwendoline softly warns.

"I want to go out there and kill anything related to that demon. So here's what I am going to do next." She stands up confidently, wiping the remainder of her tears from her face. "I am going to go out into the world, and I will track down the members of the cult that he was going on about, maybe even his demonic sister. I will make sure that they cannot hurt anyone like I have been hurt."

"This isn't what Luke wanted." Amara stands up.

"Well he isn't here anymore," she answers, her voice as cold as ice. "I just pulled a shard of glass from his heart and watched him die."

She begins to walk around the room, heading towards the door. "I will find the members and kill them."

"That isn't you talking, Evelyn, It's the grief." I jump in, worrying that she will do something that she will regret. Evelyn locks eyes with me, staring at me through her bloodied strands of hair.

"Maybe it is. But I am thinking a lot more clearly now. Luke was right when he said that we should take these people out. So get off your high horse Jessica and think logically. It's only a matter of time before a cult manages to bring him back."

"Evie," I implore Luke's favourite nickname in an attempt to calm her. "Do not do this."

"She is right Evelyn," Gwendoline joins in. "You have finished your task. You are no longer a Guardian, you do not need to hunt anyone down. In the event of Avarice becoming free then you can be called back into action, or if you have since passed into the afterlife then you will aid the next incarnation of Guardians with their job," she explains.

Evelyn turns around, hand on the door handle. "Were any of you listening out there?" She looks directly at me. "Raina said that when she died her pendant went to someone else."

"This doesn't involve us Evelyn," I try to soothe the situation,

"Someone had to replace Raina when she died. There could be a girl out there who has no idea what's going on. We need to find her, train her, and then we will attack. After all, Avarice did say his sister is out there. She is going to be out for blood."

"Is that true?" I ask Gwendoline. "Is there a water Guardian currently out there?"

She looks away, almost ashamedly. "There is a young woman out there who recent developed powers. We have sent a spirit to guide her." Our faces drop in confusion. Gwendoline quickly ushers some words out in attempt to justify their secrecy. "When Raina lost her life, she was the first ever Guardian to die prematurely, so another potential Guardian was imbued with her gifts in order to replace her, however we thought that it was not fundamental for you to know. Avarice had already started the battle and to distract you would have been perilous. You are the first ever incarnation that has fought Avarice when you are incomplete. The previous Guardians all lived long lives after they accomplished their birthright and defeated his spirit. Upon their death their powers, and pendants, mystically moved onto the next set of women where they would lie dormant until Avarice attacks. This kind of thing has never happened before. You are the first set of Guardians to defeat his body and spirit, and trap him forever."

"That's my sister for you; she's always loved to cause drama." I roll my eyes.

"What you don't understand though is that it's not only your powers that come together in harmony, it's also your personalities. The free spiritedness of the air element. The stern temperament of the fire element. The level headedness of the earth element and the innocence of the water element. All of these come together and allow you to work with each other. We didn't want to ruin the balance by introducing a new person. This new Guardian has these powers and we will ensure that she is aided by the Spirits."

"Can we help?" Amara asks.

"You have fulfilled your duty," Gwendoline repeats herself. "There are no more battles that need to be fought."

"We all nearly lost our lives today, and my best friend died in my arms, because you Spirits keep everything from us." Evelyn scoffs and opens the door. "I am going to find her, and when we are complete, we are going to hunt down every last demon that walks on this earth. Either you help me or you stay out of my way." She raises her arm until it is level with Gwendoline, and summons a seismic pulse that tears across the room, bending the air around it. Gwendoline gets hit directly in the chest, causing her to disappear in a thick puff of smoke. "I don't need interference from ghosts." The words send a chill through my body.

"Think about your family Evelyn. You cannot just disappear." I try to explain the faults in her plan.

"I'll send them a message telling them that I am okay and that they shouldn't look for me. I can send one to Luke's family too." Her plan sounds so farfetched that I am worried about her. "I can't even take his body back to them. They won't even get a chance to mourn him." Her voice begins to falter.

"Evelyn…" She silences me with a raised hand.

"Enough. You either come with me now, or you never see me again."

She walks out of the door, slamming it behind her.

Amara and I share a quick look.

"What do we do?" Amara asks, her voice shaking. "Something seems off. This whole situation with the vase, Elkwood Manor, Avarice's body… it seems like it was just too easy. All these pieces have fallen into place so easily. I think there is something we are missing. There is someone out there manipulating the whole situation. We need Evelyn back to figure it out. So tell me: what do we do?"

"I don't know. I guess we go with her, just in case anything happens. Evelyn is not the same woman that she was a few hours ago."

Amara closes her eyes and exhales before heading towards the door. My last sentence seems to weigh heavily on her.

I'm not worried what Evelyn will do.

I'm worried what she will become.

Epilogue
Mai Yun

The blaring of a car horn startles me, pulling me out of my daydream. The rain continues to pour, running down the street and pooling over the drains. I pull my hood further over my head and get back to my reading.

I can't even focus anymore. I close my book with a thud and push it to the bottom of my bag. I continue to stand under the shelter, watching the rain run off the glass roof above me.

I lean back against the wall and watch the world go on around me. An elderly gentleman sitting next to me offers me a small, toothless smile, before turning back to his newspaper. Two young children rush around, jumping in puddles and splashing each other, whilst their mother repeatedly tells them to stop.

Thank God, I know enough Italian to be able to hear what she is saying. In the three years that I have been here, I still stumble sometimes when talking to the locals. I continue to look around, taking in some of the scenery. I have never been to this bus station before, tucked away from the main city, instead residing on an out of the way road in between a row of beautiful houses.

The sound of a coach driving through the rain draws my attention to the road. Two bright yellow lights, illuminating the raindrops like diamonds, careers towards us, before coming to a halt. The doors open with a large creak and the locals all flood on board, getting out of the downpour.

I greet the driver with a soft smile before handing him the money. "Ca'Foscari University please." He punches a few buttons on his little screen and then hands me a ticket with a beaming smile.

The people of Venice are extremely warm and welcoming. I am used to moving around a lot, being born in China, and moving throughout my life. As soon as I applied to go to university, I jumped at the chance to get as far away from my family as possible. Being the daughter of a military father means that I never managed to settle down. I never had anywhere to call home, until now.

I take my seat at the back of the bus, pushing through the empty bags and outstretched legs that litter the aisle, before tucking myself out of the way on one of the rough feeling seats. Reaching into my backpack, I pull out the creased photo of myself and Sebastian.

I wish I didn't have to run away. I don't want to leave him without saying goodbye. I'm not sure it's normal for a best friend to disappear without a trace.

He can never know.

I will drop by my dormitory and pack some things then head straight for the airport. I can run away into the night and pray that no one comes looking for me.

This time last week I was a normal girl, attending class and struggling with the mountains of class work, and now something's happening to me that I can't even get my head around. I just wanted to live a normal life, work hard, meet a nice man and have two children, eventually becoming an English literature lecturer at one of the old universities.

Now I can never have any of that. I am going to have to live a life of solitude now.

Great.

I tuck the photo back into my bag and close the zip, pushing it down near my feet.

The smooth bus ride suddenly comes to a screeching halt. I lean back to avoid smacking my head against the seat in front. I lean into the aisle, watching the people pick up all their loose items that were just scattered. The bright headlights shine into the dark night, the only thing visible is the heavy downpour of raindrops.

The doors open with a weary creak as a tall figure steps through. He turns to the passengers, who are all leaning into the aisle and staring at him, offering them a wide smile and a simple 'sorry.' He hands the driver some money and begins to walk towards me.

"Is this seat taken?" he asks, gesturing to the one furthest away from me on the back row.

Wow he is cute. My head is screaming out for me to act cool and seductive but my insecurities overpower me and all I can offer is a pathetic grin and a nod, mumbling out a 'no'.

He takes his seat as I blush a deep crimson. He smirk as he plonks down, pulling some papers out of his pocket and studying them intently.

I turn away from him, hoping he doesn't see my sudden change in colour, loosing myself as I stare out of the window. The raindrops pour down heavily as the storm continues.

I press my index finger against the glass and the water begins to gather and pool around it. I run my finger upwards, and the water travels with it, following my command. I can feel each droplet, the energy that it throbs with, as I cause the water to follow my trace.

I snap my finger off the glass and tuck my hand into my pockets. I swore I would never do that again. I have already broken that promise too many times.

Reaching down my top, I pull out my pendant. I don't remember when I first got this, but in the past week I have really seemed to notice it more. The blue sapphire crystal has been glowing brighter than usual, the silver chain twinkles in the light. Rolling this around my fingers seems to soothe me.

"That's a beautiful necklace," a voice pipes up. The boy from earlier is looking directly at me.

"Thank you," I splutter, tucking it back into my shirt.

"So, where are you heading?" He strikes up a conversation. His boyish face and wide smile comes across nice enough. He doesn't *look* like he wants to hurt me.

"Back to my university. You?" I ask.

"Just heading towards the main city. I'm backpacking through here," he explains.

"That must be amazing. The freedom that you must have." I envy the control he has in his life. I still get daily phone calls by my mother.

"It's not all it's cracked up to be." A faint flicker of sadness crosses over his handsome face.

"Well," I begin, pushing some of my confidence to the surface, "If we are getting off at the same stop then we could grab a drink? Maybe I can show you around one day."

Well done me, I think I have just asked a guy out on a date! What happened to my plan to run away?

"That would be awesome." He smiles, but the downward inflection on his last word, and the way he leans in, shows me that he is asking for my name.

"Oh" I catch on. "My name is Mai. Mai Yun."

"That's a different name." He smiles, before repeating it back to himself.

"And I thought my Asian appearance would have given it away." I laugh, well, snort. I run a hand through my shoulder length black, blunt cut, hair, before explaining my name. "It's related to water." Ironically.

"I think it's a wonderful name." He cocks his head and offers one of those thousand watt smiles.

"Thank you." I blush. "And you are?" His blond hair falls messily over his forehead, with blue eyes that dazzle like the sapphire in my necklace.

He offers out his hand for me to shake, which I do, as he speaks.

"My name is Luke. Luke Morgan."